PENGUIN BOOKS

THE TRIALS OF RUMPOLE

John Mortimer is a playwright, novelist, and former practicing barrister. During the Second World War he worked with the Crown Film Unit and published several novels before turning to theater. He has written many film scripts as well as stage, radio, and television plays, including *A Voyage Round My Father*, the Rumpole plays—which won him the British Academy of the Year award—and the adaptation of Evelyn Waugh's *Brideshead Revisited*. He is the author of ten collections of Rumpole stories, and two volumes of autobiography, *Clinging to the Wreckage* and *Murderers and Other Friends*. His novels *Summer's Lease*, *Paradise Postponed*, and its sequel, *Titmuss Regained*, have been successful television series. His latest novel is *Dunster*. John Mortimer lives with his wife and two daughters in Oxfordshire, England.

BY THE SAME AUTHOR

Charade
Rumming Park
Answer Yes or No
Like Men Betrayed
Three Winters
The Narrowing Stream
Will Shakespeare (An Entertainment)
Paradise Postponed
Summer's Lease
Titmuss Regained
Dunster

Rumpole of the Bailey
The Trials of Rumpole
Rumpole for the Defence
Rumpole's Return
Rumpole and the Golden Thread
Rumpole's Last Case
Rumpole and the Age of Miracles
Rumpole à la Carte
Rumpole on Trial
The Best of Rumpole
Rumpole and the Angel of Death

Under the Hammer

With Love and Lizards (with Penelope Mortimer)

Clinging to the Wreckage
Murderers and Other Friends

In Character
Character Parts

A Voyage Round My Father, The Dock Brief,
What Shall We Tell Caroline?
The Wrong Side of the Park
Two Stars for Comfort
The Judge
Collaborators
Edwin, Bermondsey, Marble Arch, Fear of Heaven,
The Prince of Darkness

The Captain of Kopenick (trans.)
Three Boulevard Farces (trans.)
Cat among the Pigeons (trans.)
Die Fledermaus (trans.)

Famous Trials (ed.)
The Oxford Book of Villains (ed.)

John Mortimer

The Trials of Rumpole

Penguin Books

PENGUIN BOOKS
Published by the Penguin Group
Penguin Books USA Inc., 375 Hudson Street,
New York, New York 10014, U.S.A.
Penguin Books Ltd, 27 Wrights Lane, London W8 5TZ, England
Penguin Books Australia Ltd, Ringwood, Victoria, Australia
Penguin Books Canada Ltd, 10 Alcorn Avenue,
Toronto, Ontario, Canada M4V 3B2
Penguin Books (N.Z.) Ltd, 182–190 Wairau Road,
Auckland 10, New Zealand

Penguin Books Ltd, Registered Offices:
Harmondsworth, Middlesex, England

First published in Penguin Books (U.K.) 1979
First published in Penguin Books (U.S.A.) 1981
This edition published in Penguin Books 1996

10 9 8 7 6 5 4 3 2 1

PUBLISHER'S NOTE
This is a work of fiction. Names, characters, places, and incidents
either are the product of the author's imagination or are used
fictitiously, and any resemblance to actual persons, living
or dead, events, or locales is entirely coincidental.

ISBN 0 14 02.4697 5 (pbk.)
(CIP data available)

Printed in the United States of America
Set in Linotype Plantin

For Leo McKern

Contents

Rumpole and the Man of God

As I take up my pen during a brief and unfortunate lull in Crime (taking their cue from the car-workers, the villains of this city appear to have downed tools causing a regrettable series of lay-offs, redundancies and slow-time workings down the Old Bailey), I wonder which of my most recent Trials to chronicle. Sitting in Chambers on a quiet Sunday morning (I never write these memories at home for fear that She Who Must Be Obeyed, my wife Hilda, should glance over my shoulder and take exception to the manner in which I have felt it right, in the strict interests of truth and accuracy, to describe domestic life *à coté de* Chez Rumpole); seated, as I say, in my Chambers I thought of going to the archives and consulting the mementoes of some of my more notorious victories. However when I opened the cupboard it was bare, and I remembered that it was during my defence of a South London clergyman on a shoplifting rap that I had felt bound to expunge all traces of my past, and destroy my souvenirs. It is the curse, as well as the fascination of the law, that lawyers get to know more than is good for them about their fellow human beings, and this truth was driven home to me during the time that I was engaged in the affair that I have called 'Rumpole and the Man of God'.

When I was called to the Bar, too long ago now for me to remember with any degree of comfort, I may have had high-flown ideas of a general practice of a more or less lush variety, divorcing duchesses, defending stars of stage and screen from imputations of unchastity, getting shipping companies out of scrapes. But I soon found that it's crime which not only pays moderately well, but which is also by far the greatest fun. Give me a murder on a spring morning with a decent run and a tolerably sympathetic jury, and Rumpole's happiness is complete. Like most decent advocates, I have no great taste for the law; but I flatter myself I can cross-examine a copper on his notebook, or charm the Uxbridge Magistrates off their Bench, or have the old darling sitting number four in the jury-box sighing with pity for an embezzler with two wives and six starving children. I am also, and I say it with absolutely no desire to boast, about the best man in the Temple on the subject of bloodstains. There is really nothing you can tell Rumpole about blood, particularly when it's out of the body and on to the clothing in the forensic laboratory.

The old Head of my Chambers, C. H. Wystan, now deceased (also known reluctantly to me as 'Daddy', being the father of Hilda Wystan, whom I married after an absent-minded proposal at an Inns of Court Ball. Hilda now rules the Rumpole household and rejoices in the dread title of 'She Who Must Be Obeyed'), old C. H. Wystan simply couldn't stand bloodstains. He even felt queasy looking at the photographs, so I started by helping him out with his criminal work and soon won my spurs round the London Sessions, Bow Street and the Old Bailey.

By the time I was called on to defend this particular cleric, I was so well-known in the Ludgate Circus Palais de Justice that many people, to my certain knowledge, called Horace Rumpole an Old Bailey Hack. I am now famous for chain-smoking small cigars, and for the resulting avalanche of ash which falls down the waistcoat and smothers the watch chain, for my habit of frequently quoting from the *Oxford Book of English Verse*, and for my fearlessness in front of the more savage type of Circuit Judge (I fix the old darlings with my glittering eye and whisper 'Down Fido' when they grow over-excited).

Picture me then in my late sixties, well-nourished on a diet consisting largely of pub lunches, steak-and-kidney pud, and the cooking claret from Pommeroy's Wine Bar in Fleet Street, which keeps me astonishingly regular. My reputation stands very high in the remand wing of Brixton nick, where many of my regular clients, fraudsmen, safe-blowers, breakers-in and carriers of offensive weapons, smile with everlasting hope when their solicitors breathe the magic words, 'We're taking in Horace Rumpole'.

I remember walking through the Temple Gardens to my Chambers one late-September morning, with the pale sun on the roses and the first golden leaves floating down on the young solicitors' clerks and their girlfriends, and I was in a moderately expansive mood. Morning was at seven, or rather around 9.45, the hillside was undoubtedly dew-pearled, God was in his heaven, and with a little luck there was a small crime or two going on somewhere in the world. As soon as I got into the clerk's department of my Chambers at Number 3 Equity Court Erskine-Brown said 'Rumpole. I saw a priest going into your room.'

＊

Our clerk's room was as busy as Paddington Station with our young and energetic clerk Henry sending barristers rushing off to distant destinations. Erskine-Brown, in striped shirt, double-breasted waistcoat and what I believe are known as 'Chelsea Boots', was propped up against the mantelpiece reading the particulars of some building claim Henry had just given him.

'That's your con, Mr Rumpole,' said Henry, explaining the curious manifestation of a Holy Man.

'Your *conversion?* Have you seen the light, Rumpole? Is Number 3 Equity Court your Road to Damascus?'

I cannot care for Erskine-Brown, especially when he makes jokes. I chose to ignore this and go to the mantelpiece to collect my brief, where I found old Uncle Tom (T. C. Rowley), the oldest member of our Chambers, who looks in because almost anything is preferable to life with his married sister in Croydon.

'Oh dear,' said Uncle Tom. 'A vicar in trouble. I suppose it's the choirboys again. I always think the Church runs a terrible risk having choirboys. They'd be far safer with a lot of middle-aged lady sopranos.'

I had slid the pink tape off the brief and was getting the gist of the clerical slip-up when Miss Trant, the bright young Portia of Equity Court (if Portias now have rimmed specs and speak with a Roedean accent) said that she didn't think vicars were exactly my line of country.

'Of course they're my line of country,' I told her with delight.

'Anyone accused of nicking half a dozen shirts is my line of country.' I had gone through the brief instructions by this time. It seems that the cleric in question was called by the somewhat Arthurian name of the Reverend Mordred Skinner. He had gone to the summer sales in Oxford Street (a scene of carnage and rapine in which no amount of gold would have persuaded Rumpole to participate), been let off the leash in the gents' haberdashery, and later apprehended in the Hall of Food with a pile of moderately garish shirtings for which he hadn't paid.

Having spent a tough ten minutes digesting the facts of this far from complex matter (well, it showed no signs of becoming a State trial or House of Lords material) I set off in the general direction of my room, but on the way I was met by my old friend George Frobisher exuding an almost audible smell of 'bay rum' or some similar unguent.

I am not myself against a little *Eau de Cologne* on the handkerchief, but the idea of any sort of cosmetic on my friend George was like finding a Bishop *'en travestie'*, or saucy seaside postcards on sale in the vestry. George is an old friend and a dear good fellow, a gentle soul who stands up in Court with all the confidence of a sacrificial virgin waiting for the sunrise over Stonehenge, but a dab hand at *The Times* crossword and a companionable fellow for a drink after Court in Pommeroy's Wine Bar off Fleet Street. I was surprised to see he appeared to have a new suit on, a silvery tie, and a silk bandana peeping from his top pocket.

'You haven't forgotten about tonight, have you?' George asked anxiously.

'We're going off for a bottle of Chateau Fleet Street in Pommeroy's?'

'No ... I'm bringing a friend to dinner. With you and Hilda.'

I had to confess that this social engagement had slipped my mind. In any event it seemed unlikely that anyone would wish to spend an evening with She Who Must Be Obeyed unless they were tied to her by bonds of matrimony, but it seemed that George had invited himself some weeks before and that he was keenly looking forward to the occasion.

'No Pommeroy's then?' I felt cheated of the conviviality.

'No, but ... We might bring a bottle with us! I have a little news. And I'd like you and Hilda to be the first to know.' He stopped then, enigmatically, and I gave a pointed sniff at the perfume-laden haze about him.

'George ... You haven't taken to brilliantine by any chance?'

'We'll be there for seven-thirty.' George smiled in a sheepish sort of fashion and went off whistling something that someone might have mistaken for the 'Tennessee Waltz' if he happened to be tone deaf. I passed on to keep my rendezvous with the Reverend Mordred Skinner.

*

The Man of God came with a sister, Miss Evelyn Skinner, a brisk woman in sensible shoes who had foolishly let him out of her sight in the haberdashery, and Mr Morse, a grey-haired solicitor who did a lot of work for the Church Commissioners and whose idea of a thrilling trial was a gentle dispute about how many candles you can put over the High Altar on the third Sunday in Lent. My client himself was a pale, timid individual who looked, with watery eyes and a pinkish tinge to his nostrils, as if he had caught a severe cold during his childhood and had never quite got over it. He also seemed puzzled by the mysteries of the Universe, the greatest of which was the arrival of six shirts in the shopping-bag he was carrying through the Hall of Food. I suggested that the whole thing might be explained by absent-mindedness.

'Those sales,' I said, 'would induce panic in the hardiest housewife.'

'Would they?' Mordred stared at me. His eyes behind steel-rimmed glasses seemed strangely amused. 'I must say I found the scene lively and quite entertaining.'

'No doubt you took the shirts to the cash desk, meaning to pay for them.'

'There were two assistants behind the counter. Two young ladies, to take money from customers,' he said discouragingly. 'I mean there was no need for me to take the shirts to any cash desk at all, Mr Rumpole.'

I looked at the Reverend Mordred Skinner and re-lit the dying cheroot with some irritation. I am used to grateful clients, co-operative clients, clients who are willing to pull their weight and put their backs to the wheel in the great cause of Victory for Rumpole. The many murderers I have known, for instance, have all been touchingly eager to help, and although one draws the line at simulated madness or futile and misleading alibis, at least such efforts show that the customer has a will to win. The cleric in my armchair seemed, by contrast, determined to put every possible obstacle in my way.

'I don't suppose you realized that,' I told him firmly. 'You're hardly an *habitué* of the sales, are you? I expect you wandered off looking for a cash desk, and then your mind became filled with next week's sermon, or whose turn it was to do the flowers in the chancel, and the whole mundane business of shopping simply slipped your memory.'

'It is true,' the Reverend Mordred admitted, 'that I was thinking a great deal, at the time, of the Problem of Evil.'

'Oh really?'

With the best will in the world I didn't see how the Problem of Evil was going to help the defence.

'What puzzles the ordinary fellow is,' he frowned in bewilderment, 'if God is all-wise and perfectly good – why on earth did he put evil in the world?'

'May I suggest an answer?' I wanted to gain the poor cleric's confidence by showing that I had no objection to a spot of theology. 'So that an ordinary fellow like me can get plenty of briefs round the Old Bailey and London Sessions.'

Mordred considered the matter carefully and then expressed his doubts.

'No ... No, I can't think *that*'s what He had in mind.'

'It may seem a very trivial little case to you Mr Rumpole ...' Evelyn Skinner dragged us back from pure thought, 'but it's life and death to Mordred.' At which I stood and gave them all a bit of the Rumpole mind.

'A man's reputation is never trivial,' I told them. 'I must beg you both to take it extremely seriously. Mr Skinner, may I ask you to address your mind to one vital question? Given the fact that there were six shirts in the shopping-basket you were carrying, how the hell did they get there?'

Mordred looked hopeless and said, 'I can't tell you. I've prayed about it.'

'You think they might have leapt off the counter, by the power of prayer? I mean, something like the loaves and the fishes?'

'Mr Rumpole.' Mordred smiled at me. 'Yours would seem to be an extremely literal faith.'

I thought that was a little rich coming from a man of such painful simplicity, so I lit another small cigar, and found myself gazing into the hostile and somewhat fishy eyes of the sister.

'Are you suggesting, Mr Rumpole, that my brother is guilty?'

'Of course not,' I assured her. 'Your brother's innocent. And he'll be so until twelve commonsensical old darlings picked at random off Newington Causeway find him otherwise.'

'I rather thought – a quick hearing before the Magistrates. With the least possible publicity.' Mr Morse showed his sad lack of experience in crime.

'A quick hearing before the Magistrates is as good as pleading guilty.'

'You think you might win this case, with a jury?' I thought there was a faint flicker of interest in Mordred's pink-rimmed eyes.

'Juries are like Almighty God, Mr Skinner. Totally unpredictable.'

So the conference wound to an end without divulging any particular answer to the charge, and I asked Mordred to apply through the usual channels for some sort of defence when he was next at prayer. He rewarded this suggestion with a wintry smile and my visitors left me just as *S*he Who Must Be Obeyed came through on the blower to remind me that George was coming to dinner and bringing a friend, and would I buy two pounds of cooking apples at the tube station, and would I also remember not to loiter in Pommeroy's Wine Bar taking any sort of pleasure.

As I put the phone down I noticed that Miss Evelyn Skinner had filtered back into my room, apparently desiring a word with Rumpole alone. She started in a tone of pity.

'I don't think you quite understand my brother . . .'

'Oh. Miss Skinner. Yes, well ... I never felt totally at home with vicars.' I felt some sort of apology was in order.

'He's like a child in many ways.'

'The Peter Pan of the Pulpit?'

'In a way. I'm two years older than Mordred. I've always had to look after him. He wouldn't have got anywhere without me, Mr Rumpole, simply nowhere, if I hadn't been there to deal with the Parish Council, and say the right things to the Bishop. Mordred just never thinks about himself, or what he's doing half the time.'

'You should have kept a better eye on him, in the sales.'

'Of course I should! I should have been watching him like a hawk, every minute. I blame myself entirely.'

She stood there, busily blaming herself, and then her brother could be heard calling her plaintively from the passage.

'Coming, dear. I'm coming at once,' Evelyn said briskly, and was gone. I stood looking after her, smoking a small cigar and remembering Hilaire Belloc's sound advice to helpless children:

> Always keep tight hold of nurse,
> For fear of finding something worse.

*

George Frobisher brought a friend to dinner, and, as I had rather suspected when I got a whiff of George's perfume in the passage, the friend was a lady, or, as I think Hilda would have preferred to call her, a woman. Now I must make it absolutely clear that this type of conduct was totally out of character in my friend George. He had an absolutely clean record so far as women were concerned. Oh I imagine he had a mother, and I have heard him occasionally mutter about sisters; but George had been a bachelor as long as I had known him, returning from our convivial claret in Pommeroy's to the Royal Borough Hotel, Kensington, where he had a small room, reasonable *en pension* terms and coloured television after dinner in the residents' lounge, seated in front of which device George would read his briefs, occasionally taking a furtive glance at some long-running serial of Hospital Life.

Judge of my surprise, therefore, when George turned up to dinner at Casa Rumpole with a very feminine, albeit middle-aged, lady indeed. Mrs Ida Tempest, as George introduced her, came with some species of furry animal wreathed about her neck, whose eyes regarded me with a glassy stare, as I prepared to help Mrs Tempest partially disrobe.

The lady's own eyes were far from glassy, being twinkling, and roguish in their expression. Mrs Tempest had reddish hair (rather the colour of falsely glowing artificial coals on an electric fire) piled on her head, what I believe is known as a 'Cupid's Bow' mouth in the trade, and the sort of complexion which makes you think that if you caught its owner a brisk slap you would choke in the resulting cloud of white powder. Her skirt seemed too tight, and her heels too high, for total comfort; but it could not be denied that Mrs Ida Tempest was a cheerful and even a pleasant-looking person. George gazed at her throughout the evening with mingled admiration and pride.

It soon became apparent that in addition to his lady friend, George had brought a plastic bag from some off-licence containing a bottle of non-vintage Moët. Such things are more often than not the harbinger of alarming news, and sure enough as soon as the pud was on the table George handed me the bottle, to cope with an announcement that he and Mrs Ida Tempest were engaged to be married, clearly taking the view that this news should be a matter for congratulation.

'We wanted you to be the first to know,' George said proudly.

Hilda smiled in a way that can only be described as 'brave' and further comment was postponed by the explosion of the warm Moët. I filled everyone's glasses and Mrs Tempest reached with enthusiasm for the booze.

'Oh, I do love bubbly,' she said. 'I love the way it goes all tickly up the nose, don't you Hilda?'

'We hardly get it often enough to notice.' She Who Must Be Obeyed was in no celebratory mood that evening. I had noticed, during the feast, that she clearly was not hitting it off with Mrs Tempest. I therefore felt it incumbent on me to address the Court.

'Well then. If we're all filled up, I suppose it falls to me.

Accustomed as I am to public speaking ...' I began the speech.

'Usually on behalf of the criminal classes!' Hilda grumbled.

'Yes. Well ... I think I know what is expected on these occasions.'

'You mean you're like the film star's fifth husband? You know what's expected of you, but you don't know how to make it new.' It appeared from her giggles and George's proud smile that Mrs Tempest had made a joke. Hilda was not amused.

'Well then!' I came to the peroration. 'Here's to the happy couple.'

'Here's to us, George!' George and Mrs Tempest clinked glasses and twinkled at each other. We all took a mouthful of warmish gas. After which Hilda courteously pushed the food in George's *fiancée*'s direction.

'Would you care for a little more Charlotte Russe, Mrs Tempest?'

'Oh, Ida. Please call me Ida. Well, just a teeny-weeny scraping. I don't want to lose my sylph-like figure, do I Georgie? Otherwise you might not fancy me any more.'

'There's no danger of that.' The appalling thing was that George was looking roguish also.

'Of you not fancying me? Oh, I know ...' La Tempest simpered.

'Of losing your figure, my dear. She's slim as a bluebell. Isn't she slim as a bluebell, Rumpole?' George turned to me for corroboration. I answered cautiously.

'I suppose that depends rather on the size of the bluebell.'

'Oh, Horace! You are terrible! Why've you been keeping this terrible man from me, George?' Mrs Tempest seemed delighted with my enigmatic reply.

'I hope we're all going to see a lot of each other after we're married.' George smiled round the table, and got a small tightening of the lips from Hilda.

'Oh yes, George. I'm sure that'll be very nice.'

The tide had gone down in Mrs Tempest's glass, and after I had topped it up she held it to the light and said admiringly. 'Lovely glasses. So tasteful. Just look at that, George. Isn't that a lovely tasteful glass?'

'They're rejects actually,' Hilda told her. 'From the Army and Navy Stores.'

'What whim of providence was it that led you across the path of my old friend George Frobisher?' I felt I had to keep the conversation going.

'Mrs Tempest, that is Ida, came as a guest to the Royal Borough Hotel.' George started to talk shyly of romance.

'You noticed me, didn't you, dear?' Mrs Tempest was clearly cast in the position of prompter.

'I must admit I did.'

'And I noticed him noticing me. You know how it is with men, don't you, Hilda?'

'Sometimes I wonder if Rumpole notices me at all.' Hilda struck, I thought, an unnecessarily gloomy note.

'Of course I notice you,' I assured her. 'I come home in the evenings – and there you are. I notice you all the time.'

'As a matter of fact we first spoke in the Manageress's Office,' George continued with the narration, 'where we had both gone to register a complaint, on the question of the bath water.'

'There's not enough hot to fill the valleys, I told her, let alone cover the hills!' Mrs Tempest explained gleefully to Hilda, who felt, apparently, that no such explanation was necessary.

'George agreed with me. Didn't you, George?'

'Shall I say, we formed an alliance?'

'Oh, we hit it off at once. We've so many interests in common.'

'Really.' I looked at Mrs Tempest in some amazement. Apart from the basic business of keeping alive I couldn't imagine what interests she had in common with my old friend George Frobisher. She gave me a surprising answer.

'Ballroom dancing.'

'Mrs Tempest,' said George proudly, 'that is Ida, has cups for it.'

'George! You're a secret ballroom dancer?' I wanted Further and Better Particulars of this Offence.

'We're going for lessons together, at Miss McKay's *École de Dance* in Rutland Gate.'

I confess I found the prospect shocking, and I said as much to George. 'Is your life going to be devoted entirely to pleasure?'

'Does *Horace* tango at all, Hilda?' Mrs Tempest asked a foolish question.

'He's never been known to.' Hilda sniffed slightly and I tried to make the reply lightly ironic.

'I'm afraid crime is cutting seriously down on my time for the tango.'

'Such a pity, dear.' Mrs Tempest was looking at me with genuine concern. 'You don't know what you're missing.'

At which point Hilda rose firmly and asked George's intended if she wanted to powder her nose, which innocent question provoked a burst of giggles.

'You mean, do I want to spend a penny?'

'It is customary,' said Hilda with some *hauteur*, 'at this stage, to leave the gentlemen.'

'Oh, you mean you want a hand with the washing-up,' Mrs Tempest followed Hilda out, delivering her parting line to me.

'Not too many naughty stories now, Horace. I don't want you leading my Georgie astray.' At which I swear she winked.

When we were left alone with a bottle of the Old Tawney George was still gazing foolishly after the vanishing Ida. 'Charming,' he said, 'isn't she charming?'

Now at this point I became distinctly uneasy. I had been looking at La Belle Tempest with a feeling of *déjà vue*. I felt sure that I had met her before, and not in some previous existence. And, of course, I was painfully aware of the fact that the vast majority of my social contacts are made in cells, courtrooms and other places of not too good repute. I therefore answered cautiously. 'Your Mrs Tempest ... seems to have a certain amount of vivacity.'

'She's a very able business-woman, too.'

'Is she now?'

'She used to run an hotel with her first husband. Highly successful business apparently. Somewhere in Kent ...'

I frowned. The word 'hotel' rang a distant, but distinctly audible, bell.

'So I thought, when we're married, of course, she might take up a small hotel again, in the West Country perhaps.'

'And what about you, George? Would you give up your work

at the Bar and devote all your time to the veleta?' I rather wanted
to point out to him the difficulties of the situation.

'Well. I don't want to boast, but I thought I might go for a
Circuit Judgeship.' George said this shyly, as though disclosing
another astonishing sexual conquest. 'In fact I *have* applied. In
some rural area ...'

'*You* a judge, George? A *judge*? Well, come to think of it, it
might suit you. You were never much good in Court, were you,
old darling?' George looked slightly puzzled at this, but I blun-
dered on. 'It wasn't in Ramsgate, by any chance? Where your
inamorata kept a small hotel?'

'Why do you ask?' George was lapping up the port in a sort
of golden reverie.

'Don't do it, George!' I said, loudly enough, I hoped, to blast
him out of his complacency.

'Don't be a judge?'

'Don't get married! Look, George. Your Honour. If your
Lordship pleases. Have a little consideration, my dear boy.' I
tried to appeal to his better nature. 'I mean -- where would you
be leaving me?'

'Very much as you are now, I should imagine.'

'Those peaceful moments of the day. Those hours we spend
with a bottle of Chateau Fleet Street from 5.30 on in Pommeroy's
Wine Bar. That wonderful oasis of peace that lies between the
battle of the Bailey and the horrors of Home Life. You mean
they'll be denied me from now on? You mean you'll be bolting
like a rabbit down the Temple Underground back to Mrs Tempest and leaving me without a companion?'

George looked at me, thoughtfully, and then gave judgement
with, I thought, a certain lack of feeling.

'I am, of course, extremely fond of you, Rumpole. But you're
not exactly ... Well, not someone who one can share *all* one's
interests with.'

'I'm not a dab hand at the two-step?' I'm afraid I sounded
bitter.

'I didn't *say* that, Rumpole.'

'Don't do it, George! Marriage is like pleading guilty, for an
indefinite sentence. Without parole.' I poured more port.

'You're exaggerating!'

'I'm not, George. I swear by Almighty God. I'm not.' I gave him the facts. 'Do you know what happens on Saturday mornings? When free men are lying in bed, or wandering contentedly towards a glass of breakfast Chablis and a slow read of the Obituaries? You'll both set out with a list, and your lady wife will spend your hard-earned money on things you have no desire to own, like Vim, and saucepan scourers, and J-cloths ... and Mansion polish! And on your way home, you'll be asked to carry the shopping-basket ... I beg of you, don't do it!'

This plea to the jury might have had some effect, but the door then opened to admit La Belle Tempest, George's eyes glazed over and he clearly became deaf to reason. And then Hilda entered and gave me a brisk order to bring in the coffee tray.

'She Who Must Be Obeyed!' I whispered to George on my way out. 'You see what I mean?' I might as well have saved my breath. He wasn't listening.

*

Saturday morning saw self and She at the check-out point in the local Tesco's, with the substantial fee for the Portsmouth Rape Trial being frittered away on such frivolous luxuries as sliced bread, Vim, cleaning materials and so on, and as the cash register clicked merrily up Hilda passed judgement on George's *fiancée*.

'Of course she won't do for George.'

I had an uneasy suspicion that she might be correct, but I asked for further and better particulars.

'You think not? Why exactly?'

'Noticing our glasses! It's such bad form noticing people's things. I thought she was going to ask how much they cost.'

Which, so far as She was concerned, seemed to adequately sum up the case of Mrs Ida Tempest. At which point, having loaded up and checked that the saucepan scourers were all present and correct, Hilda handed me the shopping-basket, which seemed to be filled with lead weights, and strode off unimpeded to the bus stop with Rumpole groaning in her wake.

'What we do with all that Vim I can never understand.' I questioned our whole way of life. 'Do we *eat* Vim?'

'You'd miss it, Rumpole, if it wasn't there.'

*

On the following Monday I went down to Dockside Magistrates Court to defend young Jim Timson on a charge of taking and driving away a Ford Cortina. I have acted for various members of the clan Timson, a noted breed of South London villain, for many years. They know the law, and their courtroom behaviour, I mean the way they stand to attention and call the magistrate 'Sir', is impeccable. I went into battle fiercely that afternoon, and it was a famous victory. We got the summons dismissed with costs against the police. I hoped I'd achieve the same happy result in the notable trial of the Reverend Mordred Skinner, but I very much doubted it.

As soon as I was back in Chambers I opened a cupboard, sneezed in the resulting cloud of dust and burrowed in the archives. I resisted the temptation to linger among my memories and pushed aside the Penge Bungalow photographs, the revolver that was used in the killing at the East Grimble Rep, and old Charles Monti's will written on a blown ostrich egg. I only glanced at the drawing an elderly R.A. did, to while away his trial for soliciting in the Super Loo at Euston Station, of the Recorder of London. I lingered briefly on my book of old press cuttings from the *News of the World* (that fine Legal Text Book in the Criminal Jurisdiction), and merely glanced at the analysis of bloodstains from the old Brick Lane Billiard Hall Murder when I was locked in single-handed combat with a former Lord Chief Justice of England and secured an acquittal, and came at last on what I was seeking.

The blue folder of photographs was nestling under an old wig tin and an outdated work on forensic medicine. As I dug out my treasure and carried it to the light on my desk, I muttered a few lines of old William Wordsworth's, the Sheep of the Lake District,

Perhaps the plaintive numbers flow
For old, unhappy, far-off things,
And battles long ago

On the cover of the photographs I had stuck a yellowing cutting from the *Ramsgate Times*. 'Couple Charged in Local Arson Case' I read again. 'The Unexplained Destruction of the Saracen's Head Hotel!' I opened the folder. There was a picture of a building on the sea front, and a number of people standing round. I took the strong glass off my desk to examine the figures in the photograph and saw the younger, but still roguishly smiling, face of Mrs Ida Tempest, my friend George's intended.

*

Having tucked the photographs back in the archive, I went straight to Pommeroy's Wine Bar, nothing unusual about that, I rarely go anywhere else at six o'clock, after the day's work is done; but George wasn't in Chambers and I hoped he might drop in there for a strengthener before a night of dalliance with his *inamorata* in the Royal Borough Hotel. However when I got to Pommeroy's the only recognizable figure, apart from a few mournful-looking journalists and the opera critic in residence, was our Portia, Miss Phillida Trant, drinking a lonely Cinzano Bianco with ice and lemon. She told me that she hadn't seen George and said, rather enigmatically, that she was waiting for a person called Claude, who, on further inquiry, turned out to be none other than our elegant expert on the Civil side, my learned antagonist Erskine-Brown.

'Good God, is he Claude? Makes me feel quite fond of him. Why ever are you waiting for him? Do you want to pick his brains on the law of mortgages?'

'We *are* by way of being engaged,' Miss Trant said somewhat sharply.

The infection seemed to be spreading in our Chambers, like gippy tummy. I looked at Miss Trant and asked, simply for information, 'You're sure you know enough about him?'

'I'm afraid I do.' She sounded resigned.

'I mean, you'd naturally want to *know* everything, wouldn't you – about anyone you're going to commit matrimony with?' I wanted her confirmation.

'Go on, surprise me!' Miss Trant, I had the feeling, was not being entirely serious. 'He married a middle-aged Persian contortionist when he was up at Keble? I'd love to know that – and it'd make him *far* more exciting.'

At which point the beloved Claude actually made his appearance in a bowler and overcoat with a velvet collar, and announced he had some treat *in* store for Miss Trant, such as Verdi's *Requiem* in the Festival Hall, whilst she looked at him as though disappointed at the un-murkiness of the Erskine-Brown past. Then I saw George at the counter making a small purchase from Jack Pommeroy and I bore down on him. I had no doubt, at that stage, that my simple duty to my old friend was immediate disclosure. However when I reached George I found that he was investing in a bottle far removed from our usual Chateau Fleet Street.

'1967. Pichon-Longueville? Celebrating, George?'

'In a way. We have a glass or two in the room now. Can't get anything decent in the restaurant.' George was storing the nectar away in his brief-case with the air of a practised *boulevardier*.

'George. Look. My dear fellow. Look ... will you have a drink?'

'It's really much more comfortable, up in the room,' George babbled on regardless. 'And we listen to the BBC Overseas Service, old Victor Sylvester records requested from Nigeria. They only seem to *care* for ballroom dancing in the Third World nowadays.' My old friend was moving away from me, although I did all I could to stop him.

'Please, George. It'll only take a minute. Something ... you really ought to know.'

'Sorry to desert you, Rumpole. It would never do to keep Ida waiting.'

He was gone, as Jack Pommeroy with his purple face and the rose-bud in his buttonhole asked what was my pleasure.

'Red plonk,' I told him. 'Chateau Fleet Street. A large glass. I've got nothing to celebrate.'

After that I found it increasingly difficult to break the news to George, although I knew I had to do so.

*

The Reverend Mordred Skinner was duly sent for trial at the Inner London Sessions, Newington Causeway in the South East corner of London. Wherever civilization ends it is, I have always felt, somewhere just north of the Inner London Sessions. It is a strange thing but I always look forward with a certain eagerness to an appearance at the Old Bailey. I walk down Newgate Street, as often as not, with a spring in my stride and there it is, in all its glory, a stately law court, decreed by the City Fathers, an Edwardian palace with a modern extension to deal with the increase in human fallibility. Terrible things go on down the Bailey, horrifying things. Why is it I never go through its revolving door without a thrill of pleasure, a slight tremble of excitement? Why does it seem a much jollier place than my flat in Gloucester Road under the strict rule of She Who Must Be Obeyed?

Such pleasurable sensations, I must confess, are never connected with my visits to the Inner London Sessions. While a hint of spring sunshine often touches the figure of Justice on the dome of the Bailey it always seems to be a wet Monday in November at Inner London. The Sessions House is stuck in a sort of urban desert down the Old Kent Road, with nowhere to go for a decent bit of steak-and-kidney pud during the lunch hour. It is a sad sort of Court, with all the cheeky Cockney sparrows turned into silent figures waiting for the burglary to come on in Court 2, and the juries there look as if they relied on the work to eke out their social security.

I met the Reverend gentleman after I had donned the formal dress (yellowing wig bought second-hand from an ex-Attorney General of Tonga in 1932, somewhat frayed gown, collar like a blunt extension). He seemed unconcerned and was even smiling a little, although his sister Evelyn looked like one about to attend a burning at the stake; Mr Morse looked thoroughly uncomfortable and as if he'd like to get back to a nice discussion of the Almshouse charity in Chipping Sodbury.

I tried to instil a suitable sense of the solemnity of the occasion in my clerical customer by telling him that God, with that wonderful talent for practical joking which has shown itself throughout recorded history, had dealt us His Honour Judge Bullingham.

'Is he very dreadful?' Mr Skinner asked almost hopefully.

'Why he was ever made a judge is one of the unsolved mysteries of the universe.' I was determined not to sound reassuring. 'I can only suppose that his unreasoning prejudice against all black persons, defence lawyers and probation officers, comes from some deep psychological cause. Perhaps his mother, if such a person can be imagined, was once assaulted by a black probation officer who was on his way to give evidence for the defence.'

'I wonder how he feels about parsons.' My client seemed not at all put out.

'God knows. I rather doubt if he's ever met one. The Bull's leisure taste runs to strong drink and all-in wrestling. Come along, we might as well enter the *corrida*.'

A couple of hours later, His Honour Judge Bullingham, with his thick neck and complexion of a beetroot past its first youth, was calmly exploring his inner ear with his little finger and tolerantly allowing me to cross-examine a large gentleman named Pratt, resident flatfoot at the Oxford Street Bazaar.

'Mr Pratt? How long have you been a detective in this particular store?'

'Ten years, sir.'

'And before that?'

'I was with the Metropolitan Police.'

'Why did you leave?'

'Pay and conditions, sir, were hardly satisfactory.'

'Oh, really? You found it more profitable to keep your beady eye on the ladies' lingerie counter than do battle in the streets with serious crime?'

'Are you suggesting that this isn't a serious crime, Mr Rumpole?' The learned judge, who pots villains with all the subtlety of his namesake animal charging a gate, growled this question at me with his face going a darker purple than ever, and his jowls trembling.

'For many people, my Lord,' I turned to the jury and gave them the message, 'six shirts might be a mere triviality. For the Reverend Mordred Skinner, they represent the possibility of total ruin, disgrace and disaster. In this case my client's whole life hangs in the balance.' I turned a flattering gaze on the twelve honest citizens who had been chosen to pronounce on the sanctity or otherwise of the Reverend Mordred. 'That is why we must cling to our most cherished institution, trial by jury. It is not the value of the property stolen, it is the priceless matter of a man's good reputation.'

'Mister Rumpole,' the Bull lifted his head as if for the charge. 'You should know your business by now. This is not the time for making speeches, you will have an opportunity at the end of the case.'

'And as your Honour will have an opportunity *after* me to make a speech, I thought it as well to make clear who the judges of *fact* in this matter are.' I continued to look at the jury with an expression of flattering devotion.

'Yes. Very well. Let's get on with it.' The Bull retreated momentarily. I rubbed in the victory.

'Certainly. That is what I was attempting to do.' I turned to the witness. 'Mr Pratt. When you were in the gents' haberdashery . . .'

'Yes, sir?'

'You didn't see my client remove the shirts from the counter and make off with them?'

'No, sir.'

'If he had, no doubt he would have told us about it,' Bullingham could not resist growling. I gave him a little bow.

'Your Honour is always so quick to notice points in favour of the defence.' I went back to work on the store detective. 'So why did you follow my client?'

'The Supervisor noticed a pile of shirts missing. She said there was a Reverend been turning them over, your Honour.'

This tit-bit delighted the Bull, he snatched at it greedily. 'He might not have told us that, if you hadn't asked the wrong question, Mr Rumpole.'

'No question is wrong, if it reveals the truth,' I informed the jury, and then turned back to Pratt. I had an idea, an uncomfortable feeling that I might just have guessed the truth of this peculiar case. 'So you don't know if he was carrying the basket when he left the shirt department?'

'No.'

'Was he carrying it when you first spotted him, on the moving staircase?'

'I only saw his head and shoulders . . .'

The pieces were fitting together. I would have to face my client with my growing notion of a defence as soon as possible. 'So you first saw him with the basket in the Hall of Food?'

'That's right, sir.'

At which point Bullingham stirred dangerously and raised the curtain of his top lip on some large yellowing teeth. He was about to make a joke. 'Are you suggesting, Mr. Rumpole, that a basket full of shirts mysteriously materialized in your client's hand in the Tinned Meat Department?'

At which the jury laughed obsequiously. Rumpole silenced them in a voice of enormous gravity.

'Might I remind your Honour of what he said. This is a serious case.'

'As you cross-examined, Mr Rumpole, I was beginning to wonder.' Bullingham was still grinning.

'The art of cross-examination, your Honour, is a little like walking a tight-rope.'

'Oh is it?'

'One gets on so much better if one isn't continually interrupted.'

At which Bullingham relapsed into a sullen silence and I got on with the work in hand.

'It would have been quite impossible for Mr Skinner to have paid at the shirt counter, wouldn't it?'

'No, sir. There were two assistants behind the counter.'

'Young ladies?'

'Yes, sir.'

'When you saw them, what were they doing?'

'I . . . I can't exactly recall.'

'Well then, let me jog your memory.' Here I made an informed guess at what any two young lady assistants would be doing at the height of business during the summer sales. 'Were they not huddled together in an act of total recall of last night in the disco or Palais de Hop? Were they not blind and deaf to the cries of shirt-buying clerics? Were they not utterly oblivious to the life around them?'

The jury was looking at me and smiling, and some of the ladies nodded understandingly. I could feel that the old darlings knew all about young lady non-assistants in Oxford Street.

'Well, Mr Pratt. Isn't that exactly what they were doing?'

'It may have been, your Honour.'

'So is it surprising that my client took his purchase and went off in search of some more attentive assistance?'

'But I followed him downstairs, to the Hall of Food.'

'Have you any reason to suppose he wouldn't have paid for his shirts there, given the slightest opportunity?'

'I saw no sign of his attempting to do so.'

'Just as you saw no sign of the sales-ladies attempting to take his money?'

'No but . . .'

'It's a risky business entering your store, isn't it, Pratt?' I put it to him. 'You can't get served and no one speaks to you except to tell you that you're under arrest.'

I sat down to some smiles from the jury and a glance from the Bull. An eager young man named Ken Rydal was prosecuting. I had run up against this Rydal, a ginger-haired, spectacled wonder who might once have been a senior scout, and won the Duke of Edinburgh award for being left out on the mountainside for a week. 'Ken' felt a strong sense of team spirit and loyalty to the Metropolitan Police, and he was keen as mustard to add the Reverend Mordred Skinner to the notches on his woggle.

'Did you see Mr Skinner make any attempt to pay for his shirts in the Hall of Food?' Ken asked Pratt.

I read a note from my client that had finally arrived by way of the usher.

'No. No, I didn't,' said Pratt.

Ken was smiling, about to make a little scout-like funny. 'He didn't ask for them to be wrapped up with a pound of ham, for instance?'

'No, sir.' Pratt laughed and looked round the Court, to see that no one was laughing. And the Bull was glaring at Ken.

'This is not a music hall, Mr Rydal. As Mr Rumpole has reminded us, this is an extremely serious case. The whole of the Reverend gentleman's future is at stake.' The judge glanced at the clock, as if daring it not to be time for lunch. The clock co-operated, and the Bull rose, muttering 'Ten past two, members of the jury.'

I crumpled my client's note with some disgust and threw it on the floor as I stood to bow to the Bull. The Reverend Mordred had just told me he wasn't prepared to give evidence in his own defence. I would have to get him on his own and twist his arm a little.

*

'I simply couldn't take the oath.'

'What's the matter with you? Have you no religion?'

The cleric smiled politely and said, less as a question than a statement of fact, 'You don't like me very much, do you?'

We were sitting in one of the brighter hostelries in Newington Causeway. The bleak and sour-smelling saloon bar was sparsely populated by two ailing cleaning-ladies drinking stout, another senior citizen who was smoking the dog ends he kept in an old Oxo tin and exercising his talents as a Cougher for England, and a large drunk in a woolly bobble-hat who kept banging in and out the Gents with an expression of increasing euphoria. I had entrusted to Mr Morse the solicitor the tricky task of taking Miss Evelyn Skinner to lunch in the public canteen at the Sessions House. I imagined he'd get the full blast of her anxiety over the grey, unidentifiable meat and two veg. Meanwhile I had whisked the Reverend out to the pub where he sat with the intolerably matey expression vicars always assume in licensed premises.

'I felt you might tell me the truth. You of all people. Having your collar on back to front must mean something.'

'Truth is often dangerous. It must be approached cautiously, don't you think?' My client bit nervously into a singularly unattractive sausage. I tried to approach the matter cautiously.

'I've noticed with women,' I told him, 'with my wife, for instance, when we go out on our dreaded Saturday morning shopping expeditions, that She Who Must Be Obeyed is in charge of the shopping-basket. She makes the big decisions. How much Vim goes in it and so forth. When the shopping's bought, I get the job of carrying the damn thing home.'

'Simple faith is far more important than the constant scramble after unimportant facts.' Mordred was back on the old theology. 'I believe that's what the lives of the Saints tell us.'

Enough of this Cathedral gossip. We were due back in Court in half an hour and I let him have it between the eyes. 'Well, my simple faith tells me that your sister had the basket in the shirt department.'

'Does it?' He blinked most of the time, but not then.

'When Pratt saw you in the Hall of Food you were carrying the shopping-basket, which she'd handed you on the escalator.'

'Perhaps.'

'Because she'd taken the shirts and put them in the bag when you were too busy composing your sermon on the Problem of Evil to notice.' I lit a small cigar at that point, and Mordred took a sip of sour bitter. He was still smiling as he started to talk, almost shyly at first, then with increasing confidence.

'She was a pretty child. It's difficult to believe it now. She was attracted to bright things, boiled sweets, red apples, jewellery in Woolworth's. As she grew older it became worse. She would take things she couldn't possibly need ... Spectacles, bead handbags, cigarette cases although she never smoked. She was like a magpie. I thought she'd improved. I try to watch her as much as I can, although you're right, on that day I was involved with my sermon. As a matter of fact, I had no need of such shirts. I may be old-fashioned but I always wear a dog collar. Always.'

'Even on rambles with the Lads' Brigade?'

'All the same,' my client said firmly, 'I believe she did it out of love.'

Well, now we had a defence: although he didn't seem to be totally aware of it.

'Those are the facts?'

'They seem to be of no interest to anyone – except my immediate family. But that's what I'm bound to say, if I take my oath on the Bible.'

'But you were prepared to lie to me,' I reminded him. He smiled again, that small, maddening smile.

'Mr Rumpole. I have the greatest respect for your skill as an advocate, but I have never been in danger of mistaking you for Almighty God.'

'Tell the truth *now*. She'll only get a fine. Nothing!'

He seemed to consider the possibility, then he shook his head.

'To her it would be everything. She couldn't bear it.'

'What about you? You'd give up your whole life?'

'It seems the least I can do for her.' He was smiling again, hanging that patient little grin out like an advertisement for his humility and his deep sense of spiritual superiority to a worldly Old Bailey Hack.

I ground out my small cigar in the overflowing ashtray and almost shouted. 'Good God! I don't know how I keep my temper.'

'I do sympathize. He found His ideas irritated people dreadfully. Particularly lawyers.' He was almost laughing now. 'But you do understand? I am quite unable to give evidence on oath to the jury.'

*

As every criminal lawyer knows it's very difficult to get a client off unless he's prepared to take the trouble of going into the witness-box, to face up to the prosecution, and to demonstrate his innocence or at least his credentials as a fairly likeable character who might buy you a pint after work and whom you would not really want to see festering in the nick. After all fair's fair, the jury have just seen the prosecution witnesses put through it, so why should the prisoner at the Bar sit in solemn silence in the dock? I knew that if the Reverend told his story, with suitable modesty and regret, I could get him off and Evelyn would merely get a well-earned talking to. When he refused to give evidence I could almost hear the rustle of unfrocking in the distance.

Short of having my client dragged to the Bible by a sturdy usher, when he would no doubt stand mute of malice, there was nothing I could do other than address the jury in the unlikely hope of persuading them that there was no reliable evidence on which they could possibly convict the silent vicar. I was warming to my work as Bullingham sat inert, breathing hoarsely, apparently about to erupt.

'Members of the jury,' I told them. 'There is a Golden Thread that runs throughout British justice. The prosecution must prove its case. The defence has to prove nothing.'

'*Mr* Rumpole . . .' A sound came from the judge like the first rumble they once heard from Mount Vesuvius.

I soldiered on. 'The Reverend Mordred Skinner need not trouble to move four yards from that dock to the witness-box unless the prosecution has produced evidence that he *intended* to steal – and not to pay in another department.'

'Mr *Rumpole*.' The earth tremor grew louder. I raised my voice a semitone.

'Never let it be said that a man is forced to prove his innocence! Our fathers have defied kings for that principle, members of the jury. They forced King John to sign Magna Carta and sent King Charles to the scaffold and it has been handed down even to the Inner London Sessions, Newington Causeway.'

'If you'd let me get a word in edgeways . . .'

'And now it is in your trust!'

I'm not, as this narrative may have made clear, a religious man; but what happened next made me realize how the Israelites felt when the waters divided, and understand the incredulous reaction of the disciples when an uninteresting glass of water flushed darkly and smelt of the grape. I can recall the exact words of the indubitable miracle. Bullingham said, 'Mr Rumpole. I entirely agree with everything you say. And,' he added glowering threateningly at the Scout for the prosecution, 'I shall direct the jury accordingly.'

The natural malice of the Bull had been quelled by his instinctive respect for the law. He found there was no case to answer.

I met my liberated client in the Gents, a place where his sister was unable to follow him. As we stood side by side at the porcelain I congratulated him.

'I was quite reconciled to losing. I don't think my sister would have stood by me somehow. The disgrace you see. I think,' he looked almost wistful, 'I think I should have been alone.'

'You'd have been unfrocked.'

'It might have been extremely restful. Not to have to pretend to any sort of sanctity. Not to pretend to be different. To be exactly the same as everybody else.'

I looked at him standing there in the London Sessions loo, his mac over his arm, his thin neck half-strangled by a dog collar. He longed for the relaxed life of an ordinary sinner, but he had no right to it.

'Don't long for a life of crime, old darling,' I told him. 'You've obviously got no talent for it.'

Upstairs we met Evelyn and Mr Morse. The sister gave me a flicker of something which might have been a smile of gratitude.

'It was a miracle,' I told her.

'Really? I thought the judge was exceedingly fair. Come along, Mordred. He's somewhere else you know, Mr Rumpole. He can't even realize it's all over.' She attacked her brother again. 'Better put your mac on, dear. It's raining outside.'

'Yes, Evelyn. Yes. I'll put it on.' He did so, obediently.

'You must come to tea in the Rectory, Mr Rumpole.' I had a final chilly smile from Evelyn.

'Alas, dear lady. The pressure of work. These days I have so little time for pleasure.'

'Say goodbye to Mr Rumpole, Mordred.'

The cleric shook my hand, and gave me a confidential aside. 'Goodbye, Mr Rumpole. You see it was entirely a family matter. There was no need for anyone to know anything about it.'

And so he went, in his sister's charge, back to the isolation of the Rectory.

*

> Will no one tell me what she sings?
> Perhaps the plaintive numbers flow
> For old, unhappy, far-off things
> And murders long ago.

Had I, against all the odds, learned something from the Reverend? Was I now more conscious of the value of secrecy, of not dropping bombs of information which might cause ruin and havoc on the family front? It seems unlikely, but I do not know why else I was busily destroying the archive, pushing the photographs into the unused fireplace in my Chambers and applying a match, and dropping the durable articles, including the ostrich egg, into the waste-paper basket. As the flames licked across the paper and set Mrs Tempest the arsonist curling into ashy oblivion the door opened to admit Miss Trant.

'Rumpole! What on earth are you doing?'

I turned from the smoking relics.

'You keep things, Miss Trant? Mementoes? Locks of hair? Old letters, tied up in ribbon? "Memories",' I started to sing tunelessly, ' "were made of this." '

'Not really.'

'Good.'

'I've got my first brief. From when I prosecuted you in Dock Street.' This was the occasion when I tricked Miss Trant into boring the wretched Beak with a huge pile of law, and so defeated her.* It was not an incident of which I am particularly proud.

'Destroy it. Forget the past, eh? Miss Trant. Look to the future!'

'All right. Aren't you coming up to Guthrie Featherstone's room? We're laying on a few drinks for George.'

'George? Yes, of course. He'll have a lot to celebrate.'

Guthrie Featherstone, Q.C., M.P., the suave and elegant Conservative-Labour M.P. for somewhere or another who, when he is not passing the 'Gas Mains Enabling Bill' or losing politely at golf to various of Her Majesty's judges, condescends to exercise his duties as Head of Chambers (a post to which I was due

*See 'Rumpole and the Married Lady' in *Rumpole of the Bailey*, Penguin Books, 1978.

to succeed by order of seniority of barristers in practice, when I was pipped at the post by young Guthrie taking silk. Well, I didn't want it anyway*): Guthrie Featherstone occupied the best room in Chambers (first floor, high windows, overlooking Temple Gardens) and he was engaged in making a speech to our assembled members. In a corner of the room I saw our clerk Henry and Dianne the typist in charge of a table decorated by several bottles of Jack Pommeroy's cooking champagne. I made straight for the booze, and at first Featherstone's speech seemed but a background noise, like Radio Four.

'It's well known among lawyers that the finest advocates never make the best judges. The glory of the advocate is to be opinionated, brash, fearless, partisan, hectoring, rude, cunning and unfair.'

'Well done, Rumpole!' This, of course, was Erskine-Brown.

'Thank you very much, Claude.' I raised my glass to him.

'The ideal judge, however,' Featherstone babbled on, 'is detached, courteous, patient, painstaking and above all, quiet. These qualities are to be found personified in the latest addition to our Bench of Circuit Judges.'

' "Circus" Judges, Rumpole calls them,' Uncle Tom said loudly, to no one in particular.

'Ladies and gentlemen,' the Q.C., M.P. concluded, 'please raise your glasses to His Honour Judge George Frobisher.'

Everyone was smiling and drinking. So the news had broken. George was a Circuit Judge. No doubt the crowds were dancing in Fleet Street. I moved to my old friend to add my word of congratulation.

'Your health George. Coupled with the name of Mrs Ida Tempest?'

'No, Rumpole. No.' George shook his head, I thought sadly.

'What do you mean, "No"? Mrs Tempest should be here. To share in your triumph. Celebrating back at the Royal Borough Hotel, is she? She'll have the Moët on ice by the time you get back.'

---

*See 'Rumpole and the Younger Generation' in *Rumpole of the Bailey*, Penguin Books, 1978.

'Mrs Tempest left the Royal Borough last week, Rumpole. I have no means of knowing where to find her.'

At which point we were rudely interrupted by Guthrie Featherstone calling on George to make a speech. Other members joined in and Henry filled up George's glass in preparation for the great oration.

'I'm totally unprepared to *say* anything on this occasion,' George said, taking a bit of paper from his pocket to general laughter. Poor old George could never do anything off the cuff.

'Ladies and gentlemen,' George started. 'I have long felt the need to retire from the hurly-burly of practice at the Bar.'

'Comes as news to me that George Frobisher had a practice at the Bar,' Uncle Tom said to no one much in a deafening whisper.

'To escape from the benevolent despotism of Henry, now our senior clerk.' George twinkled.

'Can you do a Careless Driving at Croydon tomorrow, your Honour?' Henry called out in the cheeky manner he had adopted since he was an office boy.

Laughter.

'No, Henry, I can't. So I have long considered applying for a Circuit Judgeship in a Rural Area ...'

'Where are you going to, George? Glorious Devon?' Featherstone interrupted.

'I think they're starting me off in Luton. And I hope, very soon, I'll have the pleasure of you all appearing before me!'

'Where did George say they were sending him?' Uncle Tom asked.

'I think he said Luton, Uncle Tom,' I told him.

'Luton, glorious Luton!' Henry sometimes goes too far, for a clerk. I was glad to see that Dianne ssshed him firmly.

'Naturally as a judge, as one, however humble, of Her Majesty's judges, certain standards will be expected of me,' George went on, I thought in a tone of some regret.

'No more carousing in Pommeroy's with Horace Rumpole!' Uncle Tom was still barracking.

'And I mean to try, to do my best, to live up to those standards. That's really all I have to say. Thank you. Thank you all very much.'

There was tumultuous applause, increased in volume by the cooking champagne, and George joined me in a corner of the room. Uncle Tom was induced to make his speech, traditional and always the same on all Chambers' occasions, and George and I talked quietly together.

'George. I'm sorry. About Mrs Tempest . . .'

'It was your fault, Rumpole.' George looked at me with an air of severe rebuke.

'My fault!' I stood amazed. 'But I said nothing. Not a word. You know me, George. Discretion is Rumpole's middle name. I was silent. As the tomb.'

'When I brought her to dinner with you and Hilda. She recognized you at once.'

'She didn't show it!'

'She's a remarkable woman.'

'I was junior Counsel, for her former husband. I'm sure he led her on. She made an excellent impression. In the witness-box.' I tried to sound comforting.

'She made an excellent impression on me, Rumpole. She thought you'd be bound to tell me.'

'She thought that?'

'So she decided to tell me first.'

I stood looking at George, feeling unreasonably guilty. Somewhere in the distance Uncle Tom was going through the usual form of words.

'As the oldest member of Chambers, I can remember this set before C. H. Wystan, Rumpole's revered father-in-law, took over. It was in old Barnaby Hawks' time and the young men were myself, Everett Longbarrow, and old Willoughby Grime, who became Lord Chief Justice of Basutoland . . . He went on Circuit, I understand, wearing a battered opera hat and dispensed rough justice . . .'

The other barristers joined in the well-known chorus 'Under a Bong Tree'.

'As I remember, Ida Tempest got three years.'

'Yes,' said George.

'Her former husband got seven.' I was trying to cheer him up. 'I don't believe Ida actually applied the match.'

'All the same, it was a risk I didn't feel able to take.'

'You didn't notice the smell of burning, George? Any night in the Royal Borough Hotel . . . ?'

'Of course not! But the Lord Chancellor's secretary had just told me of my appointment. It doesn't do for a judge's wife to have done three years, even with full remission.'

I looked at George. Was the sacrifice, I wondered, really necessary? 'Did you *have* to be a judge, George?'

'I thought of that, of course. But I had the appointment. You know, at my age, Rumpole, it's difficult to learn any new sort of trade.'

'We had no work in those days,' Uncle Tom continued his trip down memory lane. 'We had no briefs of any kind. We spent our days practising chip shots, trying to get an old golf ball into the waste-paper basket with . . .'

'A mashie niblick!' the other barristers sang.

'Well, that was as good a training as any for life at the Bar,' Uncle Tom told them.

I filled George's glass. 'Drink up, George. There may be other ladies . . . turning up at the Royal Borough Hotel.'

'I very much doubt it. Every night when I sit at the table for one, I shall think – if only I'd never taken her to dinner at Rumpole's! Then I might never have known, don't you see? We could have been perfectly happy together.'

'Of course, C. H. Wystan never ever took silk. But now we have a Q.C., M.P. and dear old George Frobisher, a Circus, beg his pardon, a Circuit Judge!' Uncle Tom was raising his glass to George, his hand was trembling and he was spilling a good deal on his cuff.

'Sometimes I feel it will be difficult to forgive you, Rumpole,' George said, very quietly.

'But I do recall when dear old Willoughby Grime was appointed to Basutoland, we celebrated the matter in song.'

'George, what did I do?' I protested. 'I didn't say anything.' But it wasn't true. My mere existence had been enough to deny George his happiness.

At which point the other barristers raised their glasses to

George and started to sing 'For He's a Jolly Good Fellow'. I left them, and went out into the silence of the Temple, where I could still hear them singing.

*

Next Saturday morning I was acting the part of the native bearer with the Vim basket, following She Who Must Be Obeyed on our ritual shopping expedition.

'They've never made George Frobisher a judge!' My wife seemed to feel it an occasion for ridicule and contempt.

'In my view an excellent appointment. I shall expect to have a good record of acquittals. In the Luton Crown Court.'

'When are they going to make you a judge, Rumpole?'

'Don't ask silly questions ... I'd start every Sentence with, "There but for the Grace of God goes Horace Rumpole".'

'I can imagine what *she's* feeling like.' Hilda sniffed.

'She ... ?'

'The cat-that-swallowed-the-cream! Her Honour Mrs Judge. Mrs Ida Tempest'll think she's quite the thing, I'll be bound.'

'No. She's gone.'

'Gone, Rumpole? What did George say about that?'

> 'Cried, and the world cried too, "Our's the Treasure".
> Suddenly, as rare things will, she vanished.'

We climbed on a bus, heavily laden, back to Casa Rumpole.

'George is well out of it, if he wants my opinion.'

'I don't think he does.'

'What?'

'Want your opinion.'

Later, in our kitchen, as she stored the Vim away under the sink and I prepared our Saturday morning G and T, a thought occurred to me. 'Do you know? I'm not sure I should've taken up as a lawyer.'

'Whatever do you mean?'

'Perhaps I should have taken up as a vicar.'

'Rumpole. Have you been getting at the gin already?'

'Faith not facts, is what we need, do you think?'

Hilda was busy unpacking the saucepan scourers. Perhaps she didn't quite get my drift.

'George Frobisher has always been a bad influence, keeping you out drinking,' she said. 'Let's hope I'll be seeing more of you, now he's been made a judge.'

'I'd never have got to know all these *facts* about people if I hadn't set up as a lawyer.'

'Of course you should have been a lawyer, Rumpole!'

'Why exactly?'

'If you hadn't set up as a lawyer, if you hadn't gone into Daddy's Chambers, you'd never have met me, Rumpole!'

I looked at her, suddenly seeing great vistas of what my life might have been.

'That's true,' I said. 'Dammit, that's very true.'

'Put the Gumption away for me, will you, Rumpole?'

She Who Must Be Obeyed. Of course I did.

Rumpole and the Showfolk

I have written elsewhere of my old clerk Albert Handyside who served me very well for a long term of years, being adept at flattering solicitors' clerks, buying them glasses of Guinness and inquiring tenderly after their tomato plants, with the result that the old darlings were inclined to come across with the odd Dangerous and Careless, Indecent Assault, or Take and Drive Away which Albert was inclined to slip in Rumpole's direction. All this led to higher things such as Robbery, Unlawful Wounding and even Murder; and in general for that body of assorted crimes on which my reputation is founded. I first knew Albert when he was a nervous office boy in the Chambers of C. H. Wystan, my learned father-in-law; and when he grew to be a head clerk of magisterial dimensions we remained firm friends and often had a jar together in Pommeroy's Wine Bar in the evenings, on which relaxed occasions I would tell Albert my celebrated anecdotes of Bench and Bar and, unlike She Who Must Be Obeyed, he was always kind enough to laugh no matter how often he had heard them before.

Dear old Albert had one slight failing, a weakness which occurs among the healthiest of constitutions. He was apt to get into a terrible flurry over the petty cash. I never inquired into his book-keeping system; but I believe it might have been improved by the invention of the Abacus, or a monthly check-up by a Primary School child well versed in simple addition. It is also indubitably true that you can't pour drink down the throats of solicitors' managing clerks without some form of subsidy, and I'm sure Albert dipped liberally into the petty cash for this purpose as well as to keep himself in the large Bells and sodas, two or three of which sufficed for his simple lunch. Personally I never begrudged Albert any of this grant in aid, but ugly words such as embezzlement were uttered by Erskine-Brown and others, and, spurred on by our second clerk Harry who clearly thirsted for promotion, my learned friends were induced to part with Albert Handyside. I missed him very much. Our new clerk Henry goes to Pommeroy's with our typist Dianne, and tells her about his exploits when on holiday with the *Club Méditerranée* in Corfu. I do not think either of them would laugh at my legal anecdotes.

After he left us Albert shook the dust of London from his shoes and went up North, to some God-lost place called Grimble, and there joined a firm of solicitors as managing clerk. No doubt Northerly barristers' clerks bought him Guinness and either he had no control of the petty cash or the matter was not subjected to too close an inspection. From time to time he sent me a Christmas card on which was inscribed among the bells and holly 'Compliments of the Season, Mr Rumpole, sir. And I'm going to bring you up here for a nice little murder just as soon as I get the opportunity. Yours respectfully, A. Handyside.' At long last a brief did arrive. Mr Rumpole was asked to appear at the Grimble Assizes, to be held before Mr Justice Skelton in the Law Courts, Grimble: the title of the piece being the Queen (she does keep enormously busy prosecuting people) *versus* Margaret Hartley. The only item on the programme was 'Wilful Murder'.

*

Now you may have noticed that certain theatrical phrases have crept into the foregoing paragraph. This is not as inappropriate as it may sound, for the brief I was going up to Grimble for on the Inter-City train (a journey about as costly as a trip across the Atlantic) concerned a murder which took place in the Theatre Royal, East Grimble, a place of entertainment leased by the 'Frere-Hartley Players': the victim was one G. P. Frere, the leading actor, and my client was his wife known as 'Maggie Hartley', co-star and joint director of the company. And as I read on into R. *v.* Hartley it became clear that the case was like too many of

Rumpole's, a born loser: that is to say that unless we drew a drunken prosecutor or a jury of anarchists there seemed no reasonable way in which it might be won.

One night after the performance, Albert's instructions told me, the stage-door keeper, a Mr Croft, heard the sound of raised voices and quarrelling from the dressing-room shared by G. P. Frere and his wife Maggie Hartley. Mr Croft was having a late cup of tea in his cubby-hole with a Miss Catherine Hope, a young actress in the company, and they heard two shots fired in quick succession. Mr Croft went along the passage to investigate and opened the dressing-room door. The scene that met his eyes was, to say the least, dramatic.

It appeared from Mr Croft's evidence that the dressing-room was in a state of considerable confusion. Clothes were scattered round the room, and chairs overturned. The long mirror which ran down the length of the wall was shattered at the end furthest from the door. Near the door Mr G. P. Frere, wearing a silk dressing-gown, was sitting slumped in a chair, bleeding profusely and already dead. My client was standing half-way down the room still wearing the long white evening-dress she had worn on the stage that night. Her make-up was smudged and in her right hand she held a well-oiled service revolver. A bullet had left this weapon and entered Mr Frere's body between the third and fourth metacarpal. In order to make quite sure that her learned Counsel didn't have things too easy, Maggie Hartley had then opened her mouth and spoken, so said Croft, the following unforgettable words, here transcribed without punctuation.

'I killed him what could I do with him help me.'

In all subsequent interviews the actress said that she remembered nothing about the quarrel in the dressing-room, the dreadful climax had been blotted from her mind. She was no doubt, and still remained, in a state of shock.

I was brooding on this hopeless defence when an elderly guard acting the part of an air hostess whispered excitedly into the intercom. 'We are now arriving at Grimble Central. Grimble Central. Please collect your hand baggage.' I merged into a place which seemed to be nestling somewhere within the Arctic Circle, the air bit sharply, it was bloody cold, and a blue-nosed Albert was there to meet me.

*

'After I left your Chambers in disgrace, Mr Rumpole ...'

'After a misunderstanding, shall we say.'

'My then wife told me she was disgusted with me. She packed her bags and went to live with her married sister in Enfield.'

Albert was smiling contentedly, and that was something I could unders and. I had just had, *à coté de* Chez Albert Handyside, a meal which his handsome, still youngish second wife referred to as tea, but which had all the appurtenances of ar. excellent cold luncheon with the addition of hot scones, Dundee cake and strawberry jam.

'Bit of luck then really, you getting the petty cash so "confused".'

'All the same. I do miss the old days clerking for you in the Temple, sir. How are things down South, Mr Rumpole?'

'Down South? Much as usual. Barristers lounging about in the sun. Munching grapes to the lazy sounds of plucked guitars.'

Mrs Handyside the Second returned to the room with another huge pot of dark brown Indian tea. he replenished the Rumpole cup and Albert and I fell to discussing the tea-table subject of murder and sudden death.

'Of course it's not the Penge Bungalow Job.' Albert was referring to my most notable murder and greatest triumph, a case I did at Lewes Assizes alone and without the so-called aid of leading Counsel. 'But it's quite a decent little case, sir, in its way. A murder among the showfolk, as they terms them.'

'The showfolk, yes. Definitely worth the detour. There is, of course, one little fly in the otherwise interesting ointment.'

Albert, knowing me as he did, knew quite well what manner of insect I was referring to. I have never taken silk. I remain, at my advanced age, a 'junior' barrister. The brief in R. *v*. Hartley had only one drawback, it announced that I was to be 'led' by a local silk, Mr Jarvis Allen, Q.C. I hated the prospect of this obscure North Country Queen's Counsel getting all the fun.

'I told my senior partner, sir. I told him straight. Mr Rumpole's quite capable of doing this one on his own.' Albert was suitably apologetic.

'Reminded him, did you? I did the Penge Bungalow Murders alone and without a leader.'

'The senior partner did seem to feel ...'

'I know. I'm not on the Lord Chancellor's guest list. I never get invited to breakfast in knee breeches. It's not Rumpole, Q.C. Just Rumpole, Queer Customer ...'

'Oo I'm sure you're not,' Mrs Handyside the Second poured me another comforting cup of concentrated tannin.

'It's a murder, sir. That's attracted quite a lot of local attention.'

'And silks go with murder like steak goes with kidney! This Jarvis Allen, Q.C. ... Pretty competent sort of man, is he?'

'I've only seen him on the Bench ...'

'On the what?'

The Bench seemed no sort of a place to see dedicated defenders.

'Sits as Recorder here. Gave a young tearaway in our office three years for a punch-up at the Grimble United Ground.'

'There's no particular *art* involved in getting people into prison, Albert,' I said severely. 'How is he at keeping them out?'

After tea we had a conference fixed up with my leader and client in prison. There was no women's prison at Grimble, so our client was lodged in a room converted from an unused dispensary in the Hospital Wing of the masculine nick. She seemed older than I had expected as she sat looking composed, almost detached, surrounded by her legal advisers. It was, at that first conference, as though the case concerned someone else, and had not yet engaged her full attention.

'Mrs Frere.' Jarvis Allen, the learned Q.C. started off. He was a thin, methodical man with rimless glasses and a general rimless appearance. He had made a voluminous note in red, green and blue Biro: it didn't seem to have given him much cause for hope.

'Our client is known as Maggie Hartley, sir,' Albert reminded him. 'In the profession.'

'I think she'd better be known as Mrs Frere. In Court,' Allen said firmly. 'Now, Mrs Frere. Tommy Pierce is prosecuting and of course I know him well ... and if we went to see the judge, Skelton's a perfectly reasonable fellow. I think there's a sporting chance ... I'm making no promises, mind you, there's a sporting chance they might let us plead to manslaughter!'

He brought the last sentence out triumphantly, like a Christmas present. Jarvis Allen was exercising his remarkable talent for getting people locked up. I lit a small cigar, and said nothing.

'Of course, we'd have to accept manslaughter. I'm sure Mr Rumpole agrees. You agree, don't you, Rumpole?' My leader turned to me for support. I gave him little comfort.

'Much more agreeable doing ten years for manslaughter than ten years for murder,' I said. 'Is that the choice you're offering?'

'I don't know if you've read the evidence ... Our client was found with the gun in her hand.' Allen was beginning to get tetchy.

I thought this over and said, 'Stupid place to have it. If she'd actually *planned* a murder.'

'All the same. It leaves us without a defence.'

'Really? Do you think so? I was looking at the statement of Alan Copeland. He is ...' I ferreted among the depositions.

'What they call the "juvenile", I believe, Mr Rumpole,' Albert reminded me.

'The "juvenile", yes.' I read from Mr Copeland's statement. 'I've worked with G. P. Frere for three seasons ... G.P. drank a good deal. Always interested in some girl in the cast. A new one every year ...'

'Jealousy might be a powerful motive, for our client. That's a two-edged sword, Rumpole.' Allen was determined to look on the dreary side.

'Two-edged, yes. Most swords are.' I went on reading. 'He quarrelled violently with his wife, Maggie Hartley. On one occasion, after the dress rehearsal of *The Master Builder*, he threw a glass of milk stout in her face in front of the entire company ...'

'She had a good deal of provocation, we can put that to the

judge. That merely reduces it to manslaughter.' I was getting bored with my leader's chatter of manslaughter.

I gave my bundle of depositions to Albert and stood up, looking at our client to see if she would fit the part I had in mind.

'What you need in a murder is an unlikeable corpse ... Then if you can find a likeable defendant ... you're off to the races! Who knows? We might even reduce the crime to innocence.'

'Rumpole.' Allen had clearly had enough of my hopeless optimism. 'As I've had to tell Mrs Frere very frankly. There is a clear admission of guilt – which is not disputed.'

'What she said to the stage-door man, Mr...'

'Croft.' Albert supplied the name.

'I killed him, what could I do with him? Help me.' Allen repeated the most damning evidence with great satisfaction. 'You've read that, at least?'

'Yes, I've read it. That's the trouble.'

'What *do* you mean?'

'I mean, the trouble is, I read it. I didn't *hear* it. None of us did. And I don't suppose Mr Croft had it spelled out to him, with all the punctuation.'

'Really, Rumpole. I suppose they make jokes about murder cases in London.'

I ignored this bit of impertinence and went on to give the Q.C. some unmerited assistance. 'Suppose she said ... Suppose our client said, "I killed him" and then,' I paused for breath, ' "What could I do with him? Help me!"?'

I saw our client look at me, for the first time. When she spoke her voice, like Cordelia's, was ever soft, gentle and low, an excellent thing in woman.

'That's the reading,' she said. I must admit I was puzzled, and asked for an explanation.

'What?'

'The reading of the line. You can tell them. That's exactly how I said it.'

At last, it seemed, we had found *something* she remembered. I thought it an encouraging sign; but it wasn't really my business.

'I'm afraid, dear lady,' I gave her a small bow, 'I shan't be able to tell them anything. Who am I, after all, but the ageing juvenile? The reading of the line, as you call it, will have to come from your Q.C., Mr Jarvis Allen, who is playing the lead at the moment.'

*

After the conference I gave Albert strict instructions as to how our client was to dress for her starring appearance in the Grimble Assize Court (plain black suit, white blouse, no make-up, hair neat, voice gentle but audible to any O.A.P. with a National Health deaf-aid sitting in the back row of the jury, absolutely no reaction during the prosecution case except for a well-controlled sigh of grief at the mention of her deceased husband) and then I suggested we met later for a visit to the scene of the crime. Her Majesty's Counsel for the defence had to rush home to write an urgent, and no doubt profitable, opinion on the planning of the new Grimble Gas Works and so was unfortunately unable to join us.

'You go if you like, Rumpole,' he said as he vanished into a funereal Austin Princess. 'I can't see how it's going to be of the slightest assistance.'

The ¬heatre Royal, an ornate but crumbling Edwardian Music Hall, which might once have housed George Formby and Rob Wilton, was bolted and barred. Albert and I stood in the rain and read a torn poster.

A cat was rubbing itself against the poster. We heard the North Country voice of an elderly man calling 'Puss ... Puss ... Bedtime, pussy.'

The cat went and we followed, round to the corner where the stage-door man, Mr Croft, no doubt, was opening his door and offering a saucer of milk. We made ourselves known as a couple of lawyers and asked for a look at the scene.

'Mr Derwent's round the front of the house. First door on the right.'

I moved up the corridor to a door and, opening it, had the unnerving experience of standing on a dimly lit stage. Behind

THE THEATRE ROYAL, EAST GRIMBLE

The Frere-Hartley Players
present
G. P. Frere and Maggie Hartley

in

'PRIVATE LIVES'

by

NOËL COWARD

with

Alan Copeland
Catherine Hope

Directed by Daniel Derwent

Stalls £1.50 and £1. Circle £1 and 75p.
Matinées and Senior Citizens 50p.

me flapped a canvas balcony, and a view of the Mediterranean. As I wandered forward a voice called me out of the gloom.

'Who is it? Down here, I'm in the Stalls Bar.'

There was a light somewhere, a long way off. I went down some steps that led to the stalls and felt my way towards the light with Albert blundering after me. At last we reached the open glass door of a small bar, its dark-red walls hung with photographs of the company, and we were in the presence of a little gnome-like man, wearing a bow tie and a double-breasted suit, and that cheerily smiling but really quite expressionless apple-cheeked sort of face you see on some ventriloquist's dolls. His boot-black hair looked as if it had been dyed. He admitted to Albert that he was Daniel Derwent and at the moment in charge of the Frere-Hartley Players.

'Or what's left of them. Decimated, that's what we've been! If you've come with a two-hander for a couple of rather un-talented juveniles, I'd be delighted to put it on. I suppose you *are* in the business.'

'The business?' I wondered what business he meant. But I didn't wonder long.

'Show business. The profession.'

'No . . . Another . . . profession altogether.'

I saw he had been working at a table in the empty bar, which was smothered with papers, bills and receipts.

'Our old manager left us in a state of total confusion,' Derwent said. 'And my ear's out to *here* answering the telephone.

'The vultures can't hear of an actor shot in East Grimble but half the Character Men in *Spotlight* are after me for the job. Well, I've told everyone. Nothing's going to be decided till after Maggie's trial. We're not re-opening till then. It wouldn't seem right, somehow. *What* other profession?'

'We're lawyers, Mr Derwent,' Albert told him. 'Defending.'

'Maggie's case?' Derwent didn't stop smiling.

'My name's Handyside of Instructing Solicitors. This is Mr Rumpole from London, junior Counsel for the defence.'

'A London barrister. In the Sticks!' The little Thespian seemed to find it amusing. 'Well, Grimble's hardly a number-one touring date. All the same, I suppose murder's a draw. Anywhere . . . Care for a tiny rum?'

'That's very kind.' It was bitter cold, the unused theatre seemed to be saving on central heating and I was somewhat sick at heart at the prospect of our defence. A rum would do me no harm at all.

'Drop of orange in it? Or as she comes?'

'As she comes, thank you.'

'I always take a tiny rum, for the chords. Well, we depend on the chords, don't we, in our professions.'

Apart from a taste for rum I didn't see then what I had in common, professionally or otherwise, with Mr Derwent. I wandered off with my drink in my hand to look at the photographs of the Frere-Hartley Players. As I did so I could hear the theatre-manager chattering to Albert.

'We could have done a bomb tonight. The money we've turned away. You couldn't buy publicity like it.' Derwent was saying.

'No . . . No, I don't suppose you could.'

'Week after week all we get in the *Grimble Argus* is a little para. "Maggie Hartley took her part well." And now we're all over the front page. And we can't play. It breaks your heart. It does really.' I heard him freshen his rum with another slug from the bottle. 'Poor old G.P. could have drawn more money dead than he ever could when he was alive. Well, at least he's sober tonight, wherever he is.'

'The late Mr G. P. Frere was fond of a drink occasionally?' Albert made use of the probing understatement.

'Not that his performance suffered. He didn't act any worse when he was drunk.'

I was looking at a glossy photograph of the late Mr G. P. Frere, taken about ten years ago I should imagine: it showed a man with grey sideburns and an open-necked shirt with a silk scarf round his neck and eyes that were self-consciously quizzical. A man who, despite the passage of the years, was still determined to go on saying 'Who's for tennis?'

'What I admired about old G.P.,' I heard Derwent say, 'was his selfless concern for others! Never left you with the sole responsibility of entertaining the audience. He'd try to help by upstaging you. Or moving on your laugh line. He once tore up a newspaper all through my long speech in *Waiting for Godot* ... Now you wouldn't do that, would you, Mr Rumpole? Not in anyone's long speech. Well, of course not.'

He had moved, for his last remarks, to a point rather below, but still too close to, my left ear. I was looking at the photographs of a moderately pretty young girl, wearing a seafaring sweater, whose lips were parted as if to suck in a quick draft of ozone when out for a day with the local dinghy club.

'Miss Christine Hope?' I asked.

'Miss Christine Hopeless I called her.' This Derwent didn't seem to have a particularly high opinion of his troupe. 'God knows what G.P. saw in her. She did that audition speech from St Joan. All breathless and excited ... as if she'd just run up four flights of stairs because the angel voices were calling her about a little part in *Crossroads*. "We could *do* something with her," G.P. said. "I know what," I told him. "Burn her at the stake." '

I had come to a wall on which there were big photographs of various characters, a comic charlady, a beautiful woman in a white evening-dress, a Duchess in a tiara, a neat secretary in glasses, and a tattered siren who might have been Sadie Thompson in *Rain* if my theatrical memory served me right. All the faces were different, and they were all the faces of Maggie Hartley.

'Your client. My leading lady. I suppose *both* our shows depend on her.' Derwent was looking at the photographs with a rapt smile of appreciation. 'No doubt about it. She's good. Maggie's good.'

I turned to look at him, found him much too close and retreated a step. 'What do you mean,' I asked him, 'by good exactly?'

'There is a quality. Of perfect truthfulness. Absolute reality.'

'Truthfulness?' This was about the first encouraging thing we'd heard about Maggie Hartley.

'It's very rare.'

'Excuse me, sir. Would you be prepared to say that in Court?' Albert seemed to be about to take a statement. I moved tactfully away.

'Is that what you came here for?' Derwent asked me nervously.

I thought it over, and decided there was no point in turning a friendly source of information into a hostile witness.

'No. We wanted to see ... the scene of the crime.'

At which Mr Derwent, apparently reassured, smiled again. 'The Last Act,' he said and led us to the dressing-room, typical of a provincial rep. 'I'll unlock it for you.'

The dressing-room had been tidied up, the cupboards and drawers were empty. Otherwise it looked like the sort of room that would have been condemned as unfit for human habitation by any decent local authority. I stood in the doorway, and made sure that the mirror which went all along one side of the room was shattered in the corner furthest away from me.

'Any help to you, is it?'

'It might be. It's what we lawyers call the *locus in quo*.'

Mr Derwent was positively giggling then.

'Do you? How frightfully camp of you. It's what we actors call a dressing-room.'

So I went back to the Majestic Hotel, a building which seemed rather less welcoming than Her Majesty's Prison, Grimble. And when I was breaking my fast on their mixed grill consisting of cold greasy bacon, a stunted tomato and a sausage that would have looked ungenerous on a cocktail stick, Albert rang me with the unexpected news that at one bound put the Theatre Royal Killing up beside the Penge Bungalow Murders in the Pantheon of Rumpole's forensic triumphs. I was laughing when I came back from the telephone, and I was still laughing when I returned to spread, on a slice of blackened toast, that pat of margarine which the management of the Majestic were apparently unable to tell from butter

*

Two hours later we were in the judges' room at the Law Court discussing, in the hushed tones of relatives after a funeral, the unfortunate event which had occurred. Those present were Tommy Pierce, Q.C., Counsel for the prosecution, and his junior Roach, the learned judge, my learned leader and my learned self.

'Of course these people don't really live in the real world at all,' Jarvis Allen, Q.C., was saying. 'It's all make-believe for them. Dressing up in fancy costumes...'

He himself was wearing a wig, a tailed coat with braided cuffs and a silk gown. His opponent, also bewigged, had a huge stomach from which a gold watch-chain and seal dangled. He also took snuff and blew his nose in a red spotted handkerchief. That kind and, on the whole, gentle figure Skelton J. was fishing in the folds of his scarlet gown for a bitten pipe and an old leather pouch. I didn't think we were exactly the ones to talk about dressing up.

'You don't think she appreciates the seriousness,' the judge was clearly worried.

'I'm afraid not, Judge. Still, if she wants to sack me ... Of course it puts Rumpole in an embarrassing position.'

'Are you embarrassed, Rumpole?' His Lordship asked me.

As a matter of fact I was filled with a deeper inner joy, for Albert's call at breakfast had been to the effect that our client had chosen to dismiss her leading Counsel and put her future entirely in the hands of Horace Rumpole, B.A., that timeless member of the Junior Bar.

'Oh yes. Dreadfully embarrassed, Judge.' I did my best to look suitably modest. 'But it seems that the lady's mind is quite made up.'

'Very embarrassing for you. For you both.' The judge was understanding. 'Does she give any reason for dispensing with her leading Counsel, Jarvis?'

'She said ...' I turned a grin into a cough. I too remembered what Albert had told us. 'She said she thought Rumpole was "better casting".'

' "Better casting"? Whatever can she mean by that?'

'Better in the part, Judge,' I translated.

'Oh dear.' The judge looked distressed. 'Is she very actressy?'

'She's an actress,' I admitted, but would go no further.

'Yes. Yes, I suppose she is.' The judge lit his pipe. 'Do you have any views about this, Tommy?'

'No, Judge. When Jarvis was instructed we were going to ask your views on a plea to manslaughter.'

The portly Pierce twinkled a lot and talked in a rich North Country accent. I could see we were in for a prosecution of homely fun, like one of the comic plays of J. B. Priestley.

'Manslaughter, eh? Do you want to discuss manslaughter, Rumpole?' I appeared to give the matter some courteous consideration.

'No, Judge, I don't believe I do.'

'If you'd like an adjournment you shall certainly have it. Your client may want to think about manslaughter ... Or consider another leader. She should have leading Counsel. In a case of this ...' the judge puffed out smoke ... 'seriousness.'

'Oh, I don't think there's much point in considering another leader.'

'You don't?'

'You see,' I was doing my best not to look at Allen, 'I don't honestly think anyone else would get the part.'

*

When we got out of the judges' room, and were crossing the imposing Victorian Gothic hallway that led to the Court, my learned ex-leader, who had preserved an expression of amused detachment up to that point, turned on me with considerable hurt.

'I must say I take an extremely dim view of that.'

'Really?'

'An extremely dim view. On this Circuit we have a tradition of loyalty to our leaders.'

'It's a local custom?'

'Certainly it is.' Allen stood still and pronounced solemnly. 'I can't imagine anyone on this Circuit carrying on with a case after his leader has been sacked. It's not in the best traditions of the Bar.'

'Loyalty to one's leader. Yes, of course, that is extremely important ...' I thought about it. 'But we must consider the other great legal maxim, mustn't we?'

'Legal maxim? What legal maxim?'

' "The show must go on." Excuse me. I see Albert. Nice chatting to you but ... Things to do, old darling. Quite a number of things to do ...' So I hurried away from the fired legal eagle to where my old clerk was standing, looking distinctly anxious, at the entrance of the Court. He asked me hopefully if the judge had seen fit to grant an adjournment, so that he could persuade our client to try another silk, a course on which Albert's senior partner was particularly keen.

'Oh dear,' I had to disappoint him. 'I begged the judge, Albert. I almost went down on my knees to him. But would he grant me an adjournment? I'm afraid not. No, Rumpole, he told me, the show must go on.' I put a comforting hand on Albert's shoulder. 'Cheer up, old darling. There's only one thing you need say to your senior partner.'

'What's that, sir?'

'The Penge Bungalow Murders.'

I sounded supremely confident of course; but as I went into Court I suddenly remembered that without a leader I would have absolutely no one to blame but myself when things went wrong.

*

'I don't know if any of you ladies and gentlemen have actually attended *performances* at the Theatre Royal ...' Tommy Pierce, Q.C., opening the case for the prosecution, chuckled as though to say 'Most of us got better things to do, haven't we, members of the jury?' 'But we all have passed it going up the Makins Road in a trolley-bus on the way to Grimble Football Ground. You'll know where it is, members of the jury. Past the Snellsham Roundabout, on the corner opposite the Old Britannia Hotel, where we've all celebrated many a win by Grimble United ...'

I didn't know why he didn't just tell them: 'The prisoner's represented by Rumpole of the Bailey, a smart-alecky lawyer from London, who's never ever heard of Grimble United, let alone the Old Britannia Hotel.' I shut my eyes and looked un-interested as Tommy rumbled on, switching, now, to portentous seriousness.

'In this case, members of the jury, we enter an alien world. The world of the showfolk! They live a strange life, you may think. A life of make-believe. On the surface everyone loves each other. "You were wonderful, darling!" said to men and women alike . . .'

I seriously considered heaving myself to my hind legs to pro-test against this rubbish, but decided to sit still and continue the look of bored indifference.

'But underneath all the good companionship,' Pierce was now trying to make the flesh creep, 'run deep tides of jealousy and passion which welled up, in this particular case, members of the jury, into brutal and, say the Crown, quite cold-blooded mur-der . . .'

As he went on I thought that Derwent, the little gnome from the theatre, whom I could now see in the back of the Pit, some-where near the dock, \ as perfectly right. Murder *is* a draw. All the local nobs were in Court including the judge's wife Lady Skelton, in the front row of the Stalls, wearing her special matinée hat. I also saw the Sheriff of the County, in his fancy dress, wearing lace ruffles and a sword which stuck rather inconveni-ently between his legs, and Mrs Sheriff of the County, searching in her handbag for something which might well have been her opera glasses. And then, behind me, the star of the show, my client, looking as I told her to look. Ordinary.

'This is not a case which depends on complicated evidence, members of the jury, or points of law. Let me tell you the facts.'

The facts were not such that I wanted the jury to hear them too clearly, at least not in my learned friend's version. I slowly, and quite noisily, took a page out of my notebook. I was grateful to see that some of the members of the jury glanced in my direction.

'It simply amounts to this. The murder weapon, a Smith and Wesson revolver, was found in the defendant's hand as she stood over her husband's dead body. A bullet from the very weapon had entered between the third and fourth metacarpal!'

I didn't like Pierce's note of triumph as he said this. Accordingly I began to tear my piece of paper into very small strips. More members of the jury looked in my direction.

'Ladies and gentlemen. The defendant, as you will see on your abstract of indictment, was charged as "Maggie Hartley". It seems she prefers to be known by her maiden name, and that may give you some idea of the woman's attitude to her husband of some twenty years, the deceased in this case, the late Gerald Patrick Frere...'

At which point, gazing round the Court, I saw Daniel Derwent. He actually winked, and I realized that he thought he recognized my paper-tearing as an old ham actor's trick. I stopped doing it immediately.

*

'It were a mess. A right mess. Glass broken, blood. He was sprawled in the chair. I thought he were drunk for a moment, but he weren't. And she had this pistol, like, in her hand.' Mr Croft, the stage-doorman was standing in the witness-box in his best blue suit. The jury clearly liked him, just as they disliked the picture he was painting.

'Can you remember what she said?' The learned prosecutor prompted him gently.

'Not too fast ...' Mr Justice Skelton was, worse luck, preparing himself to write it all down.

'Just follow His Lordship's pencil ...' said Pierce, and the judicial pencil prepared to follow Mr Croft.

'She said, "I killed him, what could I do with him?" '

'What did you understand that to mean?'

I did hoist myself to my hind legs then, and registered a determined objection. 'It isn't what this witness understood it to mean. It's what the jury understands it to mean ...'

'My learned friend's quite wrong. The witness was there. He could form his own conclusion ...'

'Please, gentlemen. Let's try and have no disagreements, at least not before luncheon,' said the judge sweetly, and added, less charmingly, 'I think Mr Croft may answer the question.'

'I understood her to say she was so fed up with him, she didn't know what else to do . . .'

'But to kill him . . . ?' Only the judge could have supplied that and he did it with another charming smile.

'Yes, my Lord.'

'Did she say anything else? That you remember?'

'I think she said, "Help me." '

'Yes. Just wait there, will you? In case Mr Rumpole has some questions.'

'Just a few . . .' I rose to my feet. Here was an extremely dangerous witness whom the jury liked. It was no good making a head-on attack. The only way was to lure Mr Croft politely into my parlour. I gave the matter some thought and then tried a line on which I thought we might reach agreement.

'When you saw the deceased, Frere, slumped in the chair, your first thought was that he was drunk?'

'Yes.'

'Had you seen him slumped in a chair drunk in his dressing-room on many occasions?'

'A few.' Mr Croft answered with a knowing smile, and I felt encouraged.

'On most nights?'

'Some nights.'

'Were there some nights when he *wasn't* the worse for drink? Did he ever celebrate, with an evening of sobriety?'

I got my first smile from the jury, and the Joker for the prosecution arose in full solemnity.

'My Lord . . .'

Before Tommy Pierce could interrupt the proceedings with a speech I bowled the next question.

'Mr Croft. When you came into the dressing-room, the deceased Frere was nearest the door . . .'

'Yes. Only a couple of feet from me . . . I saw . . .'

'You saw my client was standing half-way down the room?' I asked, putting a stop to further painful details. 'Holding the gun.'

Pierce gave the jury a meaningful stare, emphasizing the evidence.

'The dressing-room mirror stretches all the way along the wall. And it was broken at the far end, away from the door?'

'Yes.'

'So to have fired the bullet that broke that end of the glass, my client would have had to turn away from the deceased and shoot behind her back ...' I swung round, by way of demonstration, and made a gesture, firing behind me. Of course I couldn't do that without bringing the full might of the prosecution to its feet.

'Surely that's a question for the jury to decide.'

'The witness was there. He can form his own conclusions.' I quoted the wisdom of my learned friend. 'What's the answer?'

'I suppose she would,' Croft said thoughtfully and the jury looked interested.

The judge cleared his throat and leaned forward, smiling politely, and being as it turned out, surprisingly unhelpful.

'Wouldn't that depend, Mr Rumpole, on where the deceased was at the time that particular shot was fired ... ?'

Pierce glowed in triumph and muttered 'Exactly!' I did a polite bow and went quickly on to the next question.

'Perhaps we could turn now to the little matter of what she said when you went into the room.'

'I can remember that perfectly.'

'The words, yes. It's the reading that matters.'

'The *what*,' Mr Rumpole?' said the judge, betraying theatrical ignorance.

'The stress, my Lord. The intonation ... It's an expression used in show business.'

'Perhaps we should confine ourselves to expressions used in Law Courts, Mr Rumpole.'

'Certainly, my Lord.' I re-addressed the witness. 'She said she'd killed him. And then, after a pause, "What could I do with him. Help me." '

Mr Croft frowned. 'I ... That is, yes.'

'Meaning. What could I do with his dead body, and asking for your help ... ?'

'My Lord. That's surely ...' Tommy Pierce was on his hind legs, and I gave him another quotation from himself.

'He was there!' I leant forward and smiled at Croft trying to make him feel that I was a friend he could trust.

'She never meant that she had killed him because she didn't know what to do with him?'

There was a long silence. Counsel for the prosecution let out a deep breath and subsided like a balloon slowly settling. The judge nudged the witness gently. 'Well. What's the answer, Mr Croft? Did she ... ?'

'I ... I can't be sure how she said it, my Lord.'

And there, on a happy note of reasonable doubt, I left it. As I came out of Court and crossed the entrance hall on my way to the cells I was accosted by the beaming Mr Daniel Derwent, who was, it seemed, anxious to congratulate me.

'What a performance, Mr Rumpole. Knock-out! You were wonderful! What I admired so was the timing. The pause, before you started the cross-examination.'

'Pause?'

'You took a beat of nine seconds. I counted.'

'Did I really?'

'Built-up tension, of course. I could see what you were after.' He put a hand on my sleeve, a red hand with big rings and polished fingernails. 'You really must let me know. If ever you want a job in Rep.'

I dislodged my fan club and went down the narrow staircase to the cells. The time had clearly come for my client to start remembering.

*

Maggie Hartley smiled at me over her untouched tray of vegetable pie. She even asked me how I was; but I had no time for small talk. It was zero hour, the last moment I had to get some reasonable instructions.

'Listen to me. Whatever you do or don't remember ... it's just impossible for you to have stood there and fired the first shot.'

'The first shot?' She frowned, as if at some distant memory.

'The one that *didn't* kill him. The one that went behind you. He must have fired that. He *must* ...'

'Yes.' She nodded her head. That was encouraging. So far as it went.

'Why the hell ... why in the name af sanity didn't you tell us that before?'

'I waited. Until there was someone I could trust.'

'Me?'

'Yes. You, Mr Rumpole.'

There's nothing more flattering than to be trusted, even by a confirmed and hopeless villain (which is why I find it hard to dislike a client), and I was convinced Maggie Hartley wasn't that. I sat down beside her in the cell and, with Albert taking notes, she started to talk. What she said was disjointed, sometimes incoherent, and God knows how it was going to sound in the witness-box, but given a few more breaks in the prosecution case, and a following wind I was beginning to get the sniff of a defence.

*

One, two, three, four ...

Mr Alan Copeland, the juvenile lead, had just given his evidence-in-chief for the prosecution. He seemed a pleasant enough young man, wearing a tie and a dark suit (good witness-box clothing) and his evidence hadn't done us any particular harm. All the same I was trying what the director Derwent had admired as the devastating pause.

Seven ... eight ... nine ...

'Have you any questions, Mr Rumpole?' The judge sounded as if he was getting a little impatient with 'the timing'. I launched the cross-examination.

'Mr Alan ... Copeland. You know the deceased man owned a Smith and Wesson revolver? Do you know where he got it?'

'He was in a spy film and it was one of the props. He bought it.'

'But it was more than a bit of scenery. It was a real revolver.'

'Unfortunately, yes.'

'And he had a licence for it ... ?'

'Oh yes. He joined the Grimble Rifle and Pistol Club and used to shoot at targets. I think he fancied himself as James Bond or something.'

'As James who ... ?' I knew that Mr Justice Skelton wouldn't be able to resist playing the part of a mystified judge, so I explained carefully.

'A character in fiction, my Lord. A person licensed to kill. He also spends a great deal of his time sleeping with air hostesses.' To Tommy Pierce's irritation I got a little giggle out of the ladies and gentlemen of the jury.

'Mr Rumpole. We have quite enough to do in this case dealing with questions of *fact*. I suggest we leave the world of fiction ... outside the Court, with our overcoats.'

The jury subsided into serious attention, and I addressed myself to the work in hand. 'Where did Mr Frere keep his revolver?'

'Usually in a locker. At the Rifle Club.'

'Usually?'

'A few weeks ago he asked me to bring it back to the theatre for him.'

'He asked *you*?'

'I'm a member of the Club myself.'

'Really, Mr Copeland.' The judge was interested. 'And what's your weapon?'

'A shot gun, my Lord. I do some clay pigeon shooting.'

'Did Frere say *why* he wanted his gun brought back to the theatre?' I gave the jury a puzzled look.

'There'd been some burglaries. I imagine he wanted to scare any intruder ...'

I had established that it was Frere's gun, and certainly not brought to the scene of the crime by Maggie. I broached another topic. 'Now you have spoken of some quarrels between Frere and his wife.'

'Yes, sir. He once threw a drink in her face.'

'During their quarrels, did you see my client retaliate in any way?'

'No. No, I never did. May I say something, my Lord ...'

'Certainly, Mr Copeland.'

I held my breath. I didn't like free-ranging witnesses, but at his answer I sat down gratefully.

'Miss Hartley, as we knew her, was an exceptionally gentle person.'

I saw the jury look at the dock, at the quiet almost motionless woman sitting there.

'Mr Copeland. You've told us you shot clay pigeons at the Rifle Club.' The prosecution was up and beaming.

'Yes, sir.'

'Nothing much to eat on a clay pigeon, I suppose.'

The jury greeted this alleged quip with total silence. The local comic had died the death in Grimble. Pierce went on and didn't improve his case.

'And Frere asked for this pistol to be brought back to the theatre. Did his wife know that, do you think ... ?'

'I certainly didn't tell her.'

'May I ask why not?'

'I think it would have made her very nervous. I certainly was.'

'Nervous of what, exactly?'

Tommy Pierce had broken the first rule of advocacy. Never ask your witness a question unless you're quite sure of the answer.

'Well ... I was always afraid G.P.'d get drunk and loose it off at someone ...'

The beauty of that answer was that it came from a witness for the prosecution, a detached observer who'd only been called to identify the gun as belonging to the late-lamented G. P. Frere. None too soon for the health of his case Tommy Pierce let Mr Copeland leave the box. I saw him cross the Court and sit next to Daniel Derwent, who gave him a little smile, as if of congratulation.

*

In the course of my legal career I have had occasion to make some study of firearms; not so intensive, of course, as my researches into the subject of blood, but I certainly know more about revolvers than I do about the law of landlord and tenant. I held the fatal weapon in a fairly expert hand as I cross-examined the Inspector who had recovered it from the scene of the crime.

'It's clear, is it not, Inspector, that two chambers had been fired?'

'Yes.'

'One bullet was found in the corner of the mirror, and another in the body of the deceased, Frere?'

'That is so.'

'Now. If the person who fired the shot into the mirror pulled back this hammer,' I pulled it back, 'to fire a second shot ... the gun is now in a condition to go off with a far lighter pressure on the trigger?'

'That is so. Yes.'

'Thank you.'

I put down the gun and as I did so allowed my thumb to accidentally press the trigger. I looked at it, surprised, as it clicked. It was a moderately effective move, and I thought the score was fifteen-love to Rumpole. Tommy Pierce rose to serve.

'Inspector. Whether the hammer was pulled back or not, a woman would have no difficulty in firing this pistol?'

'Certainly not, my Lord.'

'Yes. Thank *you*, Inspector.' The prosecution sat down smiling. Fifteen-all.

The last witness of the day was Miss Christine Hope who turned her large *ingénue* eyes on the jury and whispered her evidence at a sound level which must have made her unintelligible to the audiences at the Theatre Royal. I had decided to cross-examine her more in sorrow than in anger.

'Miss Hope. Why were you waiting at the stage door?'

'Somehow I can never bear to leave. After the show's over ... I can never bear to go.' She gave the jury a 'silly me' look of girlish enthusiasm. 'I suppose I'm just in love with The Theatre.'

'And I suppose you were also "just in love with G. P. Frere"?'

At which Miss Hope looked helplessly at the rail of the witness-box, and fiddled with the Holy Bible.

'You waited for him every night, didn't you? He left his wife at the stage door and took you home.'

'Sometimes ...'

'You're dropping your voice, Miss Hope.' The judge was leaning forward, straining to hear.

'Sometimes, my Lord,' she repeated a decibel louder.

'Every night?'

'Most nights. Yes.'

'Thank you, Miss Hope.'

Pierce, wisely, didn't re-examine and La Belle Christine left the box to looks of disapproval from certain ladies on the jury.

*

I didn't sleep well that night. Whether it was the Majestic mattress, which appeared to be stuffed with firewood, or the sounds, as of a giant suffering from indigestion, which reverberated from the central heating, or mere anxiety about the case, I don't know. At any rate Albert and I were down in the cells as soon as they opened, taking a critical look at the client I was about to expose to the perils of the witness-box. As I had instructed her she was wearing no make-up, and a simple dark dress which struck exactly the right note.

'I'm glad you like it,' Maggie said. 'I wore it in *Time and the Conways*.'

'Listen to the questions, answer them as shortly as you can.' I gave her her final orders. 'Every word to the North Country comedian is giving him a present. Just stick to the facts. Not a word of criticism of the dear departed.'

'You want *them* to like me?'

'They shouldn't find it too difficult.' I looked at her, and lit a small cigar.

'Do I have to swear on . . . the Bible?'

'It's customary.'

'I'd rather affirm.'

'You don't believe in God?' I didn't want an obscure point of theology adding unnecessary difficulties to our case.

'I suppose He's a possibility. He just doesn't seem to be a very frequent visitor to the East Grimble Rep.'

'I know a Grimble jury,' Albert clearly shared my fears. 'If you *could* swear on the Bible?'

'The audience might like it?' Maggie smiled gently.

'The jury,' I corrected her firmly.

'They're not too keen on agnostic actresses. Is that your opinion?'

'I suppose that puts it in a nutshell.'

'All right for the West End, is that it? No good in Grimble.'

'Of course I want you to be *yourself* ...' I really hoped she wasn't going to be difficult about the oath.

'No you don't. You don't want me to be myself at all. You want me to be an ordinary North Country housewife. Spending just another ordinary day on trial for murder.' For a moment her voice had hardened. I looked at her and tried to sound as calm as possible as I pulled out my watch. It was nearly time for the curtain to go up on the evidence for the defence.

'Naturally you're nervous. Time to go.'

'Bloody sick to the stomach. Every time I go on.' Her voice was gentle again, and she was smiling ruefully.

'Good luck.'

'We never say "good luck". It's bad luck to say "good luck". We say "break a leg" ...'

'Break a leg!' I smiled back at her and went upstairs to make my entrance.

Calling your client, I always think, is the worst part of any case. When you're cross-examining, or making a final speech, you're in control. Put your client in the witness-box and there the old darling is, exposed to the world, out of your protection, and all you can do is ask the questions and hope to God the answers don't blow up in your face.

With Maggie everything was going well. We were like a couple of ballroom dancers, expertly gyrating to Victor Sylvester and certain to walk away with the cup. She seemed to sense my next question, and had her answer ready, but not too fast. She looked at the jury, made herself audible to the judge, and gave an impression, a small, dark figure in the witness-box, of courage in the face of adversity. The Court was so quiet and attentive that, as she started to describe that final quarrel, I felt we were alone, two old friends, talking intimately of some dreadful event that took place a long time ago.

'He told me ... he was very much in love with Christine.'

'With Miss Hope?'

'Yes. With Christine Hope. That he wanted her to play Amanda.'

'That is ... the leading lady? And what was to happen to you?'

'He wanted me to leave the company. To go to London. He never wanted to see me again.'

'What did you say to that?'

'I said I was terribly unhappy about Christine, naturally.'

'Just tell the ladies and gentlemen of the jury what happened next.'

'He said it didn't matter what I said. He was going to get rid of me. He opened the drawer of the dressing-table.'

'Was he standing then?'

'I would say, staggering.'

'Yes, and then ... ?'

'He took out the ... the revolver.'

'This one ... ?'

I handed the gun to the usher, who took it to Maggie. She glanced at it and shuddered.

'I ... I think so.'

'What effect did it have on you when you first saw it?'

'I was terrified.'

'Did you know it was there?'

'No. I had no idea.'

'And then ... ?'

'Then. He seemed to be getting ready to fire the gun.'

'You mean he pulled back the hammer ... ?'

'My Lord ...' Pierce stirred his vast bulk and the judge was inclined to agree. He said :

'Yes. Please don't lead, Mr Rumpole.'

'I think that's what he did,' Maggie continued without assistance. 'I didn't look carefully. Naturally I was terrified. He was waving the gun. He didn't seem to be able to hold it straight. Then there was a terrible explosion. I remember glass, and dust, everywhere.'

'Who fired that shot, Mrs Frere?'

'My husband. I think ...'

'Yes?'

'I think he was trying to kill me.' She said it very quietly, but the jury heard, and remembered. She gave it a marked pause and then went on. 'After that first shot. I saw him getting ready to fire again.'

'Was he pulling ... ?'

'Please don't lead, Mr Rumpole.' The trouble with the great comedian was that he couldn't sit still in anyone else's act.

'He was pulling back ... That thing.' Maggie went on without any help.

Then I asked the judge if we could have a demonstration and the usher went up into the witness-box to play the scene with Maggie. At my suggestion he took the revolver.

'We are all quite sure that thing isn't loaded?' The judge sounded nervous.

'Quite sure, my Lord. Of course, we don't want *another* fatal *accident*!'

'Really, my Lord. That was quite improper!' Pierce rose furiously. 'My learned friend called it an accident.'

I apologized profusely, the point having been made. Then Maggie quietly positioned the usher. He raised the gun as she asked him. It was pointed murderously at her. And then Maggie grabbed at the gun in his hand, and forced it back, struggling desperately, against the usher's chest.

'I was trying to stop him. I got hold of his hand to push the gun away ... I pushed it back ... I think ... I think I must have forced back his finger on the trigger.' We heard the hammer click, and now Maggie was struggling to hold back her tears. 'There was another terrible noise ... I never meant ...'

'Yes. Thank you, Usher.'

The usher went back to the well of the Court. Maggie was calm again when I asked her:

'When Mr Croft came you said you had killed your husband?'

'Yes ... I had ... By accident.'

'What else did you say?'

'I think I said ... What could I do with him? I meant, how could I help him, of course.'

'And you asked Mr Croft to help you?'

'Yes.'

It was time for the curtain line.

'Mrs Frere. Did you ever at any time have any intention of killing your husband?'

'Never ... ! Never ... ! Never ... !' Now my questions were finished she was crying, her face and shoulders shaking. The judge leaned forward kindly.

'Don't distress yourself. Usher, a glass of water?'

Her cheeks hot with genuine tears, Maggie looked up bravely.

'Thank you, my Lord.'

'Bloody play-acting!' I heard the cynical Tommy Pierce mutter ungraciously to his junior, Roach.

*

If she was good in chief Maggie was superb in cross-examination. She answered the questions courteously, shortly, but as if she were genuinely trying to help Tommy clear up any doubt about her innocence that may have lingered in his mind. At the end he lost his nerve and almost shouted at her :

'So according to you, you did nothing wrong?'

'Oh yes,' she said. 'I did something terribly wrong.'

'Tell us. What?'

'I loved him too much. Otherwise I should have left him. Before he tried to kill me.'

During Tommy's final speech there was some coughing from the jury. He tried a joke or two about actors, lost heart and sat down upon reminding the jury that they must not let sympathy for my client affect their judgement.

'I agree entirely with my learned friend,' I started my speech. 'Put all sympathy out of your mind. The mere fact that my client clung faithfully to a drunken, adulterous husband, hoping vainly for the love he denied her; the terrible circumstance that she escaped death at his hands only to face the terrible ordeal of a trial for murder; none of these things should influence you in the least ...' nd I ended with my well-tried peroration. 'In an hour or two this case will be over. You will go home and put the kettle on and forget all about this little theatre, and the angry, drunken actor and his wretched infidelities. This case has only been a few days out of your lives. But for the lady I have the honour to represent ...' I pointed to the dock, '*all* her life hangs in the balance. Is that life to be broken and is she to go down in darkness and disgrace, or can she go back into the glowing light of her world, to bring us all joy and entertainment and laughter once again? Ask yourselves that question, members of the jury. And when you ask it, you know there can only be one answer.'

I sank back into my seat exhausted, pushing back my wig and mopping my brow with a large silk handkerchief. Looking round the Court I saw Derwent. He seemed about to applaud, until he was restrained by Mr Alan Copeland.

*

There is nothing I hate more than waiting for a jury to come back. You smoke too much and drink too many cups of coffee, your hands sweat and you can't do or think of anything else. All you can do is to pay a courtesy visit to the cells to prepare for the worst. Albert Handyside had to go off and do a touch of Dangerous Driving in the Court next door, so I was alone when I went to call on the waiting Maggie.

She was standing in her cell, totally calm.

'This is the bad part, isn't it? Like waiting for the notices.'

I sat down at the table with my notebook, unscrewed my fountain pen.

'I had better think of what to say if they find you guilty of manslaughter. I think I've got the facts for mitigation, but I'd just like to get the history clear. You'd started this theatrical company together?'

'It was my money. Every bloody penny of it.' I looked up in some surprise. The hard, tough note was there in her voice; her face was set in a look which was something like hatred.

'I don't think we need go into the financial side.' I tried to stop her, but she went on:

'Do you know what that idiotic manager we had then did? He

gave G.P. a contract worth fifty per cent of the profits : for an in-
vestment of nothing and a talent which stopped short of being
able to pour out a drink and say a line at the same time. Anyway
I never paid his percentage.' She smiled then, it was quite
humourless. 'Won't need to say that, will we?'

'No.' I said firmly.

'Fifty per cent of ten years' work! He reckoned he was owed
around twenty thousand pounds. He was going to sue us and
bankrupt the company . . .'

'I don't think you need to tell me any more.' I screwed the top
back on my fountain pen. Perhaps she had told me too much
already.

'So don't feel too badly, will you? If we're not a hit.'

I stood up and pulled out my watch. Suddenly I felt an urgent
need to get out of the cell.

'They should be back soon now.'

'It's all a game to you, isn't it?' She sounded unaccountably
bitter. 'All a wonderful game of "let's pretend". The costume. The
bows. The little jokes. The onion at the end.'

'The onion?'

'An old music-hall expression. For what makes the audience
cry. Oh, I was quite prepared to go along with it. To wear the
make-up.'

'You didn't wear any make-up.'

'I know, that was brilliant of you. You're a marvellous per-
former, Mr Rumpole. Don't let anyone tell you different.'

'It's not a question of performance.' I couldn't have that.

'Isn't it?'

'Of course it isn't! The jury are now weighing the facts. Doing
their best to discover where the truth lies.' I looked at her. Her
face gave nothing away.

'Or at least deciding if the prosecution has proved its case.'

Suddenly, quite unexpectedly, she yawned, she moved away
from me, as though I bored her.

'Oh, I'm tired. Worn out. With so much *acting*. I tell you, in
the theatre we haven't got time for all that. We've got our livings
to get.'

The woman prison officer came in.

'I think they want you upstairs now. Ready, dear?'

When Maggie spoke again her voice was low, gentle and wonderfully polite.

'Yes thanks, Elsie. I'm quite ready now.'

*

'Will your foreman please stand? Mr Foreman. Have you reached a verdict on which you are all agreed?'

'Not guilty, my Lord.'

Four words that usually set the Rumpole ears tingling with delight and the chest to swell with pleasure. Why was it, that at the end of what was no doubt a remarkable win, a famous victory even, I felt such doubt and depression? I told myself that I was not the judge of fact, that the jury had clearly not been satisfied and that the prosecution had not proved its case. I did the well-known shift of responsibility which is the advocate's perpetual comfort, but I went out of Court unelated. In the entrance hall I saw Maggie leaving, she didn't turn back to speak to me, and I saw that she was holding the hand of Mr Alan Copeland. Such congratulations as I received came from the diminutive Derwent.

'Triumph. My dear, a total triumph.'

'You told me she was truthful . . .' I looked at him.

'I meant her acting. That's quite truthful. Not to be faulted. That's all I meant.'

At which he made his exit and my Learned Friend for the Prosecution came sailing up, beaming with the joy of reconciliation.

'Well. Congratulations, Rumpole. That was a bloody good win!'

'Was it? I hope so.'

'Coming to the Circuit dinner tonight?'

'Tonight?'

'You'll enjoy it! We've got some pretty decent claret in the mess.'

*

If my judgement hadn't been weakened by exhaustion I would never have agreed to the Circuit dinner which took place, as I feared, in a private room at the Majestic Hotel. All the gang were there, Skelton J., Pierce, Roach and my one-time leader Jarvis Allen, Q.C. The food was indifferent, the claret was bad, and when the port was passed an elderly silk whom they called 'Mr Senior' in deference to his position as Leader of the Circuit, banged the table with the handle of his knife and addressed young Roach at the other end of the table.

'Mr Junior, in the matter of Rumpole.'

'Mr Senior,' Roach produced a scribble on a menu. 'I will read the indictment.'

I realized then that I had been tricked, ambushed, made to give myself up to the tender mercies of this savage Northerly Circuit. Rumpole was on trial, there was nothing to do but drink all the available port and put up with it.

'Count One,' Roach read it out. 'Deserting his learned leader in his hour of need. That is to say on the occasion of his leader having been given the sack. Particulars of Offence . . .'

'Mr Senior. Have five minutes elapsed?' Allen asked.

'Five minutes having elapsed since the loyal toast, you may now smoke.'

Tommy Pierce lit a large cigar. I lit a small one. Mr Junior Roach continued to intone.

'The said Rumpole did add considerably to the seriousness of the offence by proceeding to win in the absence of his learned leader.'

'Mr Junior. Has Rumpole anything to say by way of mitigation?'

'Rumpole.' Roach took out his watch, clearly there was a time limit in speeches. I rose to express my deepest thoughts, loosened by the gentle action of the port.

'The show had to go on!'

'What? What did Rumpole say?' Mr Justice Skelton seemed to have some difficulty in hearing.

'Sometimes. I must admit, sometimes . . . I wonder why.' I went on, 'What sort of show is it exactly? Have you considered what we are *doing* to our clients?'

'Has that port got stuck to the table?' Allen sounded plaintive and the port moved towards him.

'What are we *doing* to them?' I warmed to my work. 'Seeing they wear ties, and hats, keep their hands out of their pockets, keep their voices up, call the judge "my Lord". Generally behave like grocers at a funeral. Whoever they may be.'

'One minute,' said Roach, the time-keeper.

'What do we tell them? Look respectable! Look suitably serious! Swear on the Bible! Say nothing which might upset a jury of lay-preachers, look enormously grateful for the trouble everyone's taking before they bang you up in the nick! What do we find out about our clients in all these trials, do we ever get a fleeting glimpse of the truth? Do we ... ? Or do we put a hat on the truth. And a tie. And a serious expression. To please the jury and My Lord the Judge?' I looked round the table. 'Do you ever worry about that at all? Do you *ever*?'

'Time's up!' said Roach, and I sat down heavily.

'All right. Quite all right. The performance is over.'

Mr Senior swigged down port and proceeded to judgement.

'Rumpole's mitigation has, of course, merely added to the gravity of the offence. Rumpole, at your age and with your experience at the Bar you should have been proud to get the sack, and your further conduct in winning shows a total disregard for the feelings of an extremely sensitive silk. The least sentence I can pass is a fine of twelve bottles of claret. Have you a cheque-book on you?'

So I had no choice but to pull out a chequebook and start to write. The penalty, apparently, was worth thirty-six quid.

'Members of the Mess will now entertain the company in song,' Roach announced to a rattle of applause.

'Tommy!' Allen shouted.

'No. Really ...' The learned prosecutor was modest but was prevailed upon by cries of 'Come along, Tommy! Let's have it. "The Road to Mandalay" ... etc. etc.'

'I'm looking forward to this,' said Mr Justice Skelton, who was apparently easily entertained. As I gave my cheque to young Roach, the stout leading Counsel for the Crown rose and started in a light baritone.

> 'On the Road to Mandalay...
> Where the old Flotilla lay...
> And the dawn came up like thunder
> Out of China 'cross the Bay!'

Or words to the like effect. I was not really listening. I'd had quite enough of show business.

Rumpole and the Fascist Beast

'This is where I came in,' I said. 'I've seen it all before.'

I was sitting one Sunday in front of the gas fire at Casa Rumpole (25B Froxbury Court, Gloucester Road). I was wearing a comfortable old cardigan and carpet slippers, and sipping a G and T but the news in the paper wasn't comforting, moreover it was unpleasantly familiar to anyone who made a tentative entrance into life before the First World War, and was therefore in time to hear Hitler screeching on the wireless and see newsreels of jackboots marching into Czechoslovakia in preparation for the next.

'"BRITAIN FIRST" Rally in Brixton. Clashes with New Socialist Party. Candidate arrested.' As I said to She Who Must Be Obeyed as she came in through the front door with her mackintosh and shopping string-bag weighed down with a few unappetizing-looking goodies, it was all exactly like the bad old days.

'Rumpole! It's good news,' said Hilda. 'I've got a tin of mulligatawny soup.'

'Congratulations.' I went on reading the paper. 'Fascist marches in London. I know exactly what happens next.'

My wife took her string-bag into the kitchen, and left the door open as she unpacked her shopping. I shouted my predictions through to her.

'Next comes gas masks. Call-up. The RAF groundstaff.' Surely I was getting a bit old for the RAF groundstaff.

'And I managed to find some frozen beefburgers!' She seemed very proud of her Sunday shopping.

'Then they'll give us dried eggs. Whale steak. J. B. Priestley on the wireless. Songs by Dame Vera Lynn.' It was an appalling prospect. I dropped the paper and wandered into the kitchen to search out another bottle of gin.

'I had to go all the way down to the tube station.' Hilda was pouring tinned mulligatawny soup into a saucepan. I lit a paper spill in the gas and applied it to the end of a small cigar.

'I couldn't stand the whole damn programme round again.' I puffed out smoke. 'I suppose they've got a gramophone record of Churchill's speeches.'

'Hardly a white face to be seen. Down by the tube station.' Oh dear. 'She' does come out with these embarrassing remarks occasionally.

'Were you looking for one? I thought you were looking for mulligatawny soup.'

'My Aunt Fran would turn in her grave if she could see London nowadays.' My wife accepted a large G and T to help her through stirring the tin of soup.

'As I recall it, your Aunt Fran was married to your Uncle Percy Wystan, late Deputy Controller of the Punjabi Railway,' I reminded her.

'That is exactly what I mean!'

'She spent her life running up curries and kedgerees, supervising the punka-wallah, organizing tea parties on the backs of elephants. Your Aunt Fran would have been totally at home round our tube station.' I looked at Hilda and started to cross-examine her, a daring thing to do to She Who Must Be Obeyed. 'You didn't get the supper at Chatterjee's General Stores by any chance?'

'Everywhere else was shut.' The witness was on the defensive.

'You don't grudge Mr Chatterjee a little hospitality, do you? I mean in return for a couple of centuries, putting up with your Aunt Fran?'

Cornered, the witness had to resort to 'Don't be so silly Rumpole', a sure sign of defeat. I reckoned the score was fifteen-love to me in the first set of the evening.

*

I had for some time considered taking a pupil, someone to look up law whenever that commodity was needed, or to run round and adjourn things. Perhaps I felt the need of someone to talk to since my old friend George Frobisher had accepted a minor judgeship, and gone off to a Circus Bench somewhere in the general direction of Luton. Our Inn sent us round a list of names of those anxious to secure a pupillage, together with their life stories (Grimsby Grammar, Captain of Debates, or Eton and Oriel, doesn't wish to be connected with divorce or crime, warmly recommended by the Master of the Rolls). I passed by various candidates until I came to the name of Mr Lutaf Ali Khan. I rang the Inn and we arranged an appointment at my Chambers for 9.30 one morning. If Mr Ali Khan was to turn out to be anything like Mr Chatterjee, Hilda's useful grocer, he would be inclined, I thought, to work industriously, Sunday afternoons included.

When Mr Khan duly arrived at Chambers I was in conference. He went into the clerk's room and found the usual scene of chaos and overcrowding. Erskine-Brown was collecting papers and grumbling to our clerk Henry about the slow arrival of his fees, and Hoskins, the middle-aged father of four hungry daughters, was having a quick look at a 'break and enter' before rushing off to Inner London. Uncle Tom was looking through the obituaries in the *Daily Telegraph*. Dianne and Angela, our new assistant typist, were clattering away and Miss Trant, our budding Portia, was having a glance at a matrimonial. I rely on her account for the reception of Mr Khan in our clerk's room. He announced himself as Mr Lutaf Ali Khan and said he had an urgent appointment with my learned self. When Henry promised to ring through to my room Mr Khan beamed at them. He was eager and rather young.

'Thrilling! This is thrilling to have a chance of pupillage in the Chambers of Horace Rumpole, the legend of the Criminal Bar of England.' Uncle Tom caught his eye.

'And you, of course, sir. I will have a lot to learn from a person of your age and seniority. I expect to pick up hundreds of red-hot tips, from the whole lot of you!'

'We'll do our best to help.' Miss Trant didn't notice a particularly warm welcome from the rest of Chambers, so she advanced on him with a compensating smile.

'Thank you. You are on the secretarial side?'

'Miss Trant is a very rising young barrister,' Uncle Tom told him.

'The great fraternity of the Bar! Truly it embraces all sorts and conditions of men ... and women also,' Mr Khan said enthusiastically and then Henry rose from his desk to lead him into the presence. When he had gone Uncle Tom spoke to Miss Trant in a tone of some bewilderment.

'I don't see very clearly. It gets dark in the morning, but was that fellow some sort of Babu?'

'Indian, I'd say.' Hoskins gave his expert opinion.

'I suppose he'll pick our brains here and then go out and become Prime Minister of somewhere. Do very nicely out of it.' Uncle Tom sniffed behind the *Daily Telegraph*.

'What on *earth* does Rumpole think he's up to?' Erskine-Brown wondered, and Miss Trant gave him a look of stern disapproval.

'My old Uncle Jarvis had that fellow Gandhi in his Chambers as a pupil.' Uncle Tom was off on one of his reminiscences. 'He wore a bowler hat in those days apparently, not a loin cloth. I mean Gandhi didn't wear a loin cloth, not my Uncle Jarvis, of course.'

'What do you mean? What's Rumpole up to?' Miss Trant asked Erskine-Brown in a challenging manner.

'Taking a pupil without going through the pupillage committee in Chambers.'

'You mean taking *that* pupil, don't you?'

At which moment, Miss Trant told me, she slammed out of the clerk's room and started off down the passage. Erskine-Brown set off in pursuit, he was after all, as you may remember, her *fiancé*.

'For all I know whatever-his-name-is Khan may be a perfectly sound fellow ... but ...'

'But! But?'

'I mean ...'

'I know perfectly well what you mean,' said Miss Trant, with an anger that did her the greatest credit.

'Don't forget *Un Ballo In Maschera*.' Claude Erskine-Brown

was an Opera Buff who intended, that night, to take his *inamorata* to Covent Garden. 'It's curtain-up at 7.30.'

'Stuff *Un Ballo In Maschera*!' said the admirable Miss Trant and slammed into her room.

*

All this while I was in conference on a matter which was new to me, an alleged offence under the Race Relations Act, arising out of those very political events which had, on Sunday afternoon, made me feel that they were winding back the film of history so that we should find ourselves, in the fullness of time, reliving World War Two. My client, Captain Rex Parkin, late of the Pay Corps, was a prospective 'Britain First' parliamentary candidate, one, I profoundly hoped, whose deposit was no way safe. He had appeared at his party's rally in Brixton and made a regrettable speech in which, so ran the police evidence, he had recommended repatriation of all migrants ('We want our tinted brothers to be thoroughly *at home*. In their homes, my friends, not in ours') and he ended his speech with the gnomic utterance, 'The answer, my friends, is ... Blood.'

Someone at the meeting broke the window of an Indian grocer's shop and the gallant Captain was arrested before he, in his turn, was attacked by the New Socialists, who had armed themselves with chairs, sticks, and other mementoes from a nearby building site for the occasion.

Captain Parkin was a middle-aged humourless man who wore a neat blue suit, a Pay Corps tie, a sparse sandy moustache and the expression of someone prepared to die for his cause. He sat bolt upright on a hard chair whilst young Simmonds, an articled clerk from Parkin's solicitors' office, wallowed in my client's armchair, looked puzzled and lost documents. When Mr Lutaf Ali Khan was shown into the room by Henry there was such a sharp disapproving intake of breath from Captain Parkin that I couldn't resist taking the eager young Pakistani there and then.

'Khan! My dear fellow. You come warmly recommended from the Inn. An apt pupil ... Ready to start work, are you?'

'As soon as you say so, Mr Horace Rumpole. I am mustard keen, I must say.'

'That's the ticket! This is the client Mr ... No, sorry, *Captain*. Captain Rex Parkin.'

'And young Simmonds. Our instructing solicitor. My new pupil ...'

'Lutaf Ali Khan. At your service, Captain.'

The Captain avoided Khan's eager eye. There was an awkward silence.

'Yes. Well, why not sit down here, dear boy. Learn to take notes, I never have.'

Khan sat on the other side of Rumpole's desk, his pen poised. Captain Parkin cleared his throat.

'I would like to stress, Mr Rumpole. This is a *confidential* matter.'

'Oh, don't mind Khan. It's the only thing to do with pupils. Throw them in at the deep end. You know what we have here, Khan? A rather nasty charge under the Race Relations Act.'

'Let's see what I know about our client, the Captain. You are ex-Pay Corps.' I flicked through my brief for Khan's benefit.

'Served. Overseas ...?'

'I served my country as best I could. Given my medical condition.' The Captain looked dignified.

'Flat feet ...' I read it in the brief, and comforted the client. 'Don't worry. I was in the RAF groundstaff. We both avoided the temptations of heroism.'

'Worked after demobilization selling ... the *World Wide Encyclopedia*. Married for twenty-five years to Mavis Parkin. Owns his own bungalow "Mandalay", Durbar Lane, Bexley Heath. Employed since 1958 as a clerk in the South-East Area Gas Board ...' It sounded like a life full of incident and romance.

'Captain Parkin wishes it to be known that he's absolutely sincere.' This was young Simmonds's contribution.

'Unfortunately that isn't a defence in law. I've known quite a number of very genuine robbers. They sincerely wanted to be rich.' I continued to read. 'The answer is ... Blood.'

'Mr Rumpole. On the question of sentence ...' The Captain raised a delicate question.

'Sorry. You want to know what you might be in for?'

'The maximum. If you please, sir.'

'Two years' imprisonment. Or a fine. Or both. Section 6 of the 1978 Act.' The admirable Khan had the answer at his fingertips.

> 'And still they gazed, and still the wonder grew,
> That one small head could carry all he knew . . .

You see what a huge advantage a pupil is, Captain. Well, now you know the worst.'

And then Captain Parkin said something so unexpected, so unknown in a client, that I was left staring at him in amazement.

'I want you, sir, to ask for the maximum penalty.'

'Now Captain Perkins . . . Parkin. Now listen to me a moment, my old darling . . . Regard me,' I told him, 'as your professional attendant. Who cares for your health. Now if I were treating you for a nasty go of 'flu, Captain Perkins, I couldn't allow you to dance naked in the East wind at midnight, on a damp lawn, could I?'

'I intend, in the trial, sir, to behave as Gandhi did before the District Magistrate in Ahmadabad. I intend to argue for the maximum sentence.' Captain Parkin had risen to his feet and seemed to be standing to attention.

'Excuse me, Captain, but wasn't the Mahatma of foreign extraction?'

'One can learn at times, sir, from the enemy. Mr Gandhi asked for life imprisonment. It was the best way he could serve his cause – as a martyr.'

'Well, I suppose I have a cause too, of a sort,' I told him. 'I defend people. I don't think I could ask a judge to send a client of mine to prison. It'd be against my religion.'

'Then, sir, I am wasting your time.' Captain Parkin moved to the door. 'I'll conduct my own case. I presume I'm entitled to do that?'

'It's a free world . . . For the moment.' Before I'd got the words out the door slammed, my client had gone off on his own.

'He's a fool, Mr Rumpole. If he won't take your advice.' Young Simmonds looked intensely embarrassed.

'It's his affair entirely,' I comforted him, 'our prison system's open to all, old darling. Regardless of creed or colour.'

When I told Hilda I had a pupil, she was pleased. She remembered that her 'Daddy', old C. H. Wystan, had had a pupil, namely me. She told me to bring my pupil home to dinner one night and promised to make him a nice roast. Remembering the nonsense she had talked about the old days of the British Raj I agreed to do so.

A couple of weeks later Khan and I received another visit from Captain Rex Parkin and his distraught solicitor. It seemed that the central committee for the South-Eastern Region of the 'Britain First' Party had met at my client's bungalow 'Mandalay'. Prominent members, a Mr 'Cliff' Worseley, a local garage-owner and a Mr Sidney Cox, quantity surveyor and local party chairman, had persuaded the Captain that it was in the party's interests that the case should be fought. The Captain had told them I was an ageing junior barrister with a Pakistani pupil whereupon 'Cliff' Worseley had said that was an excellent thing as it would prove to the jury that 'Britain First' was not a racialist party. During this account Khan smiled politely, and I promised to fight the good fight and forget the Captain's former ambition to be convicted.

There were those, of course, who didn't approve of my having taken on Captain Parkin's defence. When I went into Pommeroy's Wine Bar for an evening jar I met the most distinguished member of our Chambers, Guthrie Featherstone, Q.C., M.P., who looked at me from his considerable height and in his most distinguished manner.

'Rumpole. I'm prosecuting you in the Race Relations case. Phillida Trant's my junior.'

'Sounds a formidable combination.'

'You know, Rumpole,' Featherstone went on, 'I was talking to old Keith from the Lord Chancellor's office the other day. He was surprised at you of all people ... defending a wretched Fascist beast.'

'I defend murderers. Doesn't mean I approve of murder.'

'No, but politically. I was thinking. The time may come, Rumpole, when you might think of subsiding gently on the Circuit Bench.'

'Rumpole a Circus Judge?' It was a fate which has always seemed to me considerably worse than death.

'It's not a job the Lord Chancellor's office hands out, to fellows who stand up for Fascists.'

'Oh, really?' I sank a large glass of Chateau Fleet Street and began to negotiate with Jack Pommeroy for more.

'Afraid so, Rumpole. I mean, you're not getting much younger. I don't know what your pension scheme is . . .'

My pension, as he well knew, consisted of my growing overdraft and the dwindling lease on my flat at Froxbury Court, Gloucester Road. However, I was rapidly losing patience with Guthrie Featherstone, Q.C., M.P.

'My pension scheme is about as non-existent as your friend old Keith's knowledge of Voltaire.'

'Voltaire?' The Q.C., M.P. looked puzzled.

'M. Arouet,' I explained. 'Remember what he said, "I disagree with what you say, but I will defend to the death your right to say it"? You might read that to the jury, when you're opening the little matter of the Queen against Captain Rex Parkin . . .'

*

The evening came when I took Mr Khan home to meet my wife Hilda and her roast. She Who Must Be Obeyed didn't actually scream or send for the police when she clapped eyes on my pupil, but she looked severely shaken, and matters were so tense round the festive board that I was constrained to tell one of my best stories as I carved the beef. I chose the beauty about two men charged with an act of buggery under Waterloo Bridge and tried by dear old Judge Darcy at the Bailey.

'These two men were caught misbehaving themselves under Waterloo Bridge and when he was passing sentence that exquisite old Judge Hubert Darcy said, "You two men have done an abominable act. A most disgusting and horrible act . . . And what makes it worse – you chose to do it under one of the most *beautiful* bridges in London." '

I laughed loudly at this *conte*, as I always do. Khan smiled politely, Hilda was appalled. She looked even more anxious as she pushed a laden plate of roast to Khan.

'Oh dear. I didn't realize. Can you eat beef?'

'Of course he can, Hilda. What do you think? He'd be afraid it was a reincarnation of his grandmother?' I looked at Khan reassuringly. 'Don't worry, dear boy. We got it at Sainsbury's.'

'Roast beef of old England. Perfectly fine. Suits me down to the ground.' Khan sounded enthusiastic. I tried to pour claret into his glass, but the young Pakistani put his hand over it.

'Oh, come along. If you're starting a career at the Bar, we've got to introduce you to the delights of Pommeroy's claret.'

'Well then, just a snifter.' I was glad to see him lap up the claret. I went to turn off one bar of the electric fire.

'What are you doing, Hilda, turning the place into the hothouse at Kew?'

'Don't you find England very cold, Mr Khan?' Hilda asked nervously.

'No. No, I assure you. J· is much much colder in the Punjab in the winter.'

'Wasn't your Aunt Fran in the Punjab, Hilda?'

'Oh, that was in the old days. The British Raj, you know.'

'All gone now, eh Khan? Much to the regret of our client Captain Parkin.' I gave them a bit of Kipling.

> 'Far-call'd our navies melt away
> On dune and headland sinks the fire ...
> Lo, all our pomp of yesterday
> Is one with Nineveh, and Tyre ...'

'My uncle was District Railway Officer Percy Wystan. I don't know if you ever met him?' Hilda asked, a singularly stupid question.

'Rather before my time, I'm afraid, Mrs Rumpole. All the same. We had some sensible fellows in the government then. Not these silly asses we get today.'

'Do you really think so?' She Who Must Be Obeyed seemed to be thawing slightly.

'All the same, they are your own silly asses. Isn't that the point?' I put it to Khan.

'Oh yes. But they make us blush sometimes.'

At which Hilda actually smiled and I raised a beaker to young Khan's future at the Bar.

'How can I go wrong,' Khan said, 'with such a distinguished teacher as Mr Horace Rumpole?'

'You think he's a distinguished teacher?' She was incredulous.

'Oh gosh, yes, Mrs Rumpole. Your husband's bound to end up seated on the Bench, at least at Circuit Judge level.'

'Rumpole! Do you hear that?' She was delighted.

'Never. Never in a million years . . .'

'I always thought, if you would take a bit of prosecution work, Mr Rumpole. That seems to be the path to the Bench nowadays,' Khan said, and Hilda agreed.

'Mr Khan. That's exactly what I'm always telling him.'

'I don't fancy the idea of people locked up with their own chamber-pots. Not for years on end, anyway. I wouldn't like to cross-examine them into it . . . And I don't want to sentence them to it either.'

'Someone has to do it, Mr Rumpole,' Khan said, winning more of Hilda's approval.

'Someone has to clean out the sewers. Just so long as it isn't me.'

'You know, Mrs Rumpole, I don't entirely agree with my learned pupilmaster. There are two dreadful Pakistani students in my digs and I can swear they stole my transistor radio. I'd send them inside, double-quick pronto.'

At which Hilda smiled at him sweetly. I could see that life at the Bar would hold no further terrors for Khan. The Lord Chief. The Court of Appeal. The House of Lords. The Uxbridge Magistrates. They'd all be child's play to him now. Like shooting fish in a water butt. Now he'd dealt in so masterly a fashion with She Who Must Be Obeyed.

Meanwhile Mr Khan was looking at me with serious concern.

'I honestly think Mrs Rumpole has a point though, sir. You should think in terms of a judgeship, in the years to come.'

*

Judge 'Jimmie' Jamieson was a thin, ferret-faced Scotsman of about my age. He had his wig off and was offering a silver cigarette box round to me, Guthrie Featherstone, Q.C., M.P. and Miss Trant in the privacy of his room before we started on the case of R. *v.* Parkin.

'You are an O.L., aren't you, Rumpole?' The judge asked me and I wondered if his Honour was gratuitously insulting. 'You were at Linklater's, weren't you?'

Linklater's! My old school. A wind-blasted penal colony on the Norfolk coast, where thirteen-year-olds fought for the radiators and tried to hide the lumpy porridge in letters from home.

'I haven't seen you at the O.L. dinners recently,' the judge went on.

'No.' He hadn't seen me at the Embalmers' Annual Ball, either.

'They put on a very good show for us last year, at the Connaught Rooms. – This case going to last long, is it?'

'Three days, Judge. Three or four days at the most.' Guthrie Featherstone had the time-table. Now I remembered the judge. A small trembling child from Scotland. He wore a chest protector and was incredibly mean about his tuck.

'I'm hoping to get a week's fishing in starting on Monday,' Jamieson said. 'I just wanted to get the timing from you fellows. Remember our last case, Rumpole?'

'The Paddington affray.'

'Crowds of piccaninnies scrapping with knives on Paddington Station.' The judge smiled as if at a happy memory.

'Only real worry was ... some passing white might have got hurt.'

Oh dear! Oh my ears and whiskers! We could hardly hope for a trial in the spirit of Voltaire. Miss Trant, I thought, looked especially disgusted.

*

Shortly thereafter the case was underway in one of the New Courts at the Bailey, and I was cross-examining the officer in charge.

'This broken window, of the grocer's shop, Inspector. You have no way of knowing if the perpetrator of that act had heard my client's oration, had you?'

'No, sir.'

'It might have been done by anyone at all . . . Some destructive schoolboy?'

'Let us hope he was not at Linklater's, Rumpole!' said the judge, and seemed to find it amusing.

'Now, you say my client said something . . . about blood?' I carried on, killing the laugh.

'He said "The answer is . . . blood!"' The Inspector consulted his notebook. 'I couldn't hear all that clearly.'

'Exactly! The rival factions were yelling their heads off. So he might have said "The answer is *in* the blood"?'

'Really. If my learned friend thinks there is any difference . . .' Guthrie Featherstone rose wearily.

'Let me instruct my learned friend. If he said, "The answer *is* blood", it might well be an incitement to violence.'

'I am glad my learned friend at least appreciates the point of the prosecution case . . .'

'But if he said, "The answer is *in* the blood", he was merely referring to some supposed difference in racial characteristics, and the remark was quite innocuous.'

'There is a clear distinction, is there not, Mr Featherstone?' I was half-ashamed to discover that the judge was on my side.

'If your Lordship pleases.' Featherstone subsided, and I gave the jury a friendly smile as I said:

'I am glad that my learned friend has at last grasped the nature of the defence.'

*

'Straight up, Mr Rumpole. He's got the Union Jack flying on his bungalow.'

I was in the pub opposite the Bailey to which I had inveigled my pupil Khan, who was taking a note for me in the case, for a quick shepherd's pie and a pint of draught Guinness (Khan had become quite a healthy drinker under my tuition, and a good companion both in the pub at lunchtime and in Pommeroy's after the battle of the day was done) and I had been approached by a tall, overweight individual, with a blotchy pink face, whose long tow-coloured hair hung over the rabbit-fur collar of his 'car coat'. It appeared that this unpromising individual was 'Cliff' Worseley, garage-owner of Purley and committee member of the South-Eastern section of the 'Britain First' movement. 'Cliff' had been giving me a number of details of the character and way of life of my client, Captain Parkin, including a description of the decor of his bungalow 'Mandalay', his relationship with his wife Mavis, and his addiction to home-made curries and homing pigeons.

'Union Jack on his bungalow? I don't suppose,' I asked hopefully, 'he lowers it at sunset by any chance?'

'He does Mr Rumpole! I swear to you he does,' 'Cliff' laughed delightedly. 'Is that sort of stuff any use to you?'

'I would say extremely useful.'

'Cliff' disappeared into the crowd, and I went over to the bar to find Miss Trant in sympathetic conversation with my pupil. As I arrived she went off to join her learned leader, Guthrie Featherstone, who was on the point of returning to Court.

'That woman!' Khan said looking after her. 'Is she of immoral character or what is she?'

'Why? Whatever did she say?'

'She said that she and I had the same problems. She wanted us to be friends and allies.'

'Oh, Khan ...'

'I told her that my father, who is Chief of Police in the Punjab, had gone to financial sacrifices to send me to England, and I was in no position to form any alliance with her even if I wanted to. In my country we would call that an immoral woman.'

Poor Miss Trant. The way of the liberal is extremely hard, as I found out when I came to address the jury at the end of the proceedings of R. *v.* Parkin.

*

I had worked carefully on my final speech and I joyfully incorporated all the information about my client that 'Cliff' had given me. As a matter of fact I thought it went rather well.

'Ladies and gentlemen of the jury,' I said, 'let me introduce you to a dreamer! He doesn't dream of money, or women – he dreams of the ancient days of the British Raj. Captain Rex Parkin. It's true. He's an ex-Captain of the Pay Corps. True that he's never been further East, as far as I know, than a day trip to Boulogne.'

One jury woman smiled, gradually others started to smile.

'The closest he's got to India is the weekly night out he has with his Memsahib, Mrs Mavis Parkin, in the "Star of India Curry House" in Bexley Heath.'

Someone in the jury started to laugh. I caught a glimpse of Captain Parkin's furious face in the dock and bashed on regardless.

'But Captain Rex Parkin, dreaming away amongst his pigeons and his old bound copies of the *Boys' Own Paper*, fancies himself an officer of the British Raj. The Union Jack flies daily over his bungalow "Mandalay", number 12B Durbar Lane, and is solemnly lowered every evening at sunset. Hardly appropriate dreams, are they, for the world of today? When you can hardly call out the Bengal Lancers to subdue a spot of trouble on the Ealing frontier.'

Now I was getting continuous snuffles of laughter from the jury, and behind me the prisoner at the bar was becoming increasingly restless.

'Or ride out by elephant to accept the surrender of the Maharajah of Muswell Hill?'

Captain Parkin struggled to his feet, but the Dock Officer put a hand on his arm and he subsided. He sat more or less quiet for my peroration.

'Is this a free country, members of the jury? Is this a country where Captain Parkin and other eccentrics can flourish in all their dottiness? I may not agree with what Captain Parkin said ... It's very easy to believe in free speech for those who agree with ... But someone, a wise French man, once gave us the answer ... "I disagree with everything you say, but I will defend to the death your right to say it." '

'I wish to say . . .' My client was standing rigidly to attention, apparently about to make another speech repudiating the charge of dottiness made against him by his learned Counsel.

'Sit down, Rex!' The words were only whispered but they came quite clearly from 'Cliff' in the back of the Court.

'I wish to say. I obey orders,' said Captain Parkin, and sat down and kept his mouth shut from then on.

*

Judge Jimmie Jamieson's summing-up came in for a good deal of criticism in the press and on telly, so I'll just give you the final, ill-considered, passage:

'What the defendant is alleged to have said, members of the jury, is that most of us are happier in our own homes. You may have heard the old saying, "My heart's in the Highlands, my heart isn't here". I myself am a native of another country, members of the jury. I was born in Kirkcudbrightshire. Often amid the bustle of London's traffic I long for the peace of the little village I came from and where, I hope, in my retirement, to return. I don't suppose I'd be in the least upset if anyone said that about me. Nor would I take offence if he said I have different blood in my veins. The blood of Clan Jamieson of the Glen! I don't think I can help you any further, ladies and gentlemen. You will go out and consider your verdict.'

As I have written elsewhere I regard the time when the jury is out as the worst part of a barrister's life. Your mouth is dry, your hands sweat, and, whatever the case, all your life's work seems to be on trial and waiting for a verdict. I went up to the Bar Mess on the top floor of the Old Bailey, and barristers in similar circumstances were playing draughts, or drinking coffee, or reading the *Sun*. I lit a small cigar and Miss Trant came up to me, clearly enraged.

'What did you think of that jury?'

'I thought they seemed moderately sympathetic.' In fact they seemed to be a middle-aged lot of solid citizens from the New

Cross area. I saw them nod several times at the judge's summing-up.

'Oh, did you really? Charmed, do you think they were, by your call to free speech?'

'I think they saw the point,' I told her. 'In fairness.'

'And Jimmie Jamieson wanted to pay his glowing tribute to Voltaire, too. For the first time in his life?'

'Miss Trant. You're becoming eloquent!' I looked at her with approval. No doubt she had learned her art from me, but she might turn out to be a credit to our Chambers.

'I'll tell you about that jury,' she went on remorselessly. 'I was watching their faces. They just wanted the faintest excuse to let the Fascist beast off. That's all they want.'

'Don't be ridiculous, Miss Trant. They'll decide the whole thing perfectly fairly. If they acquit it'll be because they believe in free speech.'

'Or because they're a bunch of Paki-bashers?'

I wished she wouldn't say such things. I was beginning to find them curiously unsettling. I was further unsettled when the jury came back half an hour later with a unanimous verdict 'Not Guilty'. I went over to congratulate my client, who was being 'sprung' from the dock. He looked at me with his strangely colourless eyes, standing like a ram-rod, in his parody of a military bearing, and said something to me which I shall not quickly forget.

'May God forgive you, Mr Rumpole,' he said. 'I certainly shan't.'

*

It was some months later that I learned the end of the Captain Rex Parkin story. A plump, grey-haired lady came to see me with young Simmonds, it seemed she wanted to sue certain members of the South-Eastern Committee of the 'Britain First' Party for damages for the way they had treated her husband. She asked me if she had a case, and described a meeting of the committee which took place in the living-room of their bungalow 'Mandalay' soon after I had secured her husband's acquittal. 'Cliff' Worseley was there, and Sydney Cox as chairman. I pictured the scene, the sullen faces seated round among the souvenirs of the Empire, the silent Captain Parkin sitting to attention on an upright chair, Mavis Parkin pouring coffee for the group and staying to listen to the debate. I can even imagine the offensive pomposity with which 'Cliff' put the motion.

'In a pitiful attempt to save his own skin, Rex Parkin showed the yellow streak, gentlemen. He allowed his barrister, in a so-called Court of Law, to pour scorn on the party. To make us a laughing stock! At the Old Bailey and in the National Press! Therefore I beg to move, Sydney, as deputy-chairman, and gentlemen, that Rex Parkin having proved himself unworthy of the high office we have entrusted to him, be removed as a prospective candidate of the 'Britain First' Party.

'Have you anything to say, Rex?' the chairman asked him.

'No. No. Nothing to say.'

The motion it seemed was carried and 'Cliff' Worseley was chosen as the new candidate. He stood and made a short opening address.

'Gentlemen, the need of the party is for more positive, dynamic leadership. The days of the British Raj are over. The gorgeous "Empah" on which the sun never set . . . is gone. We have work to do, gentlemen, more suited to the desperate needs of this particular moment in time . . . And in that work we must not be afraid of dirtying our hands in the interests of the party.'

Mavis watched as her husband got up, stood to attention and left the room. It seemed that he kept his pigeons in an old shed at the bottom of the garden. What his wife didn't know was that he also kept there an old army revolver and a certain amount of ammunition. She was washing up the coffee cups when she heard a shot, and saw the pigeons fly up in a white cloud. Captain Parkin, having been responsible, as he thought, for my ridiculing his party, had shot himself.

'They always wanted to get rid of him, you see. So they used that as an excuse. And it was Rex's whole life, his whole life entirely.'

I had to advise her that, so far as I could see, she had no legal remedy.

*

We were having one of our regular Chambers meetings, drinking tea out of Guthrie Featherstone's bone china tea set in Guthrie Featherstone's big room, and we were discussing the question of new tenants.

'The departure of George Frobisher to the Circuit Court Bench has left something of a gap in Chambers. Clearly we need a new tenant,' said the Q.C., M.P. 'Erskine-Brown will remind us of the candidates. There seem to be two main contenders.'

'Well, we have had an application from Owen Glendour-Owen. He wants to move up to London. He has a very sound practice in Wales. Apparently he'll bring us a large number of Welsh solicitors.'

'That's what I'm afraid of,' I grumbled.

'Really, Rumpole!' I was rebuked.

'I'm sorry. I forgot about the Race Relations Act.'

'I have seen Glendour-Owen. He seems to me to be an admirable candidate,' Featherstone told us.

'I do miss George. I can't see myself revelling in Pommeroy's Wine Bar with Glendour whatever-you-call-him.'

'The other candidate is Rumpole's pupil, Lutaf Ali Khan . . .'

'Now Khan does represent something of a special case . . .' Featherstone started innocently, but the eloquent Miss Trant was on her feet at once.

'Oh yes! I was a special case, wasn't I?'

'Now Philly . . .' Erskine-Brown tried vainly to calm her down.

'No. No, I'm going to say this. I was a special case when I joined Chambers. No one wanted a woman. I had this extraordinary difficulty getting hold of the key of the loo. And Albert had to go through the embarrassment of explaining that the barrister he was sending out to the Hendon Court might turn out to be a woman . . . Now he'll have to explain that he's a . . . a . . . what do you want me to say . . . Gentleman from Pakistan . . . ? It doesn't matter how good we are. We start out with a built-in handicap. That's what you mean by a special case, isn't it?'

'As a matter of fact what I meant was,' Featherstone explained patiently, 'we're under a good deal of pressure from the Bar Council. I also happen to know the views of the Lord Chancellor's office. Keith's tremendously keen on places being found in Chambers for ... overseas applicants.'

'I wouldn't, speaking for myself, be influenced by the wishes of the Bar Council, or even of the Chancellor's department.' Claude Erskine-Brown adopted his most judicial manner and Miss Trant barked at him.

'I'm sure you wouldn't.'

'I have given a certain amount of paper-work to Khan,' Erskine-Brown went on, 'and I happened to be in Bow Street, waiting, when I heard him do a prosecution, standing in for Hoskins.'

'You were waiting in Bow Street?' I was surprised.

'I had a licensing application,' Erskine-Brown said with dignity.

'Don't worry, old sweetheart. No one's accusing you of having been nabbed for soliciting.'

'In my opinion Lutaf Khan would make a useful and hard-working member of Chambers.' Ignoring me Erskine-Brown concluded his judgement and Miss Trant looked at him, surprised and grateful.

'He also has genuine if not particularly formed musical tastes. He can feel his way round Donizetti but I hope to help him towards Wagner. I've promised him an evening at Covent Garden, Philly.'

'He'd probably rather have another afternoon at Bow Street,' I told him.

'Thank you, Erskine-Brown,' Featherstone said. 'Thanks for your contribution. Well now, suppose we take a vote. All those in favour of the candidacy of Owen Glendour-Owen?'

'Is that the darkie?' Uncle Tom whispered deafeningly.

In the end we voted to invite my pupil to occupy a permanent seat in Chambers, and I went off to tell the news which I had no doubt, with the present shortage of places in decent sets, would overjoy him.

When I got to my room, I found Khan working hard and a letter on my desk from the Lord Chancellor's department. I opened it with somewhat mystified fingers to discover that old

Keith Hopner, Guthrie's friend, wanted to see me as soon as possible at the House of Lords. Was Rumpole tipped for High Office? I put the thought aside and turned to Khan.

'We just had a discussion of your candidacy up at the Chambers meeting and I'm delighted to tell you ... You're in.'

'No? ...' As I thought, the man was overwhelmed.

'Difficult to believe? Not at all. There was just a short discussion ... and of course you can go on sharing my room. Keep your desk over there and ...'

'This is terribly embarrassing.'

'Not at all. Be glad to have you. Look, if you'd like to start making a note of the deps in this nice little murder ...' I offered him a pile of papers that had just come in.

'The truth is ... Oh gosh. I don't want to offend Mr Featherstone and I *have* enjoyed it here. But no. No, I don't want to stay in these Chambers.'

'You don't *what*?' I couldn't believe my ears.

'I am more interested in prosecuting, Mr Rumpole. As you know, I am most keen that some of those terrible fellows get their come-uppance.'

'Yes, but Khan ... You can get prosecution briefs here. I don't do them but ...'

'Careless driving, Mr Rumpole. Take and drive away. Small potatoes. I am after the bigger fish.'

By now I must admit I was feeling ever so slightly miffed.

'Oh yes. And where exactly are you going to put down your nets?'

'I am offered a place in a Treasury Counsel's Chambers. We have a direct line there, to the Director of Public Prosecutions. With great respect, it doesn't seem to me that you fellows have too much contact ... with the Powers That Be.'

I looked at Khan amazed.

'I am sorry, Mr Rumpole. I have admired your way of doing cases ... It's your technique to laugh at them, isn't it? I suppose that's what Captain Rex Parkin found a bit too much to bear.'

'I wouldn't have thought you'd feel Captain Parkin was a great loss to society!'

'It is what is coming after him. That's what makes me more nervous.'

I let that one go, and returned to the business of his future, rather than this country's.

'It's your decision, Khan,' I told him. 'You must do exactly what you think best. But you're quite wrong if you think this Chambers has no connection with the Powers That Be.' I picked up the letter from my desk. 'I have a letter here. An invitation to the Lord Chancellor's office . . . for a little chat.'

*

Walking down the Embankment towards the House of Lords, on a sunny day with the seagulls shrieking round Boadicea's statue, I asked myself who on earth wanted to be a Circus Judge? Poor old George Frobisher did. I pitied him. I really pitied him. Working every day. Ten till four. Paying as you earn. Might as well be a bank manager. Besides which it was a lonely job, being a judge. No friends. No real mates. No companionable jars, at the end of the day, in Pommeroy's Wine Bar. I also wondered who in hell wanted to judge people. I mean what would I say to them? 'Mr Bloggs, you will go to prison for two years, and there, but for the Grace of God, Horace Rumpole goes with you'?

But when I was being led down the red-carpeted corridors of that dream palace, the House of Lords, past the portraits of old Dukes and Marquesses, my thoughts, I must confess, took a somewhat different turn. On the other hand, well, on the other hand . . . It's an easy life. I mean, you sit there, without any strain or worry. I mean, you don't give a damn who *wins*. And of course there's a bit of pension attached. Once you get your bottom on the Bench you're in for a pension. Hilda and I would be glad of a pension, I thought.

And I might even be able to do a bit of good, as a judge. Show appropriate mercy. 'Madam, you are more sinned against than sinning. The sentence will be half an hour's imprisonment which you have already served. You are free to go.' Look of cold fury on the officer in charge of the case. Being a judge might even provide Rumpole with a certain amount of harmless fun . . .

At which point I was shown into the presence of Sir Keith

Hopner, O.B.E., a large pink vision in a black jacket and pin-striped trousers, who sat in a leather chair and looked at me smiling.

'I have been thinking it over most carefully, Keith,' I told him, 'and I'm not totally opposed to the suggestion.'

'Good. That's very good. Judge Jamieson said you might be interested ...'

'*He* said that?' I was surprised he had been discussing my elevation with the primitive Scot.

'Yes. Pity about Jimmie. Pity he put his foot in it.'

'Well, one does have to be rather careful,' I sounded circumspect, 'what one says on the Bench.'

'I'm so glad you agree.'

'I've thought a lot about it,' I told him. 'But the fact is, I get rather tired these days. Not quite so young as I was, of course. Slogging from the Sessions to the Bailey and out to Chelmsford ... Plays hell with the back.'

'I hope you'll have *time* for this job,' Sir Keith was concerned.

'Well, of course. Ten till four. No home-work! Wonderful.'

'Well, it shouldn't take as long as *that*.'

'What won't?' I was puzzled.

'The little job I have in mind ... Let me explain.'

'Well. Of course I can get used to it.'

'I'm sure you can. After all, you were at "Linklater's" weren't you?'

I couldn't see what my old school had to do with it.

'Yes. But is that a qualification?'

'Didn't Jimmy Jamieson make it clear?' Sir Keith explained carefully. 'We wanted you to take on as Secretary of the "Old Linklater's" at the Bar Society. The O.L.B.S. We dine once a year, you know. In the Connaught Rooms. Come on Rumpole! We old members of school have got to stick together!'

My look of amazement turned suddenly to laughter. In fact I was still laughing as I walked back to the Temple, along the Embankment. It sounded as if the seagulls were laughing with me.

*

Rumpole and the Case of Identity

'Was this the face that launched a thousand ships
And did the stabbing in the Wandsworth Off-Licence?'

These lines passed through my mind as I sat working late in
Chambers. My wife Mrs Hilda Rumpole, known to me as She
Who Must Be Obeyed, had joined some dubious club called the
Bar Choral Society and was out in the evenings at this time, in-
dulging her fantasies in rehearsing Handel's *Messiah* as Christmas was growing remorselessly near. On my desk was a police
identikit photograph of a long-faced young man with bristling
sideburns wearing, just in case no one noticed him, a loudly
checked red-and-yellow tartan cap. This was the face, un-
reliably created from snatches of memory and a police artist's
pencil, of the man who entered an off-licence in Wandsworth
and stabbed the licensee, a small Irishman named Tosher O'Neil,
in the face and arm, making it necessary for repair work to be
carried out to the tune of twenty-seven stitches. Also on my desk
was a photograph of my client, a young man in his twenties
named David Anstey, a driver in the well-known South London
mini-cab firm 'Allbright's Cars'. Friends and fellow drivers had
told the police that David's sartorial taste ran to an unfortunate
red-and-yellow tartan cap (I wondered how many thousand luna-
tics went to football matches each weekend in such headgear). If
the prosecution could prove that this was the face Tosher remembered behind the descending knife, then David was due for a substantial visit to Her Majesty for Grievous Bodily Harm : which
would be a pity as he had an excellent work record, was just married to a young wife, and his previous slips ran to driving off other
people's Ford Cortinas, so that knifing his fellow citizens would
seem to be something of a new departure.

I was also wondering, as I read the papers in R. *v.* Anstey, how many seconds Tosher had really had to see his attacker's face; and I was brooding on the horrible difficulty, and total unreliability, of trials decided on identification evidence. Do all the middle-aged ladies who write to 'Any Answers' calling for the return of hanging understand that the fallibility of human memory would ensure that we hanged at least a few of the wrong people, or is that a risk we are bound to take in the pursuit of their favourite sport? I was thinking of all these things, and of the greater difficulty in our case: Tosher O'Neil had picked David Anstey out at an identification parade when my unfortunate client wasn't wearing a cap at all. As I turned back to compare the identikit picture with the undoubted face of the said Anstey there was a brisk knock at my door and the anxious face of Claude Erskine-Brown peered into my room.

'Rumpole . . . you're burning the midnight oil?'

'Ah, Erskine-Brown, Claude.' I decided to use him as a test for man's power of identification. 'How would you describe me, exactly?'

'You? Why on earth . . . ?'

'Let's say I'm getting unsure of my own identity. Describe Rumpole as you saw him go into Chambers this morning. Are you sure you *did* see me go into Chambers this morning? Can you swear you're not mistaken?'

'Of course I saw you coming into Chambers. Look, Rumpole . . .'

'Yes, but how *did* you know it was me?' I pressed him.

'Well, it looked like you,' he answered rudely, 'short and fat.'

'You mean well filled out. Generously proportioned. Comfortable?'

'No. Fat. Look. There's something going on down the passage and I don't like the look of it . . .' He moved closer to me in a conspiratorial fashion.

'Are you *sure* it was me?' I returned to the subject which was starting to become an obsession.

'Of course it was you. It had your muffler. And your dreadful old hat on!'

'My old hat on! Exactly. You recognized the hat!' I felt that I had hit on a vital clue to David Anstey's defence.

'Rumpole. Will you come and look at this? It's a question of Chambers security!'

Erskine-Brown had become so insistent that I had to humour him. So off we set to the room of our learned Head of Chambers, Guthrie Featherstone, Q.C., M.P. There was a light on, showing a bright streak under the door, so that it seemed that he too was burning the midnight oil. However, Claude Erskine-Brown assured me, the door was locked, and by way of evidence he turned the handle and failed to gain admittance. There did seem to be a small sound, only a whisper like the intake of breath, or perhaps my old ears deceived me and it was the sigh of some building sinking into the ground or the distant thunder of traffic on the Embankment.

'Well, what's wrong?' I asked him, for some reason we both seemed to be whispering. 'Featherstone always locks his door. He's afraid people'll come in and read his "All England Reports", and pinch his paper clips.'

At which I thought I heard another sound from behind the door, less a distant whisper than a suppressed giggle.

'What on earth's that?' Erskine-Brown looked seriously alarmed.

'Mice!' I reassured him. 'These old places are overrun by mice.'

'It was a sound . . . more like giggling.'

'Even mice – can enjoy a joke occasionally.' I put a comforting hand on Claude's shoulder. 'You're working too hard.'

'I have been snowed under lately,' the distraught man admitted.

'Pack it in, Erskine-Brown. Abandon the affidavits . . . Come and have a nightcap at Pommeroy's Wine Bar.' I steered him away down the passage. 'You ought to watch out you know. A man's got to be very careful when he starts to hear mice giggling in the night.'

*

It was some weeks prior to this night of adventure that a second typist had joined our clerk's room staff, a fairly personable brown-haired young lady named Angela who wore jeans and an American combat shirt of the sort that might have been bought second-hand from some Vietnam veteran. I can't imagine that this apparition would have produced in old C. H. Wystan (my late father-in-law and our one-time Head of Chambers) any result less dramatic than a heart attack, but Guthrie Featherstone made no protest, Henry appeared to tolerate her and Uncle Tom seemed positively charmed by her; although I did catch in Erskine-Brown's eye, when he noticed her, the gleam of an early New England settler who's brought face to face with a young, attractive and particularly burnable witch. I came into the clerk's room one lunch-time, the jury at London Sessions having convicted three cannabis dealers of mine, and told the bad news to Henry. My clients had got three years apiece.

'I suppose the judge went off and drank his large whisky and soda!' Angela spoke indignantly from behind her typewriter.

'Yes. I suppose he did.' The judge had in fact been old Bullingham, so the young lady's instinct was undoubtedly correct.

'Still, it wasn't your fault. You did your best. You were defending, weren't you?' She gave me a warm smile of approval, at which point Erskine-Brown came in with some document and asked Angela to type it. She ran a quick eye over the pleading and gave us a quotation. '"The Plaintiffs, the Gargantua Trust Property Company Ltd, are landlords of the said premises."'

'Brilliant! You *can* read it,' Erskine-Brown said with more than a hint of irony.

'"And the defendant, Mrs Parfitt, is in default of rent to the extent of £208.13. Notice to quit having been given."' Angela read with considerable disapproval and then exploded, 'Whose side are we on?'

'We are on the side, Angela, that sends us the work,' Erskine-Brown told her coldly.

'She got notice to quit. For a measly £208.13! Gargantua Trust Property Company Ltd! Well, I don't imagine they're short of a bob or two . . .'

I was observing this scene, which I was starting to enjoy as Erskine-Brown became irate.

'Angela! You're not required to judge the case. That can be left in the safe hands of the judge of the Marylebone County Court.'

'I bet Mrs Parfitt's an elderly widow,' said Angela with some considerable satisfaction.

'Of course. With twenty-three starving children. It doesn't matter what she is, Angela. Just you type it out.'

*

I had thought nothing of the mysterious incident of the light in the locked room (it's easy enough to forget to switch the light off when you lock a door) but I was a little worried, at this time, by the appearance and behaviour of our Head of Chambers, Guthrie Featherstone, Q.C., M.P. He came into Chambers very late, he looked pale and somewhat seedy, and he showed a marked lack of enthusiasm for his practice at the Bar. I put all this down to the burden of governing England, seeing us through inflation, settling Rhodesia etc. which he had assumed; but, as I sat over an early evening claret with him and Erskine-Brown in Pommeroy's Wine Bar I couldn't help feeling that Claude's incessant complaints were adding considerably to the burdens of office. When the matter of the petty cash and Dianne's salary had been brought up the Head of Chambers gave a world-weary sigh.

'All-night sitting,' he said. 'I don't know how long the old frame'll stand it.'

'Really. What great affair of State were you discussing?' I asked.

'Some earth-shaking measure for the protection of cod in Scottish waters...' Guthrie told us.

'I want to raise the matter of security in Chambers.' Poor Featherstone groaned slightly. Erskine-Brown went on remorselessly. 'The other night there were lights left on. After you'd locked up...'

'I must have forgotten...'

'And we distinctly heard a sound. Coming from your room!'

'How extraordinarily odd!' Featherstone seemed puzzled.

'Rumpole thought it might have been mice.'

'Oh, really?' The Q.C., M.P. looked at me, I thought, gratefully.

'And there's another matter I wanted to raise.'

'Another?' Here was a camel, I felt, whose back was about to be broken.

'That new girl, Angela. The one who does the typing now . . .'

'Henry says she's a bit of an asset. I know nothing about her, of course.' Featherstone sounded casual. 'But it seems that Dianne just couldn't cope single-handed . . .'

'The girl objects to typing a landlord's statement of claim. She only wants to type on behalf of the tenant. It really adds a new horror to life at the Bar, if one is going to have all one's cases decided in the typing pool.' Erskine-Brown completed the indictment and Featherstone gave him another uneasy smile.

'I really don't see how you can dignify those two girls, Dianne and "Angela", did you say her name was? with the title of "typing pool". Anyway, Henry tells me she's extremely good. It seems she's pretty well indispensable. But perhaps you'll head a small committee, Claude, to deal with the question of mice in Chambers.'

Shortly after this Erskine-Brown went off to some musical evening with Miss Phillida Trant, and Henry called in for a quick Cinzano Bianco and a complaint to his Head of Chambers.

'It's that new girl, Angela, Mr Featherstone. Quite frankly she's getting on my wick.'

At which I was amazed to hear Guthrie Featherstone say,

'Really, Henry? Mr Erskine-Brown was just saying what an enormous help she is, typing his pleadings.'

Henry turned to me for support.

'She wants to turn our clerk's room into a co-operative, sir. She thinks the girls should chip in to my percentage of Chambers' fees.'

'Workers' participation, Henry,' Featherstone closed his eyes wearily, 'it's bound to come.'

At which Henry gave me a look which said more clearly than

words, 'not in these Chambers it bloody isn't', and I was left to brood on the strange duplicity of Guthrie Featherstone, Q.C., M.P.

*

'Would I wear me cap, Squire? Would I? Not if I was going to cut up some geezer in an off-licence. That'd be like leaving me visiting card.' I was with my client, young David Anstey, and Jennifer, a pleasant and hard-working solicitor's clerk, in the interview room at Brixton Prison.

'Mr Anstey,' I told him. 'If I ever get you out of this hotel, you might consider reading for the Bar. Because, old darling, you have put your finger on the bull point of the defence! Why would anyone wear a comical cap when out on an errand of mayhem and malicious wounding? Unless...'

'Unless they wanted to be recognized!' Jennifer suggested.

'Unless they wanted *someone* to be recognized...' I lit a small cigar. Outside the glass box of the interview room I could see other barristers interviewing other clients in other glass boxes, until the series ended in the screws' office, with its pleasant collection of cacti in pots. Outside in the yard other screws were exercising malignant Airedales.

'I'm not worried, Squire,' Dave Anstey sounded unhealthily optimistic. 'I'm just not worried at all. I'm in the clear.'

'No one in Brixton's in the clear, old darling,' I told him. 'Not till they hear the magical words "Not Guilty".' I sat down, for the purpose of reading my brief. 'Now, this little alibi of yours... It entirely depends on the evidence of your guv'nor?'

'He's very good to me, Mr Rumpole. And to the wife, since we got married. He bought all our home for us. Very generous-minded individual. "Freddy Allbright will see you right." That's his motto. Biggest mini-cab owner in London.'

'You were with him all the evening of Tuesday, March the fourth?' The stabbing in the off-licence had taken place at about a quarter to nine.

'I come back from a trip to Wembley at 8. Then Freddy took me for a curry. We was together until 10.30. Then I went home to the wife.'

Alibis always sound so delightfully healthy, but they crack up dreadfully easily. I asked Dave how his kindly employer could possibly fix the date of one out of a long line of curries.

'It was the evening before his wife's birthday. He'd got Mrs Allbright a gift.'

'What exactly?'

'It was an evening bag. Highly tasteful. For his Ladies' Night down at the Masons. He even showed it to me. Look, Mr Rumpole, it's cast iron, my alibi.'

Whatever the truth about his defence, Dave Anstey it seemed had total faith in it. As for me, I'm not sure that I like cast iron alibis. They're the sort that sink quickest, to the bottom of the sea.

*

To wash away the sour taste of Brixton nick I went for a glass of Chateau Fleet Street (as a matter of fact the metallic flavour of this particular claret gives it a slight prison flavour, as if the grape had been grown on the sunless side of Wormwood Scrubs: I exaggerate, of course; this is a libel on Pommeroy's Wine Bar, whose budget Bordeaux has elevated my evenings and kept me astonishingly regular for years). As I arrived in the bar I was greeted by Erskine-Brown who was waving a crumpled copy of *The Times* newspaper, and by Miss Phillida Trant, who had been booked as junior to 'Soapy Joe' Truscott of Treasury Counsel, to appear on behalf of Her Majesty the Queen in the case of David Anstey. No sooner had I drawn up a stool and ordered a bottle of the cooking claret and three glasses than Erskine-Brown shoved his newspaper under my nose, open at the uninspiring account of yesterday's debates in Parliament.

'Just take a look at the end. I've marked it in red.' Erskine-Brown was almost too excited for coherent speech.

'After the defeat of the motion to Preserve the Ancient Grasslands, the House rose at 10.30,' I read aloud. 'Earth-shattering news, is it, Claude? What, am I meant to flee the country? Put myself out to pasture in some newly preserved grasslands?'

'Guthrie Featherstone clearly told me that last night he was at an *all-night sitting* on the Cod Fisheries (Scotland) Bill.' Erskine-Brown had apparently reached the punch-line.

'Well, I don't see what's peculiar about that ...' I gave him a blankish look.

'It sounds to me like the collapse of an alibi.' Miss Trant, our Portia, seemed to have sniffed a *prima facie* case.

'Exactly!' Erskine-Brown chimed in. I did my best to give their excitement a douche of cold water.

'Not at all. My God, I can see where you're headed, Miss Trant. The Portia of the Prosecution! Suspicious of everyone.' The claret arrived, I gave them each a glass and some soothing words. 'It's perfectly natural for Q.C., M.P.s to forget which day it is. Poor devils, they must be constantly under the delusion that they've been discussing cod in Scotland until the small hours. If you take my advice, Miss Trant, you'll keep your mind on the off-licence stabbing. I was meaning to ask the prosecution. Who owns that off-licence, by the way?' I was looking for a motive for the Wandsworth stabbing, so I casually asked the question which was almost fatal to the defence.

'Who *owns* it?' Miss Trant frowned. 'I don't know. I could find out for you.'

'Oh, do do that, Miss Trant. It might be so much more important than the busy life of our learned Head of Chambers.'

*

That evening an event of unearthly, not to say spooky significance occurred in Casa Rumpole, 25B Froxbury Court in the Gloucester Road. I was sitting by the electric fire, reading the depositions in a promising little indecent assault and taking a bedtime bracer of the old and Tawney, when the house was riven by the sound of a rich contralto voice raised in what seemed to be some devout ditty.

'The Lord God Omnipotent ...
The Lord God Omnipotent ...
The Lord God Omnipotent ...

sang what I first took for the ghost of some member of the Bach Choir, justifiably murdered long ago in Froxbury Court. Then I remembered that my wife was in the kitchen, the apparent source of the sound. Had She Who Must Be Obeyed taken leave of her senses?

'*Hilda!* What on *earth's* going on?'

'I'm doing the *Messiah*,' Hilda said enigmatically, making a non-singing entrance with two cups of steaming Nescafé.

'What the hell for?'

'The Bar Choral Society.' She put down the coffee as though I should have known all about it. 'Marigold Featherstone rang me up and asked if I'd be interested. They take on wives.'

'An assembly of barristers' wives. Giving tongue. How perfectly ghastly!' I lapped up port, this was no moment for coffee.

'In praise of God, Rumpole. It is going to be Christmas.' Hilda installed herself on the other side of the electric fire.

'Sometimes I wonder if God enjoys Christmas all that much.'

At which Hilda put down her cup and saucer and leant forward to say, extremely seriously, 'Marigold Featherstone's not a happy woman.'

'Perhaps it's the *Messiah* getting her down. It's been known to have that effect on people.

'It's Guthrie Featherstone.' Hilda shook her head sadly. 'If you ask my opinion, that marriage is dying for lack of attention.'

'Hilda! You shock me. You don't stand there at choir practice when you should be giving praise to the Lord, gossiping away about Featherstone's marriage?'

'It's not gossip, Rumpole. I told you. She's not a happy woman. Of course, it's enormously difficult being married to a politician . . .'

Or a part-time contralto . . . That was what I felt like saying. Actually I remained mute of malice.

'Their marriage is cracking up, Rumpole. And it's all *your fault.*'

'My fault?' I was astonished. I had only met Marigold Featherstone occasionally at a Chambers 'do'. An ex-nurse who had once played tennis for Roedean, she was not exactly Rumpole's bottle of claret.

'Guthrie's out late. Of course he has his all-night sittings. But even when he hasn't . . . it seems you keep him in Pommeroy's Wine Bar for hours. Boozing.'

'I do?' I only rarely took a glass with Guthrie, and, whenever I did, he was in and out of the bar like a rabbit in a hurry.

'Marigold asks him where he's been and he says, "Old Rumpole kept me talking about Chambers business in Pommeroy's. I simply couldn't get away from him." '

'*Old* Rumpole? Is that what he calls me?' If our learned Head of Chambers was going to use me as an alibi he might at least have been polite about me.

'I suppose that's what you were getting up to tonight.'

I had, it was true, whiled away a couple of hours in Pommeroy's, a place notable for the absence of Guthrie Featherstone, Q.C., M.P.

'Well, there wouldn't have been much point in coming back here, would there? Not while you were hitting high notes with Marigold Featherstone.'

'You want to be very careful, Rumpole. You want to be careful you don't break up *two* marriages.' On which line She returned to the kitchen to keep an urgent appointment with the washing-up. As the plates clattered I heard her, over again, carolling:

'The Lord God Omnipotent ...
The Lord God Omnipotent ...
The Lord God Omnipotent ... e ... e ... e ... ent
Reigneth!'

Oh well, I thought, thank God He's doing something at last.

*

In due course we assembled, myself, 'Soapy Joe' leading for the prosecution, Miss Trant, junior for the prosecution, Dave Anstey and Jennifer my solicitors' managing clerk, before Mr Justice Vosper, a pale and sarcastic judge who has never learnt to sit quietly, but always wants to take part in the proceedings, usually as a super-leader for the prosecution. Tosher O'Neil, scarred down one side of his face, a living piece of evidence for the sympathetic jury, was in the witness-box, concluding his examination-in-chief by Miss Trant.

'Can you describe the man who attacked you?'

'He had this red cap on ...'

'Apart from the red cap?'

'Yes. Apart from the red cap. Come on, Portia,' I muttered at her. It didn't put her off.

'Well, he was tall. Big-built.' The witness gave the man in the dock a meaningful look.

'Like about twenty million others,' I muttered, and found the judge staring in my direction, with some distaste.

'Did you say something, Mr Rumpole?' his Lordship asked.

'Nothing at all, my Lord.'

'What about his hair? What you could see of it.' Miss Trant asked.

'He had long sideburns. Sort of brown colour. What I could see of it.'

Miss Trant whispered to her leader to check she had asked all the relevant questions, and I heaved myself to my hind legs to cross-examine.

'If you look at my client, Mr O'Neil, you can see quite clearly. He has no sideburns at all.'

'No. No, he hasn't.'

'Mr Rumpole. I'm sure you don't need reminding. We live in the age of the electric razor.' Mr Justice Vosper was really the worst sort of judge; the judge who makes jokes.

'My Lord?'

'Sideburns can be shaved off. If it's convenient to do so.' Vosper J. didn't actually wink at the jury, but they gave him a conspiratorial smile.

I re-attacked the witness O'Neil.

'You told us his sideburns were sort of brown. Sort of ginger-brown? Greyish-brown? Blackish-brown? Or just brown-brown?'

Tosher didn't answer, so I pressed on.

'You know, we have heard the evidence of Mr Smith who was waiting for a bus outside the off-licence. He told us about a man with a red tartan cap and *black* sideburns.'

'I ... didn't have a lot of time to notice him. It was that quick.'

'That quick! You only saw him, didn't you, for a matter of seconds?'

'Yes.'

'So my client stands on trial for a couple of seconds . . .'

'It will no doubt be considerably longer, by the time *you're* finished, Mr Rumpole.' Vosper could never resist that sort of remark; the jury gave him an obedient titter, and I said, 'if your Lordship pleases' as coldly as possible, then I asked the witness,

'You've never met Dave Anstey?'

'Never in my life.'

'So far as you knew he had absolutely no motive for attacking you?'

'Not as far as I know.'

'Mr Rumpole. As you know perfectly well, motive is quite irrelevant in a criminal prosecution.' Mr Justice Vosper was giving me a rough ride. I began to long for a 'Not Guilty' verdict, if only to see his Lordship's look of bemused disappointment.

Outside the Court, when we broke for lunch, a large man smelling of Havana cigars, wearing a camel-hair overcoat and several obtrusive rings came up to me smiling cheerfully. He was accompanied by a blonde and extremely personable young woman, lapped in an expensive fur coat.

'How're we doing, Mr Rumpole?' the man asked, and the lady announced herself as 'Dave's wife. Betty Anstey'.

'Betty's only been married to Dave six months,' the man said. 'Lovely girl, isn't she, Mr Rumpole? Particularly lovely girl . . .'

'You are . . . ?'

'Freddie Allbright. "Allbright will see you right." That's my motto, Mr Rumpole. In mini-cars as in everything else.'

'Our alibi witness?' I asked Jennifer.

'I've got the alibi ready, Mr Rumpole. Ready to go whenever you want it.' Freddie Allbright smiled, ready, it seemed, to see us right at any time.

'Can't talk to witnesses, you know.' It silenced him. 'I expect we'll call you on Monday.' I asked Mrs Anstey if she'd been in Court. She shook her head tearfully.

'I can't go in there, Mr Rumpole. I really can't. Not to have everyone staring at me because of David. Dave's all right, is he?'

'As well as can be expected,' I told her. 'I'm sure he'd appreciate a visit, down the cells.'

'I promised the young lady a lunch, Mr Rumpole,' Freddie told me. 'Better get our skates on, Betty love. Don't want some lawyer snitching our table at the Savoy, do we, Mr Rumpole?'

'No. No, I'm sure you don't.'

I watched Betty put her arm in Freddie's and they walked away. I was trying to think of the implications of this vision when Miss Trant came alongside with some rather odd news.

'I've got that information for you,' she said helpfully. 'The landlord of the off-licence. It's a company called "Allbright Motors".'

'Thank you, Miss Trant.' I wished I hadn't asked.

*

I didn't myself have lunch in the Savoy that day. In fact I didn't even have a slice of cold pie in the pub opposite. I went straight down to the cells with Jennifer and voiced my anxieties to our client Dave Anstey.

'If an alibi comes unstuck, everything comes unstuck.' I looked at him thoughtfully and lit a small cigar. 'They may not believe *you*, just because they don't believe your alibi . . .'

'They'll believe Freddie, Squire. Freddie's got no axe to grind.' Dave seemed imperturbably cheerful.

'Hasn't he?'

'Has he, Mr Rumpole?' Jennifer frowned.

'Freddie Allbright owns the off-licence where Tosher was cut.'

'Never!' Dave seemed genuinely surprised to hear it.

'You didn't know that?'

'Straight up, Squire, I didn't . . . Does it make any difference?'

'I don't know. Tosher picked you out at the ID parade. You'd never seen him before.'

'Never in my life. Straight up.'

'*Someone* must have told him . . . about you and your remarkable head-gear. You trust Freddie Allbright?' Dave's answer was so enthusiastic that I almost began to doubt my own doubts.

'You must be joking. The things the Guvnor's done for me! Big bonus when we married. Canteen of cutlery, must have cost him two hundred nicker . . .'

'And a fur coat?' I asked him. But Dave Anstey didn't know anything about his wife's fur coat. And Jennifer seemed worried at my apparent distrust of our case on the alibi.

'If we don't call the alibi evidence,' she wondered, 'won't the prosecution comment? They've got Mr Allbright's statement.' She's a thoughtful girl Jennifer, with more sense of a trial than her employers who were no doubt lunching in the West End at length, setting up launderettes and discos: I gave her the benefit of my learned opinion.

'Let Soapy Joe comment till he's blue in the face. He'll be left with a weak case of identification.'

However any thought of giving our alibi a miss was clearly repugnant to our client.

'I want the Guvnor called,' he said. 'Freddie's been like a father to me.'

'Think about it, Dave. Then I'll need your written instructions before I call Mr Freddie Allbright.' I moved to the door. Dave looked up at me, he was frowning:

'What sort of coat exactly?'

'God knows! No doubt some rare animal gave up its life for it.'

'My Betty works, don't she? She saved up for it.' Dave had apparently convinced himself. 'You got to call the Guvnor, Mr Rumpole.'

'Please. Think about it, Dave.'

*

I was also thinking about it; and I was starting to get a glimmer of what later turned out to be the truth about the Anstey case as I called into Chambers the next morning to collect my brief, and a fresh supply of small cigars, on my way to the Bailey. When I got into my room I sniffed a female perfume and saw a familiar well-turned-out figure sitting in my client's chair. Although familiar I couldn't place my visitor at first, but the look of a rather attractive horse matched with the brisk tone of a ward sister left me in no doubt.

'I'm Marigold Featherstone. You remember me?'

'Of course. I'm just on my way down to the Bailey,' I dived for the brief and cheroots. 'Guthrie's room's along the passage.'

'He's not in. Whenever I ring up Chambers he's not in.'

'Perhaps, if I could give him some sort of message ...' I went to the door in a meaningful manner. At which point Marigold, wife of our Head of Chambers, dropped her bombshell.

'Mr Rumpole. Do you handle divorce?'

'Only rarely. And with a strong pair of tongs. Look, I must rush, I'm ...'

'I want you to act for me. If it should come to that.'

'Come to what, Mrs ... Marigold?' I paused, somewhat weakly.

'Divorce! Guthrie's behaving extremely oddly. He's never there.'

I could see that the woman was outraged, and I tried to cheer her up.

'Well, that can be an advantage, I suppose. In married life. Speaking for myself, I'm married to someone who's always there. Now, if you'll excuse me ...'

However Mrs Marigold Featherstone wouldn't let me go until she had given evidence.

'I saw Guthrie in Sloane Square. I saw him from the top of a bus. He was arm-in-arm with a girl. They were looking into Peter Jones's window. When I tackled him, he denied it.'

'Well now. How can you be sure it was Guthrie?' Instinctively I started to test the evidence. 'I mean from a bus what did you see? The top of his head ... For how long ... a couple of seconds?'

'I'm *sure* it was Guthrie.' The witness was almost too positive. 'He had his black jacket on, and striped trousers.'

I renewed the cross-examination. 'Ah, Mrs Feather ... Ah, Marigold. Now that's where mistakes are so easily made. You see, just *because* he had a black jacket on, you thought it was your husband! It's so easy to put a black jacket on, isn't it, or a red-and-yellow tartan cap. Do I make myself clear?'

'Not in the least.' Marigold frowned.

'Anyway. I'm a friend of Guthrie's. We stay out together late, boozing in Pommeroy's Wine Bar. That's where he is, a lot of the time.' I was beginning to feel anxious for the fate of the wretched Q.C., M.P.

'So he tells me.' Marigold did not sound friendly.

'And I'm in his Chambers. So I couldn't possibly act for you if it comes to divorce. It'd be extremely embarrassing,' I assured her.

Marigold's answer sounded like a brisk rebuke to a probationer nurse on the subject of bed-pans.

'If it comes to a divorce, Mr Rumpole,' she said, 'I want it to be as embarrassing as possible.'

*

Marigold's fell purpose was not, I was later to discover, the only trouble into which our Head of Chambers had been getting himself. It appeared that he had reached the stage of life when men are said to get hot flushes (I can't remember going through it myself) and suffer from the delusion that they embody the least admirable qualities of Don Juan and the late Rudolf Valentino. I heard that when Miss Phillida Trant, who is in fact, beneath a business-like exterior, extremely personable, went into Featherstone's room to borrow a book he invited her to lunch in Soho. When she told him, as was the case, that she was going out with Erskine-Brown (a contemporary phrase which I take to mean 'staying in' with Erskine-Brown) the rogue Guthrie said that Erskine-Brown never took her anywhere interesting, and asked if she had, in fact, ever been taken to 'Fridays', a dark cellar off Covent Garden where he said the B.P.s (Featherstone's appalling phrase, apparently it means Beautiful People) met nightly to jig about to loud music in the dark. This painful interview ended by Guthrie trying to remove Miss Trant's spectacles, in the way he said James Stewart always did, to reveal the full beauty of girl librarians in the films of the thirties.

It is a matter of history that, one night after a prolonged experience of *Rigoletto* at the Royal Opera House, Miss Trant did persuade her escort Erskine-Brown to take her down the inky entrance of 'Fridays'. There they saw, or thought they saw, a disturbing spectacle which was only described to me later. At that time I had no thoughts in my head except for those concerning the defence of Dave Anstey, and the perils we might face when we tried to prove his alibi.

*

When I got down to the Old Bailey I saw Betty Anstey, proudly wrapped in the fur in which I was beginning to suspect she slept, waiting outside our Court. I drew the usher aside and asked him as a particular favour to call her into Court when I tipped him the wink, and on no account give her the chance of taking off her coat. I then went into the ring and, having had firm instructions from Dave to do so, breathed a silent prayer, fastened my seat belt, and called Freddie Allbright Esq. in support of our alibi. Freddie walked confidently into the witness-box, large and neat in a blue suit, with a spotted blue tie and matching handkerchief, and smiled towards the dock (which smile was returned by Dave with a simple faith in good things to come).

At first we were rolling fairly smoothly. I established a curry dinner sometime in March, and then I asked an apparently helpful Freddie Allbright about the time.

'8.45. 'Course I was with Dave at 8.45. I took him for a meal at 8, and we was together till 9.30.' So far so good, I moved stealthily towards the clincher.

'Now, can you fix the date?'

' 'Course I can. My wife's birthday . . .' Well, nothing to worry about as yet.

'What's the date of that?'

'March the fifth. Same every year. I'd got her an evening bag, and I told Dave about it when I met him the next day.' Freddie was still smiling as he said it, but I felt as if I'd stepped into a lift-shaft some moments after the lift had gone. Was there a chance that we misunderstood each other?

'The *next* day?' I asked, apparently unconcerned.

'Right. The next day when we went for the curry.' There was no chance. Dave was looking stricken and incredulous – and the judge was making a careful note. He looked up, and asked with casual pleasure.

'That would be March the sixth?'

'That's right, my Lord.' Freddie agreed eagerly.

'I wanted to ask you about the day *before* your wife's birthday.' I felt like a surgeon trying to sew up an ever-expanding wound.

'March the fourth? Oh, I don't know what Dave was doing then. No. I tell a lie.'

'Do you, Mr Allbright?' I asked him. I hoped I sounded dangerous. Freddie only asked me an innocent question.

'Was that the Tuesday, March the fourth?'

'Yes.'

'Then Dave had *that* night off.' Freddie hammered the last nail in our coffin. 'I remember he'd been off a couple of nights before we went for the curry.'

Dave seemed about to shout from the dock. Wise Jennifer ssshed him. The judge leant forward to emphasize the hopelessness of our position. He addressed our broken reed of a witness.

'So you don't know what Mr Anstey was doing on the night of the fourth?'

'Haven't a clue, my Lord.' Freddie smiled charmingly.

The judge turned to me and put the boot in, gently but with deadly accuracy.

'You may like to remind the jury, Mr Rumpole, that the stabbing in the off-licence took place on the fourth of March.'

'I leave that to you, old darling. You're obviously loving it,' was what I thought of saying. Instead I asked the usher to present Mr Allbright (of 'Allbright's will see you right', not in Court they won't) with his signed statement in support of our alibi.

'Mr Allbright!' I put it to him. 'Did you not sign that document making it clear that you were with Mr Anstey on the evening of the *fourth* of March? '

'I may have done. Yes.'

At which Soapy Joe arose, his hands clasped together, his voice humble and low, and made a typically Soapy interjection.

'My Lord, is my learned friend entitled to cross-question his own witness?'

'If the witness is hostile. Yes.' I argued the law.

'Does my learned friend suggest that the witness is hostile to *him*?' said his Soapiness.

'No. I suggest that the witness is hostile to the *truth*!' I looked at the jury who were beginning to sense a Scene in Court and stirred with modified excitement.

'If the witness has signed a previous inconsistent statement you may cross-examine him,' said Vosper J. judicially and added I thought maliciously, 'if you think that's a *wise* course, Mr Rumpole.' The jury smiled at what they felt might have been a joke. Soapy Joe subsided, and I said I was obliged to his Lordship and began to attack the traitor in the witness-box. The time for half-measures was over. Now it was all or nothing.

'Mr Allbright. Is your company the landlord of the off-licence where Tosher was stabbed?'

'It might be.' My first shot had ruffled the Allbright feathers a little.

'What do you mean by that? Is your business empire so vast you can't be sure where your boundaries lie?'

'We've got the lease on the off-licence. Yes.'

'So Tosher was working for *you*.'

'He might have been.'

'And what was he doing? Putting his hand in the till. Not paying his dues? Did you have to send someone to teach him a lesson?'

Now the jury was interested. Freddie played a safe delaying shot. He looked puzzled.

'Someone?'

'Who are you suggesting *someone* might be, Mr Rumpole?' Mr Justice Vosper was weighing in on behalf of the witness. I ignored him and spoke directly to Allbright.

'Someone you sent in a cap like that worn by my client Dave Anstey.'

Even Vosper J. was quiet at that. I saw Dave looking lost in the dock and Freddie Allbright attempting a disarming smile.

'Now why would I do a thing like that, Mr Rumpole?'

I didn't answer him straight away. I was whispering a word of instruction to the usher who left the Court. I then turned again to the witness.

'Mr Allbright. Are you friendly with my client's wife, Betty?'

'I'm like a father to both of them. Yes.' Freddie smiled at the jury. They didn't smile back.

'Whilst my client's been in custody, have you been seeing Betty Anstey regularly?'

'I've tried to take her out of herself, yes,' Freddie admitted after a helpful pause.

'Has taking her out of herself included buying her an expensive fur coat? The one she's wearing now?'

The usher opened the door. Betty came in, nestling in her slaughtered article of wild life. Dave looked at her from the dock. She avoided his eye. Freddie improved the effect of this scene on the jury by saying:

'I may have lent her a bob or two, to tide her over.'

'Yes. Thank you, Mrs Anstey.' I let Betty go with the bob or two of fur on her back, and some nasty looks from the ladies in the jury following her. When the Court was quiet again I unloosened the broadside.

'Mr Allbright,' I thundered. 'Has your object in this case always been to have Dave Anstey convicted?'

Freddie gave another answer which, from his point of view, could only be described as a bad error of judgement. 'No. I wanted to help Dave.'

'Is that why you've gone back on your alibi statement? Because you wanted to *help* him?'

'Or have you gone back on it because you are trying to tell us the truth?' The judge was doing his best in a tricky situation.

'Look. I put March the fourth first because Dave asked me to,' Freddie explained.

'*Mr Anstey* asked you to?' the judge was delighted.

'He said that was the date of the stabbing, like. Look, I'm sorry I can't help you, Mr Rumpole . . .'

'I'm sorry I can't help *you*, Allbright. In your attempt to get your mistress's husband put inside for a long period of years . . .'

'Mr Rumpole. Is there any basis for that suggestion?' Justice Vosper was losing what I believe is known nowadays as 'his cool'.

'If there isn't perhaps my learned friend will call the lady to rebut it. She's still outside Court.' I let the jury notice the lack of enthusiasm from Soapy Joe and went on. 'You sent your hireling, wearing that entirely recognizable cap, to teach Tosher a lesson. So Tosher identified him . . .'

'May I remind you, Mr Rumpole,' the judge sighed wearily, 'when your client was picked out at the identification parade, he wasn't wearing a cap.'

'Of course not, my Lord.' I turned on the witness.

'Perhaps you'd care to tell us, Allbright . . . who was it gave Tosher his instructions?'

Freddie looked in silence at the unsympathetic jury. I went on, more in sorrow than in anger, to pry into this wretched conspiracy.

'Didn't Tosher know who you wanted fitted up with this little enterprise in the off-licence?'

' "Fitted up" is hardly a legal term, Mr Rumpole,' the judge tried the flippant approach. 'It makes it sound like a cupboard.'

I thought I'd teach Vosper J. to make jokes in Court.

'Then shall we say "framed", Allbright?' I said. 'It sounds like a picture. In this case the wrong picture entirely!'

*

The cross-examination of a hostile Allbright was, of course, only the beginning of a long and hot struggle with the judge which ended after two more days, with Rumpole suggesting to the jury that they had the alternative explanation of the events in the off-licence and they could not be certain that the case put forward by Soapy Joe on behalf of Her Majesty was certain to be correct.

'If you find Dave Anstey guilty,' I told them, 'the other man, the other man in the tartan cap sent by Freddie Allbright to enforce his dominion over the garages and off-licences of his part of Wandsworth, that "other man" will not go away or disappear, but he will return to haunt our dreams with the terrible possibility of injustice . . . It is your choice, members of the jury. Your choice entirely.'

After a nerve-wracking absence of five hours, and by a majority of ten to two, the jury opted for unhaunted dreams and decided to give Dave the benefit of the doubt and spring him from the dock. When I said 'goodbye' to him he was looking lost.

'Where do I go now, Mr Rumpole?'

'Not to Brixton at least.'

'I got no marriage, Squire. I got no job. I can't believe in anyone no more.'

'You'll get a job, Dave. You'll find another girl.'

'Not in Wandsworth I won't. Freddie'll see to that. He's got Wandsworth sewn up, has Fred Allbright. He's highly respected in this area.'

I was surprised by the tone in which he still spoke of his former employer.

'Cheer up, Dave. There is a world outside Wandsworth.'

Mr Anstey shook his head and went away looking as if he rather doubted that. I knew what I needed then, and went to find it in Pommeroy's Wine Bar, where I also saw the members of our clerk's room, Henry, Dianne and Angela in a corner and, at the bar, Erskine-Brown and Miss Trant. My former prosecutor gave me a smile of congratulation.

'We thought we had you chained up, padlocked into a tin trunk and sunk in the bottom of the sea,' she said. 'But with one leap Houdini was free.'

'Out five hours. It was a damned-close-run thing.'

'It was a smashing cross-examination, a lesson to us all,' Miss Trant told her *fiancé*.

'It's high time,' said Erskine-Brown, 'that a little justice was done to you, Rumpole.'

'Justice?'

'It's a rotten shame. You should have been Head of Chambers long ago. It was yours as the senior man. Everybody thought so.'

It was true that there had been a time when I was expected to be Head of Chambers; but Guthrie Featherstone, the newly arrived Q.C., M.P., put in for knee breeches and a pair of silk stockings and so got the blessing of my old Dad-in-law C. H. Wystan as the most desirable successor.*

'I can't remember you voting for me at the time, Erskine-Brown,' I reminded him.

*See 'Rumpole and the Younger Generation' in *Rumpole of the Bailey*, Penguin Books, 1978.

'Well, Guthrie Featherstone arrived. And he took silk and ...'

'Popped in betwixt the election and my hopes.'

'It was a rotten shame, actually!' Miss Trant agreed.

'Of course, in those days ... we didn't know the truth about Guthrie Featherstone ...' Erskine-Brown said darkly.

'Oh, no? And what is the truth about Guthrie Featherstone, Q.C., M.P.?' I challenged him.

'Claude quite honestly thinks he's lost his marbles.' Miss Trant shook her head sadly.

'He made a pass at Philly!' Erskine-Brown sounded incredulous.

'Well, actually, he simply asked me out to lunch.'

But Erskine-Brown looked darkly across the room at Angela and almost whispered. 'And he's quite simply having it off with that female Communist in the typing pool.'

'Young Angela? You astonish me!' I raised an unbelieving eyebrow.

'We must have a reliable Head of Chambers,' Erskine-Brown insisted. 'Not someone who's about to be involved in an unsavoury scandal!' I wondered what a savoury scandal would be: a scandal fried on toast, perhaps, with an anchovy and a dash of Worcester Sauce?

'Everyone's noticed things about Guthrie,' Miss Trant said.

'Things?'

'Definite signs of unreliability. The point is ... We'll ask Guthrie Featherstone to resign and make way for *you*, Rumpole, as Head of Chambers.' Erskine-Brown the kingmaker was, it seemed, about to make me a definite offer.

'I do think you'd make an absolutely super Head!' Miss Trant seconded the motion with flattering enthusiasm. At which moment Featherstone looked into the bar, waved at us and left immediately for an unknown destination. When he had gone I gave my learned friend Erskine-Brown a warning.

'Guthrie Featherstone, Q.C., M.P. isn't an experienced Labour-Conservative M.P. for nothing. He hogs the middle of the road just in case anyone's trying to pass him. Perhaps he's not the resigning kind.'

'Then we simply move out from under him. To one of the new sets of Chambers in Lincoln's Inn,' Erskine-Brown smiled. 'I've sounded out Henry . . . and Hoskins, and Owen Glendour-Jones.'

'Tell me, Erskine-Brown. Have you had any time for your practice with all this sounding?'

'No one's going to work with a Head of Chambers who's having it off with a revolutionary from the typing pool.'

At which point Miss Angela Trotsky got up and left the bar. Was it at a signal from our Head of Chambers?

'I'd just like to know *why* you're making this extraordinary allegation?' I asked Erskine-Brown for further and better particulars.

'Claude and I saw Guthrie Featherstone dancing. In "Fridays",' Miss Trant came out with a surprising piece of news.

'The Q.C., M.P. dancing? What's your evidence for that?'

'The evidence of my own eyes!' Erskine-Brown said proudly.

'The evidence of people's own eyes can, as Miss Trant knows, be extremely unconvincing. Did you see his face? What about the sideburns?'

'We didn't see his face exactly . . .' Miss Trant said.

'He had his back to us. But *she* was there!' said Erskine-Brown.

'The Communist menace of the clerk's room?'

'And Guthrie was wearing some sort of multi-coloured green-and-yellow shirt. With flowers on it.' Erskine-Brown brought out the full horror of the offence.

'Then it couldn't have been Guthrie Featherstone!' I assured him.

'Of course it was!'

'Mistaken identity. Guthrie Featherstone simply doesn't wear multi-coloured shirts with flowers on them.' I drained the blushing beaker of Chateau Fleet Street. 'As for the other matter. I'll think about it.' At which point I left Counsel for the prosecution of Guthrie Featherstone.

*

After Court the next evening I was in Guthrie Featherstone's room, awaiting an interview with our Head of Chambers. A cupboard door was squeaking, swinging open. I got up to shut it and looked into the cupboard. All I saw was Guthrie Featherstone, Q.C.'s gear hanging on hangers. On another hanger I blinked at the sight of a ghastly green-and-yellow shirt, with a floral pattern. I shut the cupboard door quickly as Featherstone entered the presence.

'Henry said you wanted to see me . . .' he started.

'Don't you want to see *me*?'

'Not particularly.' He looked extremely tired.

'I would say, you needed a little help.'

'I'm perfectly all right. Thank you, Rumpole.'

'Are you? They're closing in! Your wife Marigold wants to start a divorce. She consulted me.'

'*You!* Whatever did she consult *you* for?' Featherstone sounded shaken.

'No doubt to cause the maximum havoc. Young Erskine-Brown alleges he saw you dancing.'

The extraordinary thing was that Featherstone then smiled, apparently delighted with the accusation.

'With Angela?'

'Claude Erskine-Brown suspects you of having a Red in the bed, so far as I can gather.'

The accused Featherstone went to sit at his desk. He seemed perfectly relaxed as he made a full verbal confession.

'All right. It's all true. It's all perfectly true, Rumpole.'

'You plead guilty?' I must say I was surprised.

'As a matter of fact it's all terribly innocent,' he rambled on. 'Jumping about in "Fridays" till two o'clock in the morning. Then back for an hour or two in Angela's ridiculously narrow bed in Oakley Street. Then off to breakfast in the House of Commons.'

'That must be the worst part about it!'

'What?'

'Breakfast in the House of Commons.' I gave him a critical look-over. 'You're obviously not cut out for that type of existence.'

'The physical strain *is* exhausting.' Guthrie sighed.

'I imagine so. It must come as a terrible shock to a man only used to somnolent parliamentary debates and a little golf.'

'Golf! It happened when I was playing with Mr Justice Vosper. You know him?'

'Only in Court. Never on the green.'

'He was talking about the Death Penalty.'

'With nostalgia, I assume.'

'I sliced a drive into the rough,' Featherstone reminisced. 'I went behind a patch of low scrub and there were a boy and girl making love, not undressed, you understand. No great white bottoms waving in the air. Just kissing each other, and laughing. I felt there was an entire world I had totally missed. I told the judge I'd been taken ill, and left the course.'

'Taken ill? Of course you had.' I had no illusions about Guthrie's complaint.

'I spent the afternoon just wandering about Richmond. In search of adventure.'

'You drew a blank, I should imagine.'

'Next morning I came into Chambers and saw Angela. She's twenty-one, Rumpole, can you imagine it?'

'With difficulty. Tell me. What is that military uniform she affects?'

'An American combat shirt. It's a sort of joke. To show her pacifist convictions.'

'Most amusing! So you set out, quite deliberately, to destroy your position in Chambers?'

'Deliberately?'

'Of course. Locking yourself in this room. What on earth was that for?'

'We couldn't go back to Oakley Street. Her flatmate was entertaining a man from the BBC World Service . . .'

I remembered, with some humiliation, the night I'd played the unlovely role of eavesdropper with Erskine-Brown.

'Barristers' Chambers have been put to many uses, Featherstone, but only rarely as a setting for French farce! Oh, you were very determined, weren't you? Telling Marigold the most transparent lies. Carefully informing Miss Trant and therefore Erskine-Brown of the disco or Palais de Hop where you are apparently to be found nightly, tripping the light fantastic!' (I went to the cupboard and threw it open, dramatically displaying the incriminating evidence.) 'Keeping your dancing apparel in the cupboard.'

'Angela gave me that for my birthday,' Featherstone looked at the shirt with a tired affection. 'I couldn't take it home to Marigold.'

'What do you intend to do with it?' I asked with some contempt. 'Send Henry round to the launderette?'

'I don't know, Rumpole. What do you suggest?'

'I suggest you give it to the deserving poor. Look, Featherstone. My dear Guthrie.' I tried to bring some common sense to bear on the subject. 'You can't do it!'

'Do what, exactly?'

'Escape! You came to us as the ready-made figure of respectability. Q.C., M.P. Pipped me to the post as I remember it, for Head of Chambers – and remarkably gratified to get it. What are you going to do now? Abandon us, like a lot of ageing wives, leave us to rot on Bingo and National Assistance, while you go prancing off down Oakley Street in a remarkably lurid Paisley blouse! You can't do it. It's quite impossible. Out of the question!'

'Why *can't* I?' Featherstone was sitting behind his desk, smiling up at me.

'Because it was decided differently for you! When your mother gave proud birth to another Featherstone. When you became the youngest prefect at Marlborough. When you humbly asked the Lord Chancellor for a pair of knee breeches and took Marigold's advice on a suspender belt for your silk stockings. And when you got yourself elected Head of Chambers! It's all mapped out for you, Guthrie! The tram-lines are leading to Solicitor General in the next middle-of-the-road Conservative-Labour government, and the High Court Bench, and death of Sir Guthrie Featherstone, a judge of courteous severity, and flags fluttering at half-mast over the Benchers' dining hall . . .'

'I don't *have* to do all that.' Guthrie stood up, defiant.

'What's the alternative? Hanging round the Pier Hotel, waiting for the man from the BBC to go on night duty. Scratching a living writing "Advice from a Barrister" in the Sunday papers. Come off it, that's someone else entirely. That's not our Guthrie Featherstone.'

He took all this quietly, and stood looking at me. Finally he made the most extraordinary counter-accusation.

'You're jealous!'

'Am I?' I was, I confess, puzzled.

'Just because *you* can't escape . . .'

'Can't I? Of course I can. I am a free soul.' I resented the accusation. 'A free soul entirely.'

'Just because you're tied hand and foot by the Income Tax and the VAT-man and when Henry's going to find you another brief, and "She Who Must Be Obeyed".'

'Featherstone! Is that any way to speak of Mrs Hilda Rumpole?'

'I don't know. You do.'

'That, sir, is a husband's privilege. Anyway. Why do you say I'm jealous?'

'I don't know. Is it because you want to be the only anarchist in Chambers?'

Featherstone moved away and lit a cigarette. I stood and looked at him, thoughtful, and if I'm honest I must say worried. Was there a certain truth in what he said? Had Guthrie Featherstone put his finger on the Achilles Heel of Rumpole? Did I need *him* to make me feel a free, roving spirit. With Guthrie gone should I be reduced to a mere barrister, perhaps a deadly respectable Head of Chambers, calling meetings about the regrettable failure of learned friends to switch the light off in the loo, and their extravagance with the soap? I decided to deny his allegations.

'I don't need your sort of adventure to be a free soul, Featherstone. I can be bounded in the Temple and count myself a king of infinite space.' I went to the door, using that moment to remind him of a case in which he was prosecuting. 'Remember we've got a case on next week. Importation of cannabis. You're against me.'

'Prosecuting?' He sounded doubtful.

'That is . . .' I looked at him accusingly, 'unless you've "Gone Dancing".'

*

I am not especially proud of what I did then, but the chance of Guthrie Featherstone appearing as the Protector of Society against the insidious attacks of the drug culture seemed too good to miss. Before the Q.C., M.P. rose to open the prosecution, I had phoned Chambers and asked Harry to send Angela straight down to the Old Bailey as I had urgent need of her services as a shorthand note-taker. When I got to Court I was delighted to see our Head of Chambers standing erect as a pillar of the Establishment, saying exactly what I required him to say.

'In this case I appear with my learned friend Mr Owen Glendour-Jones to prosecute and the defence is represented by my learned friend Mr Horace Rumpole. Members of the jury, this case concerns the possession of a dangerous drug – cannabis resin.' Guthrie began promisingly. At which moment the glass door swung open to admit that girlish GI Angela. She came to my side and I asked her to sit and take a note of Guthrie's opening speech. Intent on his work he seemed not to have noticed her arrival. As he carried on I could feel Angela's indignation glowing behind me.

'Cannabis, whatever you may have read in the papers, members of the jury, is a dangerous drug. Prohibited by Parliament,' said Featherstone. 'Oh, it may be very fashionable for young people to say that it does less harm than a whisky and soda, or that smoking cannabis in some way makes you a better, purer soul than squares like us, members of the jury, who may prefer an honest pint, or in the case of the ladies of the jury, a small gin and tonic? You will hear a lot in this case about the defendant feeling it his mission to "turn us all on", as if we were electric lights. The fact remains, says the prosecution, that the dealer in cannabis resin is merely a common criminal, engaged in breaking the law for sordid commercial gain . . .'

The Court door banged. The outraged Angela, by now totally disillusioned with her swinging lover, had gone. We never saw her round the Temple or the Bailey again.

*

Christianity has no doubt brought great benefits to humanity, but in my opinion Christmas is not one of them. With a sickening of the heart I began to notice, as I went quietly about my life of crime, the dreadful signs of the outbreak of Christmas fever. My take-away claret from Pommeroy's was wrapped in paper decorated with reindeer and robins, Henry and Dianne began to put up holly in the clerk's room. Soon we should have to struggle down Oxford Street so that I could buy She the lavender water she never uses, and She could buy me the tie I never wear. Paper streamers went up in the list office at the Bailey, and there was plastic holly in the gate room at Brixton nick. In time more decorations were hung in Featherstone's room in Chambers, where was held our annual Christmas thrash (wives and girlfriends invited, warm gin and vermouth and Dianne traditionally far from steady on her pins before the end of the evening). I had gone through a drink or two at this gathering when I found myself in the centre of a group which consisted solely of Erskine-Brown and Miss Trant. I took the opportunity of telling them that I would take no part in a Chambers revolution; and that having looked carefully into the allegations against Guthrie Featherstone I found that the prosecution had not made out its case, indeed I believed the unfortunate Guthrie had this in common with Dave Anstey. They were both victims of cases of mistaken identity.

'What're you up to now, Houdini?' Miss Trant asked suspiciously.

'It may be. It may very well be,' I suggested, 'that there has been someone, a totally different someone, masquerading as Guthrie Featherstone!' I looked towards Featherstone, well-turned-out in a grey suit, who had arrived, escorting a smiling Marigold. 'All I can tell you for certain is,' I went on to the plotters, 'our respected Head of Chambers is clearly not the person you saw whooping it up in the disco. Look at him now, graciously escorting his lovely wife to our Christmas celebration. Look at him carefully, Erskine-Brown! Observe him closely, Miss Trant. Is that the man you saw? Certainly not! Do I make myself clear?'

'Not in the least, Rumpole,' Erskine-Brown grumbled and frowned displeased. I moved off. Marigold was enjoying a stimulating sherry. I came up to her. 'Mrs Featherstone. Marigold. I owe you an apology . . .'

'Mr Rumpole?'

'Keeping your husband out late boozing in Pommeroy's. Disgusting behaviour! I have put a complete stop to it.'

'So I've noticed.' Marigold smiled graciously. 'The all-night sittings seem to have dropped off lately, too. I get Guthrie for dinner nowadays.'

'How delicious!' I gave her a small bow and She Who Must Be Obeyed hove into view, clutching a large G and T.

'Rumpole!' She trumpeted.

'You know She . . . you know my wife, of course.' I did my best to introduce her.

'Of course,' Marigold inclined her head. 'We sing together.'

'You're coming to the *Messiah*, Rumpole,' Hilda said.

'Oh yes, Mr Rumpole,' Marigold added her pennyworth. 'Do come. We make a jolly brave stab at the "Hallelujah Chorus".'

'Do you really? How very sporting of you. I hate to miss it: but you see, the pressure of work in Chambers . . .'

'You *are* coming to the *Messiah*, Rumpole!' In She's mouth it was an announcement, not an invitation. Further conversation was precluded by Henry calling for silence for our Head of Chambers.

'I'm not going to make a speech . . .' Featherstone began to general applause. 'I just wanted to welcome you all . . . Members and wives and girlfriends who are members also . . .' Here he raised his glass to our Portia, Miss Trant. 'To our annual Christmas "do". We have had a pretty good year, Henry tells me, in Chambers . . .' In fact Henry was wearing a new suit as a small tribute to his ten per cent. Featherstone boomed on, 'And we have managed to stick together throughout this year . . .'

'Except for one departure in the typing department,' I reminded him tactlessly.

Featherstone ignored this and continued, 'Glendour-Jones has joined us, since the departure of George Frobisher for the Circuit Court Bench. I only want to say . . .'

' "That he which hath no stomach to this fight" . . .' I felt it was time to put some force into this oration, so I almost shouted King Harry's call to battle.

'Did you want to say something, Horace?' Featherstone smiled and I cantered on, after draining my glass.

> 'Let him depart; his passport shall be made,
> And crowns for convoy put into his purse:
> We would not plead in that man's company
> That fears his fellowship to plead with us.'

'What on earth's your husband talking about?' I heard Marigold whisper to She.

'It's Shakespeare. He does it all the time at home. I wish he wouldn't do it when we're out. So dreadfully embarrassing.'

'When people speak of a split in Chambers or of the possibility of any other head but our distinguished Q.C., M.P. . . .' I turned my eyes on the subversive Erskine-Brown, 'they are making a grave error, and a terrible mistake . . . Like the mistakes in identity which may do such terrible injustice in our Courts. My learned leader, Guthrie Featherstone, Q.C., M.P. is a man fashioned by nature to be Head of Chambers. He couldn't possibly be anything else. So we Old Bailey Hacks, we common soldiers at the Bar, will attack a New Year, under his leadership, crying together, "God for Guthrie, Henry and Dianne!" '

I moved to Featherstone, put a hand on his shoulder.

'Sorry, old darling,' I said quietly. 'You're lumbered with it!'

Rumpole and the Course of True Love

Love, although the staple diet of the *Oxford Book of English Verse*, and the subject which seems the concern of the majority of its contributors, has not, so far, much disturbed the even course of these memoirs, which have been mainly concerned with blood-stains, mayhem, murder and other such signs of affection. I cannot help thinking that the time occupied in the course of an average lifetime in the pursuit of love has been greatly exaggerated. Dr Donne and Lord Byron, I am convinced, spent many more of their spare moments asleep, or staring aimlessly into the middle distance, or having a lonely chop and an early night than they would have us believe. The days spent by Rumpole, for instance, in the hectic pursuit of passion during the course of an average lifetime at the Bar, if laid end to end, would hardly fill out a summer holiday.

I was, it is true, extremely fond of Miss Porter, my *fiancée*, the daughter of my old Oxford tutor, but our engagement had to be broken off by reason of her inappropriate and quite unexpected death. She was a docile young woman, with a gentle uncomplaining voice, and had I married her I would no doubt have been spared the more military aspect of home life with She Who Must Be Obeyed, whose tone of voice often seems more suited to the barrack square than to the boudoir. I stumbled, rather than plunged, into marriage with She (Mrs Hilda Rumpole) as the result of a gentle push from her father, old C. H. Wystan, my one-time Head of Chambers, and was rash enough to propose to her when my gills were awash with champagne during a distant Inns of Court Ball (we all make mistakes during our early years at the Bar). It can hardly be said that hectic passion has been the keynote of my married life with She Who Must

Be Obeyed, although I remember a holiday we took around 1949 in Brittany when She showed an unwonted enthusiasm for the stuff (I have always put it down to the shellfish). Although embarrassing at the time this holiday did ultimately produce the enduring benefit of my son Nicholas Rumpole, with whom I found considerable rapport and formed what I sincerely hope is a lasting friendship.

It would be idle, of course, to pretend that the Rumpole heart has been forever chilled and that those lyrical effusions which fill so much of my old *Oxford Book* (Sir Arthur Quiller-Couch edition) have no resonance for me. I was deeply taken with a comrade-in-arms, young 'Bobby' O'Keefe who looked, in those days, as pert and exquisitely rounded as ladies on the cover of *Reveille*. I met 'Bobby' when she was in the WAAF and I was doing my best to serve my country in the Air Force groundstaff, but her sudden marriage to Pilot Officer Sam 'Three Fingers' Dogherty broke off this potentially inconvenient romance.

I should also add, in the interests of honesty, that there is a girl with copper-coloured hair and an engaging smile behind the urn in a café opposite the Old Bailey who brightens my breakfasts, with whom I enjoy what can only be described at light banter (although my heart sinks unaccountably when she tells me about her boyfriend who is apparently in the weight-lifting business).

So much for love and Rumpole. I must now deal with the disastrous effects of this disease on the learned Head of my Chambers, Guthrie Featherstone, Q.C., M.P. and on a client of mine, Ronald Ransom, teacher of English Language and Literature at the John Keats Comprehensive School in the wilds of Hertfordshire.

The John Keats was, so my client Ransom told me, the very model of a modern comprehensive school: designed to enhance the name of State Education, and to empty the public schools of all but a hard core of sado-masochists and the children of Asiatic bankers. The John Keats was, it seemed, so free and yet so self-disciplined, so well-equipped and yet so 'caring' (unlike my old public school where they certainly didn't care whether you lived or died), and so genuinely 'civilized' that many Labour M.P.s and even some Cabinet Ministers bought homes in that part of Hertfordshire, so that they could enjoy the double advantage of an excellent education for their children, and an easy conscience when presenting themselves as men of the people.

The John Keats Comprehensive was enlightened in its teaching methods. In History, so Ransom told me, the social life of the medieval village, or the economic basis of the Industrial Revolution were taught, rather than the dates of the Kings and Queens of England. The Domestic Science students could run up a reasonable 'moussaka' or 'salade Nicoise'; the Literature classes spent a great deal of time extemporizing short playlets on the hopelessness of life in a comprehensive school; Sex Instruction took place from an early age, and the John Keats pupil graduated from basic intercourse in Junior Three, to 'The Value of Foreplay' and 'The Toleration of Sexual Minorities' in the Sixth.

There's no doubt that my client Ransom enjoyed his life and work at the John Keats Comprehensive. He had been brought up by a strict Methodist family in Scotland and sent to a grimly academic school, where Shakespeare had been reduced to a grammatical exercise and the construing of Virgil was no more exciting than lower mathematics. Neither that, nor his teachers' training college, had led him to hope of an educational establishment where art was held to be more important than exams, where Mahler was thought to be more exciting than football, and where *Romeo and Juliet* was discussed as a poetic and sexual experience and not picked over for familiar quotations. His pleasure in his work was in no way diminished by the fact that there sat in the front row of his classroom, eagerly drinking in his explanation of the convoluted passions of Dr John Donne, and deeply grateful for his soft Scottish reading of Andrew Marvell's impatient verses to his coy mistress, a Miss Francesca Capstick, the moderately bright daughter of a local bank manager. It was to her that he addressed Marvell's dire warning not to hang about until 'worms should try, that long-preserved virginity', and she was, of course, the reason for his ending up in my Chambers one summer morning. Miss Capstick was, at the time relevant to the offence, fifteen years and eleven months old.

I had, later, an opportunity of examining Miss Capstick in some detail. She was by no means the blousy, tarty sort of girl who misleads men as to her age with make-up or hair dye. In fact she wore no make-up, her hair was long, brown and very clean, her eyes were large and gentle, her voice quiet, at times hardly audible. Her face can be seen in a hundred reproductions among the nymphs attendant upon Botticelli's 'Primavera'; she was called 'Frank' by her friends and chewed gum during some part of her evidence.

*

> 'I wonder by my troth, what thou, and I
> Did, till we loved? were we not weaned till then,
> But sucked on country pleasures, childishly?
> Or snorted we in the seven sleepers' den?'

The Headmaster of the John Keats read out the verses with initial anger and disgust which turned, Ransom told me, to the sincere guttural trill of a Radio Three poetry reader. The Head always produced the school play and fancied himself as some mute inglorious Gielgud who had got lost in the State Education system. He therefore could not read the immortal words, even in a document he felt to be incriminating, without giving them a little rhythm, a touch of projection.

> 'Twas so, but this all pleasures fancies bee
> If any beauty I did see
> Which I desired and got,
> Twas but a dream of thee,'

Ransom supplied helpfully.

'That's not the point.' The Headmaster threw the letter down on his desk and started to pace the room with the nervous rage he had tried to get into his Sixth Formers' rendering of the quarrel scene in *Julius Caesar*. 'The point is that you were writing these amorous ravings to a young girl who has not yet had the maturing experience of attempting O-levels. Francesca Campstick.'

'Her name's Francesca Capstick and I'm teaching her John Donne. So naturally I sent her that quotation.'

'And since the night at the Festival Hall, and the cannelloni and Orvieto at "Luigi's", I realize I love you spiritually and physically more than anyone I've ever loved in my life before.' The Headmaster had now repossessed himself of the letter. 'Is that a quotation from John Donne?'

'No. As a matter of fact, it's a quotation from me.'

'I rather thought it was.' The Headmaster was quick as a bloodhound on the scent, although it was not a difficult deduction to make as the letter was undoubtedly in his English master's handwriting. 'You see, I've got your letter!'

'Yes,' said Ronnie. 'And I rather wonder who gave it to you.'

'A ... A well-wisher.'

'A well-wisher of yours, or mine?'

'I think, perhaps, a well-wisher of Francesca's. And what exactly does that passage mean?'

'It means we went to the Royal Festival Hall, where we heard a Vivaldi concert conducted by Neville Marriner, and afterwards we went to "Luigi's" in Covent Garden where we had cannelloni and a bottle of Orvieto.'

'Anything else?' By this time, apparently, the Headmaster was playing the sneering role of the minor inquisitor from *St Joan*.

'Anything else? Oh yes.' Ronnie kept his head admirably. 'Francesca had a large cassata ice and I had a cup of black coffee and a Strega.'

By this time, Ransom told me, the Headmaster was trembling. No doubt if he had been running an old-fashioned blood-and-thunder type of academy he might have remained more calm. He might even have torn up Ransom's letter and told him to take girls *en masse* to Vivaldi in the future, rather than give them individual attention. But as the Head of a Progressive school he no doubt feared that he was only a whisper away from anarchy, one false step and he would have a Maoist take-over in the PE period, strip-shows in the art classes and group tactile experience during Religious Instruction. Accordingly he pressed Ransom with cross-examination, ever a dangerous weapon in the hands of the amateur.

'And what does this mean?' he asked again, brandishing the letter. ' "I realize I love you physically and spiritually more than anyone I've ever loved in my life before."?'

'It means exactly what it says,' Ransom told him. 'Francesca is an extremely sensitive and intelligent girl as well as being physically beautiful. What it does *not* mean is that I have ever been to bed with her.'

'Well,' the Headmaster said, and Ransom told me the gleam in the old Thespian's eye was undoubtedly salacious. 'We will have to see what Miss Clapstick says about that.'

'I'm sure she'll tell you exactly the same thing,' Ransom answered, as subsequently recorded in the deposition of the Headmaster's evidence. 'And she may even tell you that her name is "Capstick" as well.'

'I'm glad you reminded me of that,' said the old trooper, hogging the curtain line. 'As I also mean to write to her father.'

What Miss Capstick did tell the Headmaster led to a letter from the Headmaster to Capstick *père* regretting that, as there were bad apples in every barrel, so there were black sheep, or persons who took the message of the poets too literally, even among the teaching staff of the John Keats Comprehensive. When Mr Capstick the bank manager received the bad news it led to his visiting the Old Bill. In due course Inspector David Hewitt of the local Constabulary rang up Ronald Ransom and asked him if he might find it convenient to call in at the Station the next morning, that is if he wanted to spare himself the embarrassment of a couple of the local rozzers tramping in to finger his collar just as he was explaining the saucier passages in *Measure for Measure* to a crowded classroom of delighted adolescents.

That particular chain of events led inevitably to a conference in my room in Chambers at Number 3 Equity Court, and to my asking Ransom that unavoidable but always embarrassing question, 'Well, did you do it?'

♣

'I can't fight the case.' Ransom was a pleasant-looking young man, I'd say in his late twenties, a dark-haired, blue-eyed Scot. He wore an old tweed jacket which he'd probably had since he was a student and a tie that might, for all I knew, have been hand-woven by some admirer in evening classes.

'That doesn't sound exactly like an answer to my question.'

'Well, she told the old boy I did, didn't she?'

It was a question and not an answer and seemed to me to show traces of a fighting spirit; so I eagerly prepared for battle.

'Fantasy! That's why she said that. Pure fantasy!'

'You really think so?'

'Well, of course. I mean, children...'

'She's almost sixteen.'

It was that 'almost' that had landed him on the windy side of the law. I tried again. 'Young people ... persons, reading poetry. Well, naturally it stimulates the imagination. I will have to educate the trial judge, who may well consider the All England Law Reports the height of erotic fantasy. I will have to explain to him exactly how poetry affects the mind.'

'How about the body?' As a client this gentle young Scot seemed unlikely to prove helpful.

'We'd better forget about the body. Judges in this class of case don't really like to be reminded that the body exists. "This case," we shall say (I was already framing some of the better phrases for my final speech), "this case, members of the jury," (I stood up and lit, with relish, a small cigar) "this case exists entirely in a young girl's imagination, an imagination over-stimulated by indulgence in the love poems of John Donne. When I was a lad, members of the jury, when some of us were lads, we read about brave Horatius, and imagined we were fighting to keep the bridge and defend, single-handed, the City of Rome. Young Fanny Chopstick..."'

'Capstick.'

'Whatever her name is ... "reads about being someone's enthusiastic mistress and so she imagines she is *precisely that*!"' I paused for a moment to consider whether this was a proposition sound in law and logic. Given a reasonably educated jury (I'd settle for one member with the *Guardian* sticking out of his pocket) I decided that it was.

'You'd have to cross-examine her?' Ransom asked me.

'Gently. To point out the vividness of her imagination.'

'I couldn't have her put through that in Court, Mr Rumpole.'

I looked at him, at his almost embarrassingly honest eyes, his frayed jacket and homespun tie. 'May I remind you, Mr Ransom,' I said, 'of the present overcrowded conditions in our prisons. Are you seeking to add to the congestion?'

'I know, but . . .'

'And may I also remind you of the unpopularity with the other inmates of anyone convicted of offences with young girls. It's so easy to spill boiling cocoa on someone's head. I believe it's known as "cocoaing the S.O.s".'

'What's an S.O., Mr Rumpole?' Ransom sounded detached.

'A sexual offender.' I could have also told him that an unpopular prisoner could fairly easily choke to death on a rock-cake.

'The client,' up spoke Mr Grayson, the local Hertfordshire solicitor, an anxious and kindly looking individual who in fact had the *Guardian* not sticking out of his pocket, indeed, but nestling in his pile of papers in the case of the Queen against Ronald Ransom (and it was most definitely *not* the sort of case, in my opinion, in which Her Majesty should have let herself get involved). 'The client wants to keep out of prison.'

'Well,' I smiled. 'How unusual!'

'It wouldn't be prison, would it?' Ransom looked alarmed for the first time. 'I mean, she was nearly sixteen . . .'

'She *is* sixteen now,' Mr Grayson added.

'*Now* is hardly the point,' I told them. 'Whether Mr Ransom goes to prison or not would depend, in my opinion, entirely on the judge concerned. Now, at the Bailey if we drew "Pokey" Peterson, who happens to be paying maintenance to an ageing ex-wife, and who has just married a young lady from the chorus at Churchill's Club, well, you'd probably get a conditional discharge; but if fate span the wheel and sent us Mr Justice Vosper, I'm afraid you'd be into the slammer before you can say "the

expense of spirit in a waste of shame". So if it's merely a question of sparing a young girl's feelings . . .'

'It is. It's a question of that,' Ransom answered me.

'Then think of yourself. Your job.'

'I don't care about the job really. I'd like to try and write
something. I've never had the time.'

'You may get the time now. Possibly eighteen months.'

Ransom was kind enough to laugh at this pleasantry. 'You're
too ruthless a questioner, Mr Rumpole,' he flattered me. 'And I
think too much of Francesca to have her put through the mill by
you. I'm definitely pleading guilty. But surely they won't send
me to prison, will they?' For the first time his eyes avoided me.

'I told you. It depends entirely on the judge. Now, if you can
tell me who we're likely to get . . .'

'Oh, I can tell you *that*,' Mr Grayson announced our in-
credible, our earth-shattering good fortune just as if it were the
date, or the probable length of the hearing. 'It's in our local
Circuit Court. We'll have His Honour Judge Frobisher.'

His Honour Judge George Frobisher! His Honour old George.
His Honour my oldest, my dearest friend, in whose company I
have sunk more bottles of Pommeroy's plonk and solved more
knotty clues in *The Times* crossword than with any other person, alive or dead. Old George with whom I spent almost forty
years in Chambers until he was elevated, or demoted as I would
prefer to call it, to a position on the Circuit, or Circus Bench.
Dear old George, who confided in me when he was thinking of
committing an unpremeditated act of matrimony with a lady
who, I recalled, had a touch of arson in her past.* I had crossed
swords with old George in friendly duels in almost every Court
in England, from the Uxbridge Magistrates to the Family Division, and from London Sessions to Lewes Assizes; and for the
life of me I couldn't remember any occasion when George had
emerged victorious. Old George Frobisher, it has to be said, is
the dearest of fellows, the kindest of companions and the best of
listeners; he is sound on his law and takes a good note of the
evidence; but in Court he stands up with all the eager self-

*See 'Rumpole and the Man of God'

confidence of a rabbit with a retiring disposition caught in the headlights of an oncoming car. He was also, at the Bar, frenetically incapable of making up his mind; not only on vital issues, such as whether to put his client into the witness-box, but on minor matters, such as whether to start his final speeches, 'Members of the jury' or 'Ladies and gentlemen of the jury'. (Sometimes he compromised and called them both.) He was also extremely suggestible, and many is the County Court claim I have been able to settle with old George on extremely favourable terms, and many are the prosecutions charges I have been able to persuade him to drop like a hot potato. In short, I have never had, in Court or out of it, the slightest trouble with old George.

'You don't mean to tell me ...' I was almost, I swear it, laughing with delight. 'You don't mean to tell me our judge is my old friend George Frobisher?'

'His Honour Judge George Frobisher, yes,' Mr Grayson replied, in a tone of what I thought was quite unnecessary awe.

'Then I promise you, more, I give you my word,' I was happy to assure Mr Ronald Ransom, 'your chances of being cocoaed are nil. What is more, you will never be banged up, even in an open prison. Plead guilty if you feel you have to. We shall have absolutely no trouble with old George.'

*

The good fortunes of my client Ransom seemed to be increasing daily. One early morning in the following weeks I called into my breakfast café opposite the Old Bailey, and was disappointed to find that the attraction by the tea urn was noticeably absent (a chill, perhaps, or exhaustion after a night out with the weight-lifter). Sitting there, however, nursing a cup of coffee, shivering slightly and looking distinctly green about the gills was Miss Phillida Trant, our talented Chambers' token tribute to sexual equality, the Portia of Number 3 Equity Court.

'Hullo, Rumpole,' she said. 'I hear you're going to be agin me out in the wilds of Hertfordshire. Case of R. *v* Ransom. Spot of unlawful carnal knowledge.' The trouble with lady barristers, you will have noticed, is that they talk more like men barristers than men barristers do.

'Good heavens,' I said. 'Miss Trant! You don't look in the least bit well. Are you sickening for something?' I wasn't coming straight to the point, you notice, which was my firm determination to keep Ronald Ransom out of the cooler. I was determined to try a little circuitous politeness first.

'Yes,' she said. 'I'm afraid I am.'

'Can I get you something?' I asked solicitously. 'They do a particularly good bacon and egg on a fried slice here.' At which news Miss Trant went, if possible, even greener.

'No, thank you,' she said. 'As a matter of fact, I've just thrown up in the loo at Blackfriars Station.'

'It's gastric 'flu.' I sat down beside her and lit a small cigar which didn't seem to help matters; Miss Trant coughed and waved her hand in the air. 'There's a lot of it about.'

'It's not gastric 'flu,' Miss Trant told me. 'I'm up the bloody spout.'

I didn't know whether congratulations or commiserations were in order. Accordingly I took a gulp of coffee, with an expression of deep sympathy and respect.

'I don't know why I'm telling *you*,' she said. 'I haven't even told Claude yet.' Claude, I remembered, was the baptismal name of Erskine-Brown, the pompous young specializer in mortgages and company law, and the member of our Chambers least sympathetic to Rumpole, to whom Miss Trant had been rash enough to get herself engaged. 'I suppose I'm telling you because, well, you've brought me up in the law, haven't you? You're a sort of father figure. Ever since you gave me such a terrible beating in the Dock Street Magistrates Court.'*

I am no longer proud of the way in which I induced Miss Trant, who was prosecuting, to bore the Dock Street Magistrate to such a state of irritation, by quoting law to him by the yard, that he gave judgement for Rumpole. Accordingly I asked with

* See 'Rumpole and the Married Lady' in *Rumpole of the Bailey*, Penguin Books, 1978.

some sympathy, 'The proposed nipper does emanate from Erskine-Brown, I suppose?'

'Oh yes,' Miss Trant nodded vigorously. 'The trouble is, I can't seem to bring myself to tell him. He'll want to marry me or something.'

'You don't want to get married?'

'I've got three new firms of solicitors,' Miss Trant told me, 'and a six-month-long firm fraud starting in Portsmouth in November. Of course I don't want to get married! What would I want to get married for?'

The trouble, as I say, with lady barristers is that they're so much keener on being barristers than barristers are.

'Claude'll want me to stay at home,' Miss Trant went on pathetically, 'and mix up Ostermilk.'

'Well,' I told her judicially, 'I see your problem, Miss Trant. But I suppose it'll have to come out in the end.'

'Yes,' she said, 'that's what I'm afraid of.'

The conversation seemed to be weaving unhealthily towards the gynaecological, an area of life I have always strictly avoided. 'Well, yes,' I said. 'Now about this wretched school-teacher, poor old Ronald Ransom . . .'

'It's not going to take long, is it?' Miss Trant put on her glasses again and looked at me anxiously. 'I'm prosecuting a larceny at the Bailey the week after.'

'I thought about three weeks.' Ransom's luck seemed to be holding out marvellously. 'Unless of course I can twist his arm and get him to plead guilty.'

'Is there any hope of that?' Miss Trant sounded eager.

'I suppose anything's possible.' I looked thoughtful. 'Of course, I'd have to be sure he wouldn't get sent to prison.'

'Why on earth should he get sent to prison?' Miss Trant looked at me, surprised. 'She was almost sixteen. Anyway, in my opinion, the bloody girl asked for it.'

Only one thing is certain in the dubious world of the law. No one is harder on a lady than a lady barrister.

*

Ronald Ransom and Miss Phillida Trant weren't the only ones

for whom the course of true love was not running particularly smoothly at that time. I have written already* of the unfortunate time when the learned Head of our Chambers, Guthrie Featherstone, Q.C., M.P., had apparently lost his marbles (in Erskine-Brown's vivid phrase) and taken up with a junior typist in our clerk's room of such pronounced left-wing views that she declined to type a statement of claim on behalf of a landlord in a possession case. She would only type on behalf of tenants, defendants, abandoned wives and other unprivileged persons. It is true that I had managed, with what I can say without boasting was consummate legal skill, to extricate Featherstone from this unfortunate situation. However, with that longing for self-immolation which seizes persons who plead guilty, or make long statements to the police, Guthrie Featherstone had, in an intimate moment, over an up till then cheerful dinner at 'L'Étoile', confessed the whole affair to his wife Marigold, who had been predictably furious and left the table with her *poulet à l'estragon* practically untouched.

After the confession Marigold's mood ranged from the martyred to the vindictive in varying degrees of unbearability, so that the unfortunate Guthrie often arrived at Chambers looking less like a suave and successful Q.C. (for undoubtedly he was still successful) than a man who spends his nights watching over a dynamite factory in which all the employees are allowed to smoke.

Now it was about this time that I was defending a rather beguiling young man called Higgins on a long series of safe-breakings and warehouse-enterings. The evidence against him consisted of a swollen bank account for which no particular explanation could be given and a collection of heavy tools and comic masks in his car. It was alleged to appeal to Higgins's sense of comedy to enter enclosed premises wearing a Mickey Mouse or Count Dracula mask to prevent identification.

This case was being prosecuted, competently enough, by my learned Head of Chambers, and as we sat together chattering before the judge came into Court, I happened to remark that Guthrie wasn't looking quite up to snuff. In fact he seemed to

*See 'Rumpole and the Case of Identity'.

be in a mood of deep despondency. He explained, in answer to my solicitous inquiry, that his wife Marigold was still cutting up extremely rough and had what the poor man described as 'a touch of the nervy'.

'She's threatening to divorce me, Rumpole.'

'Not *still?*'

'I just couldn't face the whole stink of a divorce at the moment. I mean, a divorce just plays havoc with your chance of getting your bottom o: to the Bench.'

At last all was explained. Since I had put Guthrie Featherstone back on the road to respectability he had gone the whole hog and was hell bent on a scarlet-and-ermine trimmed dressing-gown.

'You want to get your bottom there, of course ...'

'It's not me so much. It's Marigold.'

'Marigold?'

'My wife, Marigold.'

'Oh, *that* Marigold.'

'She's fired off an ultimatum. Unless I can make the High Court Bench she's going to up sticks and file a petition.'

'Seems a bit desperate.'

'She *is* desperate.'

'But my dear Guthrie. My dear old Featherstone. What are you going to do about it? I mean, you can't just knock on the Lord Chancellor's door and ask ...'

'Vosper J. has a bit of influence in appointments ...'

I was sure he had. Mr Justice Vosper was a man who could well be capable of ordering muffins after a death sentence, if muffins and death sentences still existed, but he was a powerful figure in the judicial hierarchy and his influence on appointments, among many other factors, would ensure that there would never be a Mr Justice Rumpole known to history.

'I'm playing golf with Vosper at the weekend, and with old Keith from the Lord Chancellor's office,' Guthrie answered proudly.

It seems that Marigold Featherstone had driven her desperate spouse a long way down the Primrose Path that leads to the eternal isolation in the Judges' Lodgings. However, I wanted to be helpful.

'If you're playing golf with Vosper J.,' I said, 'it might be as well not to win.'

'That thought, Rumpole, had occurred to me.'

Another thought had occurred to me also. It was a wheeze that I thought could be put to some good purpose in the defence of my client Higgins.

'I suppose,' I said casually, 'that if you *really* want the High Court Bench, you have to start doing your cases in a different sort of way.'

'What sort of way do you mean by that exactly, Rumpole?' Guthrie asked anxiously.

'Well. I mean, you have to stop being too much the advocate. Stop trying to win too hard. You'll have to show yourself above the dust of the arena. You have to adopt the *judicial attitude.*'

'The judicial attitude, of course, yes. You think I should adopt it?' Guthrie was swallowing the Rumpole plan, hook, line and sinker.

'I don't think you can start too soon,' I told him.

Shortly after that the judge (who was, of course, given Rumpole's usual run of bad luck, dear old Vosper J.) arrived and put his bottom on its accustomed place on the Bench, and Guthrie Featherstone rose to make his final speech for the prosecution which came out, to my great satisfaction, as a sterling attempt to adopt 'the judicial attitude'.

'Of course, members of the jury,' said Guthrie, 'as prosecuting counsel I adopt an attitude which is quite fair and, I hope, judicial. The prosecution has to prove its case, and if it doesn't do so the defence is entitled to succeed.' I saw my client Higgins look at Guthrie with a wild surmise. It was rather as if a heretic, dragged before the Inquisition, had been told he'd just won a holiday in the Bahamas. 'If you think he might possibly have won the money in his bank account at the races, even if he has forgotten the name of the horse and even the track concerned, then you must acquit him! If you think he may have been tak-

ing those various animal masks to a children's party at a Dr
Barnardo's Home, or if you think he possibly needed those heavy
tools to put up the "Do-It-Yourself Shelving" to accommodate
his *Encyclopaedia Britannica*, then the prosecution will not have
proved its case and the defendant. Higgins is entitled to be
acquitted. In all things we must be judicial, totally fair and keep
a balanced view. We must keep ourselves calm, you know, and
above the dust of the arena . . .'

'What on earth was the matter with that brief what prosecuted
me?' asked a puzzled Mr Higgins as he later left the Court without a stain on his character. 'Is he ill or something?'

'Not ill,' I assured him. 'Just suffering the terrible consequences
of love.'

*

'The course of true love never did run smooth.' I was talking,
in a rare moment of conversational amity, to Mrs Hilda Rumpole. 'And what's more, there's such a lot of it about these days.'

'A lot of what about, Rumpole?'

'Love. Miss Trant, the Portia of our Chambers, is apparently
expecting offspring.'

'She told you *that*? Whatever for?'

'I think she was trying to explain why she couldn't fancy two
eggs and a fried slice.'

'I suppose that man Claude Erskine-Brown's responsible.'
Hilda referred, of course, to Miss Trant's *fiancé*, not one of Rumpole's greatest fans.

'I imagine so. The poor little thing's probably lying in the
womb boning up on the law of landlord and tenant. They'll
expect it to get a place in Chambers.'

'Oh. And are they expecting to get married at any time? Or
will she be too busy with the baby?' Hilda seemed, most un-
justly, to be somehow blaming me for the moments of passion
which seemed to have transported Miss Trant and Erskine-
Brown after some particularly hectic rendering of *Lohengrin*. I
thought I would deflect her displeasure by feeding her another
juicy gobbet of Chambers gossip.

'And Marigold wants Featherstone to be a judge. Apparently

she means to divorce him if he doesn't get a red dressing-gown.'

'Marigold Featherstone,' said She judicially, 'has had a lot to put up with.'

'Poor Guthrie's looking in a terrible way. He's reduced to having to play golf with Vosper J. and old Keith from the Lord Chancellor's office.'

'Guthrie Featherstone will make a splendid judge.' She came to a firm decision, 'I'll have to have a talk about this with Marigold. We're meeting at choir practice tomorrow. You'll be coming to the *Elijah*, won't you, Rumpole?'

It will be remembered that Hilda and Marigold had joined a dreaded group of lawyers' wives who insisted on adding endless Oratorios to the other horrors of Yuletide. I fielded the invitation by neatly changing the subject.

'And speaking of love . . .'

'Were we, Rumpole?'

'Of course we were. I'm doing an Unlawful Carnal Knowledge in Hertfordshire tomorrow. Before old George Frobisher. Who is now,' I reminded her, 'a Circuit Judge.'

'Oh well, George Frobisher,' Hilda sounded dismissive. 'You'll be able to wrap him round your little finger, won't you, Rumpole?'

*

Hilda had, with rare discernment, voiced my own opinion as to how a case before His Honour Judge Frobisher would go. As I saw it my client was prepared to plead guilty if there were no question of his being called upon to visit Her Majesty; so when we arrived at the local Court I requested an interview with His Honour, and roped Miss Trant, for the prosecution, into what I hoped would prove a fruitful and friendly meeting. The news came back that the learned judge would be delighted to receive us both, and we proceeded down a passage in the new Hertfordshire Palais de Justice, a place with a lot of glass, light-polished wood and a strong smell of rubber floor-covering, and were shown into the presence of my dear old friend and sweetest of men, George Frobisher, our late stable-mate at Number 3 Equity Court in the Temple.

'George. My dear old friend. Judge George Frobisher,' I greeted him.

'Good to see you, Rumpole. I've been looking forward to the day when you came before me.'

'I'm sure you have, George. I'm sure you have. Of course, I may not be before you today for very long.'

'Oh, really?'

'I have had a word with my learned friend, with the opposition, who happens to be, by a happy coincidence, our old stablemate. You remember Miss Trant? The Portia of our Chambers?'

'Miss Trant. Glad, of course, to have you before me too.'

'Thank you, Judge,' said Miss Trant. So far all so very amiable.

'And we've been able to put our heads together, well, we had breakfast together as it so happens. They do a pretty good egg and bacon and fried slice in that little café opposite the Old Bailey ... And we've been able, Miss Trant and I, to come to a certain view about this case.'

'Have you?' George sounded curiously uninterested. 'Of course, I've come to no sort of view at all. I find it far better in this job not to come to any sort of view before one has heard the evidence.'

'And how do you enjoy it, George?' I was going to play the whole business slowly, and in the friendliest possible way.

'Enjoy what, Rumpole?'

'The job.'

'Lonely. It gets extremely lonely sometimes. Yes. Life is very lonely nowadays. I must say that it is.'

'Give you a decent lunch here, do they?' I tried to sound solicitous.

'Sandwiches!' George said sadly. 'The usher brings in sandwiches. It's usually cheese and tomato, but on Fridays for some reason he always brings one sardine.'

'Probably got a Catholic usher there, George,' I suggested.

'Perhaps he is,' George gave a faint smile. 'You know, that hadn't occurred to me.'

'Well, sandwiches are no good to you, George. No good to you at all. Bring you in a glass of plonk from the off-licence, does he?'

'There's a machine in the front hall that expels some sweet warm liquid in a plastic cup. I'm never quite sure whether my usher pushes the button marked Tea, Cocoa, Coffee, or Oxtail Soup.'

'George. The conditions of your work sound squalid in the extreme.'

'Not squalid, Rumpole. Not squalid really.' George looked extremely depressed. 'Just extremely lonely. Of course, I always led a lonely sort of life in the evenings in my diggings at the Royal Borough Hotel, Kensington. But I had the companionship of you fellows in Chambers during the day.' He looked at Miss Trant. 'Fellows' clearly meant her as well.

'And our drinks together in Pommeroy's Wine Bar when the day's work was done.'

'Of course, . .umpole. I look back on those evenings with considerable nostalgia.'

'The high spot, wouldn't you say, George, of your life at the Bar?' I established all he owed to Rumpole.

'Well ... Of course I won't say that being awarded a Circuit Judgeship hasn't struck me as something of an achievement,' George said modestly.

'But as nothing compared to those happy pints of plonk we downed at Pommeroy's, eh George? As nothing compared to the bottles of Chateau Fleet Street we consumed together whilst battling with the powerful but anonymous brain behind *The Times* crossword.'

'They were certainly good times, Rumpole.'

'The best,' I assured him. 'I would certainly say the best. I miss you, George, now that they've fitted you up with a mauve dressing-gown.'

'And of course, Rumpole, I miss you too. That goes without saying. It's good to have you here. You said you didn't expect to be here long?'

'No. No, George. Not long at all.'

'Pity.'

'From my point of view, yes. But for my client . . .'

'Rumpole says it's going to be a plea,' Miss Trant seemed anxious to press on with the meeting.

'Really?' George looked surprised. 'That's not like you, Rumpole.'

'I know.' Miss Trant smiled. 'He always taught me never to plead guilty.'

'I'm not saying it will be a plea. I'm saying it *might* be. Look here, George. My silly old client . . .'

'The young schoolmaster?' George's tone was somewhat cold.

'Yes. The schoolmaster.'

'Of course, he was *in loco parentis* . . .' George started to ramble. I cut him short.

'Let's cut out the Latin, George, and get down to some sort of reality. Ransom doesn't want to put the girl through the ordeal of being cross-examined by me. Which I think is very decent of him. Particularly, as you may remember, as I do have some sort of skill, in the art of cross-examination.'

'Indeed, Rumpole,' George smiled politely, 'we all admired it. Didn't we, Miss Trant?'

'Gosh, yes!' Miss Trant agreed. 'I had a client who once compared Rumpole's cross-examination to being hit by a steam-roller at ninety miles per hour.'

'You're all very kind. Well, my client is quite prepared to spare the girl that, which must earn him a considerably lower tariff.'

'Must it?' To my amazement George sounded unconvinced.

'And bearing in mind that the girl no doubt consented, on her own evidence.'

'Did she?'

'That's perfectly clear, Judge,' Miss Trant supported me. 'In fact, the prosecution will go so far as to say she led the man on. The first letter, you will see from the depositions, was the one she wrote to him and left in his locker in the staff-room. It contains the quotation from *Romeo and Juliet*.'

'I wonder if there isn't really too much poetry taught in schools nowadays,' George frowned unhappily.

'She was inciting him though. That's Miss Trant's point, George,' I tried to point out patiently.

'It's one thing to be tempted, Rumpole. But you don't have to give in to it.'

> ' 'Tis one thing to be tempted, Escalus,
> Another thing to fall.'

I helped him out. 'Shakespeare's *Measure for Measure*. Is that what you're trying to remember, George?'

'Perhaps it is, Rumpole. Perhaps it is.'

'But those lines were spoken by Angelo in the play. A dreadful judge of whom the author said that his urine was congealed ice. You're not like that, are you, George?' I wanted to shame my old friend into a quick decision.

'I hope not, Rumpole. I sincerely hope not. Mind you, I have been having a little trouble with the water-works lately, pardon me, Miss Trant ...' He was clearly rambling again. I was determined to put an end to it.

'Well then. Don't let's have this nonsense about "It's one thing to be tempted'. The fact is, this young girl was never for a moment seduced.'

George looked mildly at both of us and spoke most politely. 'You two no doubt have all the law at your fingertips. But that's absolutely no defence, is it?'

'No, it's not a defence. But it must be mitigation.' Miss Trant was doing her best.

'Thank you, Miss Trant,' I smiled at her. 'Of course it is, George. Powerful mitigation!'

'Then no doubt you will raise it, Rumpole. At the proper time?'

'The proper time?' I was giving George the message loud and clear; but he didn't seem to be getting it.

'At the end of the case. If your client's found guilty.'

'George. The proper time is now.' I tried to explain, as if to a child. 'Look, my friend, my dear old friend ...' Then I lost patience. 'Oh, pull yourself together, George. Look. The girl would have been sixteen in another month. She's over sixteen now!'

'Is that a defence? Remind me. What's your client's age?' The man was being singularly obtuse. I chose an answer from literature.

'Do you know how old Juliet was when she met Romeo?'

'No, I don't. But no doubt you'll be making use of the fact in your speech to the jury.'

'She was under fourteen! You remember her old Nurse?'

'Not personally.' George smiled, I thought foolishly.

> 'Even or odd, of all days of the year
> Come Lammas Eve at night shall she be fourteen,'

I reminded him.

'You remember so much more Shakespeare than I do, Rumpole. I've always admired you for it.'

'That was how old Juliet was, at the time she married Romeo and went to bed with him.'

'And came to a rather unpleasant end, if I remember. What was it, locked up in a tomb and taking poison?' If he was trying to catch me out on Shakespeare I could get the better of him.

'All because of that idiotic monk. We don't want *you* making any mistakes like that, George.'

'I try not to make mistakes in this job, Rumpole. One can only do one's best.'

'When you spoke of locking up, of course nothing of that sort would be appropriate here.' I tried to make the position clear.

'Wouldn't it, Rumpole?'

'Of course it wouldn't.' I was trying to keep my temper.

'The prosecution wouldn't regard this as an offence th   warrants a prison sentence.' Miss Trant offered her help. I was grateful for it.

'But then it's really nothing to do with the prosecution, is it?' George was smiling at her.

'Well, not strictly . . .'

'It's *my* job to decide on sentence. I must say, I never find it at all easy. Particularly when it comes to prison.' George was passing from the obtuse to the obnoxious.

'That must come as a great comfort to those you bang up. To know it caused you a little difficulty, George,' I told him.

'But I must say, if your client's found guilty . . .'

I tried to explain the situation for the last time. 'I told you. He's prepared to plead. And face a conditional discharge.' George looked impassive. I went on, 'Or at the most a suspended sentence. Damn it all, he'll lose his job, George!'

'It's his job, I must confess, that's worrying me, Rumpole.' George frowned. 'His job was to look after this girl.'

'This young woman,' I corrected him.

'This minor. Not to fill her up with Vivaldi and cannelloni and take her to bed in some maisonette in Fitzjohn's Avenue, borrowed from friends.'

'They're a couple from the BBC. Highly respectable people.'

'They weren't respectable if they knew what was going on.'

'They didn't.'

'Then your client was abusing their hospitality, as well as his position as a school-teacher.'

'George. Abelard was Éloise's tutor.'

'Éloise and Abelard aren't on trial in this Court,' George said firmly. 'If they were I might have something rather unpleasant to say to them.' George stood up unexpectedly. 'Well, I'm sorry I can't do more for you. And I'm sorry your visit won't be a longer one, Rumpole.'

'It may be longer,' I told him. 'I'm not pleading guilty un-less . . .'

'Rumpole,' George interrupted me. 'You know perfectly well I can't come to any sort of bargain.'

'Just tell me, George . . .' I was almost pleading with him, 'George, we know each other well enough!'

'Well enough for me to tell you both this,' George actually interrupted me, 'I can't possibly hold out any promises. If Ransom's found guilty I'll have to consider sentence, very carefully. I couldn't rule out the possibility of prison. I couldn't rule it out at all. Does that help you?'

'You know bloody well it doesn't!' I wanted George to be in no doubt. 'Come along, Miss Trant.' At the door I turned to wish my old friend ill. 'Enjoy your sandwiches!'

*

'Sandwiches! I hope they choke him! Thank God it's not Friday. He won't even get sardine.' I was reporting to Ransom and Grayson the solicitor in the corridor outside the Court.

'I thought he was a friend of yours, Mr Rumpole.' Ransom frowned.

'He was a friend. I suppose he is one still. The bloody mauve dressing-gown. It's gone to his head!'

'I don't want Francesca to suffer,' Ransom was playing the old gramophone record.

'All right then,' I told him, 'you suffer. Do you want to go away? Maybe for a year? Maybe eighteen months, locked in with a gay mugger, watched over by an underpaid screw with a fifteen-year-old daughter of his own, spending your time slopping out and volunteering for pills to decrease your libido? Because if that's what you want, my friend George is prepared to offer it to you. On a plate!' I paused for my words to take effect, looked at Ransom, and then I said, 'Of course, if you tell me that you actually bedded the young lady.'

'No. No, I don't tell you that,' Ransom answered slowly.

'Then we plead "Not Guilty". We teach old George a lesson he'll never forget. And we win this case!'

'How do we do that, Mr Rumpole?' Grayson seemed to be merely asking for information.

'By having a go at Miss Francesca Capstick.'

'Please, Mr Rumpole. Treat her gently,' Ransom still insisted.

'I shall treat her as gently as if I were a steam-roller, going at ninety miles per hour,' I reassured him. 'How much is known about her?'

'Nothing at all is known about her. By *me*,' Mr Grayson said.

'You mean *someone* might know?'

'Well, Hughie . . . Hughie might know a good deal.'

'Who is this invaluable grass?'

'My son Hughie,' Grayson admitted. 'He goes to John Keats. He knows most of Francesca's friends.'

So we had a dependable source of information for the cross-examination of Francesca. Even then, it seemed, Ransom's luck was holding well.

*

The proceedings in R. *v.* Ransom were opened kindly and gently by Miss Trant. She told the ladies and gentlemen of the jury that there was no question but that Francesca was a willing party, she was almost sixteen at the time, and they must be careful of accepting her evidence unless it was corroborated in a material particular. She then called the Headmaster who was apparently anxious to get away (no doubt to an urgent meeting of the British Drama League). I thought the most interesting part of his evidence was the fact that a whole bundle of Ransom's letters (poetic effusions which left the issue as to whether he had in fact committed an offence under Section 6 of the Sexual Offences Act 1956 quite unresolved) together with copies, or drafts of Francesca's letters to him, appeared as if by magic, fastened with an elastic band, on the Headmaster's desk, and were waiting for him when he came back from Assembly (a reading from *Lord of the Rings* and a snatch of Joan Baez on the record-player). Who, I wondered, had been kind enough to present the Ransom-Capstick correspondence to the Headmaster, and who had abstracted it from its beautiful recipient?

When the witness went on to describe the interview he had with Miss Capstick on the vital issue, Rumpole pushed himself to his hind legs to protest.

'Your Honour.'

'Yes, Mr Rumpole.' George, my old friend, sounded curiously aloof.

'Any statement made by this young lady is not evidence. I object . . .'

'Very well,' said the co-operative Miss Trant. 'I won't press the matter.' Good old Portia. I sat down, delighted, when George did something totally unexpected.

'The evidence of a complaint is admissible, surely,' he said. 'In a sexual case. To negative consent.'

'But everyone agrees she consented! Consent is not an issue here.' I almost added, 'Come on, George. You never had any instinctive grasp of the rules of evidence.' (He probably found it more convenient to look it all up in a book.)

'It is my responsibility to rule on the evidence and I do so now,' said George pompously. The whole business of becoming a judge seemed to have done absolutely nothing for his personality. 'The evidence of a complaint is admissible. Yes. What was the question, Miss Trant?'

I sat in a fury which I did absolutely nothing to conceal while Miss Trant asked her questions, and the answers revealed that Miss Capstick had 'complained' that she had been taken to a concert, an Italian meal and to bed in a place in Fitzjohn's Avenue where 'the defendant' had borrowed a room. 'Intimacy had also taken place' in Ransom's Ford Capri while parked in a wood near St Albans, at Francesca's house whilst her parents were away for the weekend and, in what must have been a hasty moment of extreme danger and discomfort, in a corner of the art-room during the course of a school dance. All this had happened within two weeks. Ransom and Francesca, it seemed, had taken the advice of Andrew Marvell in the poem they had read together.

> 'Thus, though we cannot make our sun
> Stand still, yet we will make him run ...'

*

At the lunch break I saw Francesca leaving Court with her parents and a sixteen-year-old, spotty-faced youth with ginger hair, glasses, a long scarf and a scowl of perpetual bad temper. I was standing with my client as the group passed us; all, including Francesca, looking self-consciously in the opposite direction. However, after they had gone by I saw the youth turn his head to look back at Ransom with a smile which I can only describe as unpleasantly triumphant.

'It's agonizing!' Ransom said. 'Hearing the letters read out. Hers and mine. It was love, that's all it was. Does it have to be dragged out in Court and cheapened?'

'I'm afraid it does,' I told him, and led the way to the bleak pub opposite, where we sat on tartan-covered benches, listened to piped music and consumed Scotch eggs and gassy beer. 'By the way, who was that unpleasant-looking youth with Francesca? Not her brother?'

'Someone in her class,' Ransom told me vaguely. 'His name's Mowersby. C. J. Mowersby.'

'Charlie?'

'I don't know. He always puts C.J. on the top of his essays.'

'Any good, are they?'

'What?'

'His essays.'

'Absolutely appalling. C. J. Mowersby can't wait to give up English language and literature and take up computer-programming as his special subject. Why on earth are you interested in him?'

'He looked as if he hated you.'

'Probably because I wrote on one of his essays, "Poetry is emotion recollected in tranquillity; not quotations collected for a quick O-level." I remember writing that.'

'C. J. Mowersby is not an admirer of poetry?'

'As far as I can tell, he's not an admirer of anything. Except computers.'

'And Francesca?'

'She talks to him of course. She talks to everyone. She's such a wonderful, friendly sort of kid.'

'Yes, of course. There's no particular reason why he should be with her family at this trial?'

'None I can think of.'

Ransom returned to his theme of the horrors of having the tender emotions of a young Juliet such as his pupil dragged out in Court to be coarsely prodded and examined by the hard hands of such as Rumpole; and I asked Grayson to instruct his son Hughie, our undercover-agent at the John Keats Comprehensive, to give us all the dirt on Mowersby, C.J.

As we went back to Court the Mowersby youth was lurking alone on the steps that led up to the public gallery. He gave my client another look of undisguised contempt.

'You must have done more to him,' I suggested, 'than write a snide remark on his Wordsworth essay.'

'Well. I may have suggested to the Headmaster that his attitude was simply bloody-minded in Poetry Appreciation. I remember Mowersby saying in a seminar on the metaphysicals that all my bloody understanding of John Donne didn't mean I could knock up more than four thousand a year. I believe I told the H.M. that Mowersby was quite unsuitable for John Keats and might be asked to continue his education elsewhere.'

'So he's come to sit at your trial,' I said, 'like an old woman knitting by the side of the guillotine.'

After Court that day Mr Grayson drove me to his house where young Hughie Grayson was delighted to knock off his biology prep and give me an hour on the life and loves of Form Five B. By the end of our little chat I felt I had lived through a peculiarly sultry chapter in the History of the Italian Renaissance, around the time when the Borgias were at the height of their sexual potency. I also knew why C. J. Mowersby was so greatly enjoying our trial.

*

'The bundle of letters left on the Headmaster's desk consisted of letters from Mr Ransom and copies of your letters to him.' I was cross-examining Francesca. She looked pretty and demure, she answered softly, and was unostentatiously chewing gum.

'That's right. I kept them in a bundle together.'

'You kept copies of the letters you wrote to him?'

'Yes.' Her voice sank another few decibels.

'Speak up, please.'

'Yes, I did. I kept copies.'

'Why?'

'I don't know. I suppose I just wanted to.'

'Was it because you were in love with Mr Ransom?'

Francesca removed her chewing-gum delicately, stuck it under the rail of the witness-box, shrugged slightly and answered, 'I just kept copies.'

'And this correspondence started with a letter from you?'

'Did it?'

I fished out the first incriminating document and waved it at her. 'It's the first letter in date order you wrote to Mr Ransom, "And all my fortunes at thy foot I'll lay," you wrote, "And follow thee my Lord throughout the world".'

'It comes from the play we were doing. *Romeo and Juliet.*'

'Exactly! And what did you mean by all your "fortunes"?'

There was a pause. Then she shrugged again. 'I don't know.'

'You weren't offering your teacher your pocket money or your savings certificates?'

'Not exactly.' She smiled politely, as if she thought I had made a joke.

'You were offering your love.'

'That's what I *said*,' she qualified her answer.

'Offering to do *anything* for him.'

After only a second's hesitation she answered, 'Yes.'

'And to follow him wherever he asked you to go?'

'Your client wasn't *bound* to take advantage of that offer, Mr Rumpole,' George put his oar in, as I thought quite unnecessarily.

'Oh no, your Honour. I just wish to establish who made the first approach.' I turned to the witness. 'Miss Capstick. Have you any idea how this bundle of letters got on to the Headmaster's table?'

'No. No idea.' She was starting to look bored, as if I were a particularly dull geography lesson.

'Presumably you kept them safely?'

'Yes.'

'Did you keep them at home?'

A small hesitation, then she said, 'No.'

'Because you didn't want your parents to find them?'

'I didn't keep them at home.'

'So you kept them at school. In your locker, perhaps?'

'No. No, I gave them to a friend of mine to keep for me.'

'May we hear the name of this friend?'

But George put in another unhelpful word. 'Really, Mr Rumpole. Is that relevant?'

'Perhaps not, my Lord. I'll leave it for the moment.' I turned back to Francesca and again attempted, not too successfully, to engage her interest. 'You have a good many friends at school, haven't you?'

'Of course I have.'

'Of course. You're a very popular girl.' She didn't look in the least flattered and I picked up the copy of her first letter again. 'When you wrote this first letter to Mr Ransom, did you have any particular friends at that time?'

'Girlfriends, do you mean?'

'You know I don't mean girlfriends,' I pressed her and she looked slightly more interested.

'You mean anyone I was going out with?'

'Going out with so often means staying in with, doesn't it?'

'Really, Mr Rumpole...' George tried to protest.

I ignored him and repeated, 'Doesn't it?'

'You mean Charles?'

'Yes.' Now at last something was cooking. I hoped it was C. J. Mowersby's goose.

'You mean I was going out with Charles ... Yes, I was. What about it?' She smiled at the jury. They didn't smile back.

'Is Charles Mowersby in Court? Perhaps he'd stand up.' I looked round and saw the sullen, spotty 1ace in the gallery. He didn't move. 'Perhaps he'd stand up,' I repeated. The unappealing youth lumbered to his feet. 'Is that Mr C. J. Mowersby?'

'That's Charles. Yes.' Unsmiling and sullen as ever, Mr Mowersby resumed his seat.

'He's the one you were going out with. When you wrote the letter, swearing to follow your Lord Mr Ransom throughout the world?'

'Yes.'

'Tell me. The school term's still on, isn't it? Do you know why Mr Mowersby is here?'

'I suppose he's interested.'

'Yes. Yes, I suppose he is.' I picked up the letters again. 'Before you wrote your first letter to Mr Ransom had you been on a school holiday in France, camping with Charles Mowersby?'

'With all our class. Yes.'

'Camping. Sleeping under canvas?'

'I was sharing a tent with my girlfriend.'

'Exactly. A girl named Mary Pennington?'

'With Mary. Yes.'

'Did a boy called Hugh Grayson go on that holiday with you?' I was now prepared to divulge the source of my information.

'Hughie did. Yes. He was sharing a tent with Charles.'

'Exactly. And on the first night did you ask Mary Pennington to go into Hughie Grayson's tent so that Charles Mowersby could come into yours?'

There was a long pause. The jury looked at her stonily, but Miss Capstick said, 'I might have done ...' clearly, almost defiantly.

'Did you spend the night with Charles Mowersby? Did you sleep with him?'

This time the answer was quiet, inaudible. 'What did you say?'

'Mr Rumpole. I'm really wondering what the relevance ...' Once again George needed ignoring. I kept my eyes on the witness.

'What did you say?'

'I said I might have done.'

'And did you say to Mr C. J. Mowersby of Form Five B of the John Keats Comprehensive "I'll follow thee my Lord throughout the world"?'

'No, I didn't.'

'Why not?'

'Charles doesn't like poetry.'

'Charles doesn't like poetry. And he doesn't like Mr Ransom either, does he?'

'Mr Rumpole ...' It was George again. I carried on regardless.

'Does he?' I asked, with some determination. 'Because Mr Ransom writes rude remarks on his essays on Wordsworth, and Mr Ransom reported him to the Headmaster, and Mr Ransom thought that Mr C. J. Mowersby might be invited to continue his education elsewhere. So Charles doesn't like your schoolteacher?'

'He doesn't like him. No.'

'He hates him.'

'Perhaps.'

By now even George had given up and the jury were clearly interested.

'The friend you gave your bundle of letters to for safe keeping. Was that Mr Mowersby, by any chance?'

The witness-box is an odd sort of place. Sometimes people feel unable to lie in it. Francesca said, 'Yes.'

'And it was Mr Mowersby who gave them to the Headmaster?'

'It might have been.'

'Mr Rumpole. Suppose all this is true . . .' George was burbling on again and I turned on him and almost shouted.

'Suppose all this is true? Then this whole charge is nothing but a pretence, a cruel joke, played on my client by this . . . this young woman who wanted to help her boyfriend get his revenge!' I said to Francesca quietly, 'Your first letter . . . your letter full of Juliet's love. Didn't Charles suggest you write that?'

'He wanted to show Mr Ransom up.' At last, she gave me the answer I wanted.

'For what? For a fool who'd have his head turned by young girls writing poetry?'

'Something like that. Yes.'

'So Charles suggested you write that letter?'

'He found the bit out of the play. Yes.'

'Really! That must have been the first time Mr Mowersby showed an interest in literature.' The jury gave an obedient titter. 'And did you hand my client's replies to Mowersby as you got them?'

'More or less.'

'And I suppose he was delighted with the way things were going? He had a nice little bundle of trouble for Mr Ransom to drop on the Headmaster's table?'

'I suppose he did. He never wanted me to go to the concert though.' She answered quickly and I stopped to think of the next question.

'You mean the concert at the Festival Hall?'

'Charles never wanted me to go to that.' I felt a sort of danger, but ignored it and pressed on.

'You're not going to say you acted independently for once in your life?' By now Francesca was answering quite confidently, as if she were telling me some not very interesting school gossip.

'I'd found out Charles was taking Mary Pennington out. Hughie Grayson told me he'd seen them together at *Saturday Night Fever*.'

I looked up again at the sullen, spotty face in the gallery, the glasses, the muffler, the ginger hair: I tried to imagine Charles Mowersby in the role of a demon lover and failed utterly.

'So, well . . . I went to the concert.'

'But not to bed with my client?' I said it with all possible determination. She didn't answer, and that encouraged me to go on. 'Not to bed with the man on whom you were playing an elaborate practical joke, just so your boyfriend could get him into trouble with the Headmaster? Your victim! Your poor, wretched gull. You didn't go to bed with *him*, did you?'

There was a pause. Francesca sighed, and then said patiently, as though explaining things to an idiot, 'I told you. I'd heard Charles was taking out Mary Pennington. So that's how it happened.'

'How what happened?'

'How I had it away with Mr Ransom.'

'You mean sexual intercourse?' George asked, showing himself to be unexpectedly up in contemporary English.

'Yes,' said Francesca.

'Because you were annoyed with Charles. You did *that*?' I tried to sound incredulous.

'I wasn't annoyed. I was furious with him.'

'Because of that, you say, you made love to my client?'

'That was the reason. Really.'

'Without love?'

'Yes.'

'Did you enjoy the experience?'

'Not much. He kept on spouting poetry.'

I looked at my client's face. I knew that nothing, no prison sentence that George had it in his power to award, would now hurt him more than the words that his young Juliet, Miss Francesca Capstick, had just spoken. I took a deep breath and began again, 'I put it to you that what you have just told us is a deliberate and wicked lie. You never went to bed with my client.'

'I did. We did it again too...'

'Just as your letter to him was a wicked and deliberate lie, aimed to deceive him, your evidence has been completely invented to deceive this jury.' I went on like that for the rest of the afternoon. But my heart was no longer in it.

*

Guthrie Featherstone played golf with Mr Justice Vosper and Keith from the Lord Chancellor's office, but his luck was out. Vosper got stuck in some sort of sand dune, Keith hit his ball into a river, and Guthrie committed the unpardonable and quite unintentional social blunder of holing out in one on the thirteenth; so for the moment his heavy hints on his willingness to exchange the hectic struggle of the front row for the peace and comfort of the Judicial Bench went unheeded.

Worse still, Hilda told all my gossip to Marigold Featherstone, who told Guthrie, who summoned Erskine-Brown to him and said that the last thing he needed was to be Head of a Chambers in which irregular unions and unsanctified births were a common occurrence. As his own marriage would founder unless he got a judgeship, he begged Erskine-Brown to pop the question to an ever-increasing Miss Phillida Trant.

At first his proposal was received somewhat coldly, but when Erskine-Brown insisted that he was particularly fond of children, Miss Trant asked him if he would be prepared to baby-sit if she were kept late at London Sessions, and when he showed willing Claude was accepted without more ado. The happy couple were married in the Temple Church and we had a reception in a tent in Temple Gardens. Old George Frobisher came and we sank our noses into glasses of non-vintage Pommeroy's Shampoo.

'Sorry to have had to put that fellow Ransom away,' George said. 'I really had no alternative. Was two years too much?'

'Two days would have been too much. You know that, George.'

George ignored this and gulped champagne. 'I heard they're

not prosecuting that young boy Mowersby. No doubt that's a wise decision. It's different, isn't it, for the young?'

'You mean they're so much more grown-up, and experienced?'

'But your client was her schoolmaster. He was in charge of her.'

'No, George. She was in charge of him. Totally.'

'Are you angry with me, Rumpole?'

'I was. Exceedingly.'

'It wasn't my fault.'

He was right, of course. It wasn't George's fault. It was the fault of life, the fault of love, the fault of poetry, the fault of youth, the fault of the law. Not George's fault at all. Ronald Ransom had thanked me for all I'd done, but I knew he hated me for it. As for Miss Francesca Capstick, she left the Court arm-in-arm with C. J. Mowersby. It was the only time I ever saw him smile.

Rumpole and the Age for Retirement

'Sir Mathew told the Police Federation that the work of crime detection was becoming more and more frustrating. "And when you catch them," he said, "there's always some clever dick of a bent barrister who earns his living by finding a legal loophole for the crook to wriggle out of." '

The wireless set in the kitchen at Casa Rumpole, where I was moodily chewing a slice of burnt toast and drinking a cup of instant before setting off for the Ludgate Circus Palais de Justice, crackled with indignation as it reported the words of some highly placed copper who was intent, as highly placed coppers are nowadays, on repealing Magna Carta, abolishing Habeas Corpus, reversing the presumption of innocence and substituting a brief hearing before the sergeant in the local Station (from which all lawyers would, of course, be barred) for the antiquated and unsatisfactory system of trial by jury. As I went for the ancient hat and well-used mackintosh I heard that Sir Mathew had regretted 'the recent serious epidemic of acquittals at the Old Bailey, which was a glaring example of the injustice caused by underworld legal vultures'.

Oh dear, and a very big 'oh dear' at that. Rumpole's occupation, that of making sure that citizens of all classes are not randomly convicted of crimes they didn't do just so that the prison statistics may look more impressive, seems to have fallen into disrepute. I felt more than usually unappreciated as I burrowed down the Gloucester Road tube on my mole-like journey to irritate the constabulary and pour sand in the gear-box of justice, and when I emerged, blinking, into the daylight of the Temple Station I was beginning to wonder if it was not time to abandon the up-hill struggle. Was it possible that Rumpole should retire from the Bar?

Of course I have nothing to retire on, except an overdraft at the National Westminster Bank and a dribble of uncollected fees. But now my son Nick has gone off to seek a Newer World, being something pretty high up in the University of Baltimore (Sociology Department) and living with his wife Erica in some luxurious ranch-style edifice, with a swimming-pool in what my daughter-in-law mysteriously refers to as the 'Back Yard' (I always thought of a back yard as a place for dustbins, bicycles and possibly a cage for ferrets), Hilda and I are more or less alone in the world.

'It little profits that an idle king ...' I quoted to myself as I climbed into the frayed black gown and crowned myself with the antique wig, and poor old Alfred Tennyson's words seemed more than usually apposite:

'By this still hearth, among these barren crags,
Matched with an aged wife, I mete and dole
Unequal laws unto a savage race,
That hoard and feed and sleep and know not me ...'

I recalled the poor old Laureate's words again that day when, delivered of my final speech in a case where I was defending a certain Melvin Glassworth on a well-aimed charge of conspiracy to steal various works of art and valuable antiques, I sat in Number 3 Court at the Old Bailey, listening to the summing-up of that singularly unattractive judge, Mr Justice Vosper. Just as a gambler at Monte Carlo may be bankrupted by a long run on the black when all his savings are staked on the red, so I had suffered the misfortune of facing Vosper J. in three cases running at the Bailey. This judge, who in my considered opinion has a great deal in common with Shakespeare's Angelo (they both urinate congealed ice), suffered all the worst faults of a judge; he was unable to keep quiet, he invariably acted as leading counsel for the prosecution, and he could never resist trying to make a joke instead of leaving the comedy to Rumpole. Anyway there we sat, Counsel for the prosecution relaxed, the jury looking young and serious (they had all no doubt heard the wise words of the Head Copper on the wireless that morning) and Mr Melvin Glassworth, a plumpish, pinkish man who smelt of various toilet preparations, sweating slightly in the dock as he saw the doors of the prison house begin to close. I shut my eyes and from afar became aware that the words now falling from his Lordship, might be construed as discouraging Rumpole's continued activity about the Courts of Justice.

'Finally, members of the jury, allow me to remind you,' said his Lordship, 'you decide this case on the facts and not on the speeches of Counsel, however eloquently they address you.' In other words his message was 'Beware of Rumpole, the Old Bailey Hack'. 'Counsel for the defence in this case,' the judge went on, 'has chosen to challenge the police evidence as he is entitled to do. But you are entitled to form your own view of the evidence, quite independent of the view of learned Counsel, however long he may have been practising at the Bar.' Why didn't he just tell them 'Rumpole's past it?' 'We all enjoy Mr Rumpole's speeches. We always find his little jokes *most amusing*. But you and I have a more serious duty to perform ...' I knew he was delighted that I was only there to provide light relief. Bring on the dancing Rumpole.

'Of course, if by any chance you think there is a reasonable doubt in this case you will follow Mr Rumpole's advice and acquit the defendant Glassworth of this serious charge of conspiracy to steal these valuable works of art.' Here his Lordship smiled tolerantly at the jury, in the full knowledge that they would agree that this was a truly laughable suggestion. 'But if you think that the prosecution case is unanswerable ...' In other words, Vosper J. was saying, if you have an ounce of common sense, 'then it is your plain duty, in accordance with your oath, to find the defendant guilty as charged.' And bugger Rumpole, he might have added. 'So will you please go now and consider your verdict. The only question for you is whether Melvin Glassworth is guilty as charged ... Mr Jury Bailiff ...'

Whereupon the usher rose in the well of the Court, held up a Bible and swore to take the jury to some convenient place to consider this simple question, and I prayed silently that they would consider the feelings of an old man and stay out for a decent interval, or at least more than five minutes. Meanwhile I went out into the corridor, lit a small cigar with the nervous hand and the dry mouth I always experience when the jury goes out to consider its verdict, and was immediately accosted by a bulky man of about my own age, wearing a lightweight checked summer sports-jacket, who addressed me in a low, rumbling, transatlantic accent.

'Mr Rumpole,' he said, 'I have heard a lot about you, sir. Your fame has spread to the States.'

'I can't believe it.'

'Oh yes, sir. You know, I practised as an attorney myself. For many years. Of course, I didn't wear the rug.'

I thought he must be referring to some sort of plaid, perhaps for use in cold courts, and I was confused.

'The *what*?'

'The headpiece. The horse-hair peruque.'

'Oh this.' I slapped my antique wig. 'Of course, we're invisible without it. Unless we've got it on the judge can't see us. Sometimes I'm tempted to remove the wig and disappear entirely from view.'

'I can understand, sir. Exactly how you feel.' The gravelly voice was sympathetic. 'The learned judge seemed to regard you as a senior citizen.'

'I'm not all *that* senior.' I was defensive. 'And he's not all that learned!'

'I long ago gave up the dust of conflict for the Groves of Academe. What do you call an academic lawyer here?'

As bad language is not encouraged from members of my learned profession round the Bailey I didn't tell him.

In the ensuing silence he pulled out his wallet and presented me with an embossed card.

'Professor Kramer. Head of the Department of Law', it announced, 'in the University of Baltimore.'

Baltimore! My son's university; but the usher came bustling up to put an end to further inquiry.

'Mr Rumpole,' he said urgently, 'they're coming back, Mr Rumpole.'

'How extremely rude of them.' I turned to Professor Kramer. 'My son Nick's at Baltimore. Teaching Sociology. He's got his own small Department now. And a new house. 1106 East Drive, Baltimore. You know it? Of course, Nick's the brain of the family.'

'They've got a verdict, Mr Rumpole,' the usher intoned.

'Look, I've got to go now, Professor . . .'

'Kramer, Julius Kramer. I shall be in touch! Back to the dust of battle, Mr Rumpole. I have to tell you. It's just great to be out of it!'

*

The jury came back and announced their unanimous decision, the judge announced the three-year sentence he'd been planning throughout the trial, and I went down to the cells to say goodbye to Mr Melvin Glassworth. Taking your leave of a convicted client is one of those awkward social occasions which I would give anything to avoid, but which are as mandatory as an invitation to the Palace (not that I have ever had an invitation to the Palace; but I have kept many disappointed engagements down the cells at the Bailey). However disastrous the result or excessive the sentence you rarely get blamed for losing a case; the prisoner may be almost relieved that it wasn't as bad as he feared, and he is always numb; it's only after a week in chokey that the shock wears off, the pain starts, and the customer faces up to the reality of stone walls and banging up and stinking chamber-pots and tears, I have no doubt, start to prick behind his eyes.

As I have said, you rarely get blamed. Mr Melvin Glassworth was, however, the exception that proves the rule. When my solicitor, Mr Bernard, and I went down to the cells he was red-faced, sweating more than ever, and extremely angry. It was no good suggesting that three years for a theft worth at least twenty-thousand nicker was not outrageous, so Rumpole lit a small cigar, and contented himself into looking genuinely grieved. Mr Bernard provided cold comfort by pointing out that it was only two really, with time off for good behaviour.

'Oh, what's two? A long weekend in the country. Is that what you're trying to tell me? I suppose you want me to be grateful.' Mr Glassworth mopped his forehead with a purple silk handkerchief that smelt of old pear drops. 'I'm a man of a certain fastidiousness,' he told us. 'I have to have two shirts a day, me! Two clean shirts is not an indulgence as far as I'm concerned. It's a necessity! Do they still have slopping out?'

'I'm afraid they do,' I had to tell him. He moved away from us; I was afraid that the tears were coming now.

'I have spent my life in the acquisition of beautiful objects,' Mr Glassworth said. That, of course, was really the problem. 'Slopping out. How can I live through it, me!' He went on, 'And the sickening sexual advances of beefy warders!'

'I shouldn't count on that, old darling,' I said, not quite sufficiently under my breath.

'What did you say?'

'Nothing ... I'm sorry.'

'*You're* sorry! *You* can go home.' Mr Glassworth's misery exploded in anger. 'Have a bath with a decent tablet of Imperial Leather. Dry on a warm fleecy towel. Use talcum powder and *eau de toilette*, you!'

'I don't actually ...' But there was no real point in establishing my bathroom habits.

'Attacking the police! That wasn't a smash hit with the jury, was it? And those little jokes in your final speech, they didn't exactly bring the house down!'

'The judge went too far in his summing-up, Melvin. We can think about an appeal.' Mr Bernard was soothing, but Melvin Glassworth turned on me, unappeased.

'You know what you ought to be thinking about, you. Retirement!' he said. 'That's what you ought to do! Bloody retire!'

*

My next appearance before Mr Justice Vosper took place after old Uncle Percy Timson found Jesus Christ unexpectedly in his lock-up garage.

I have written elsewhere of the Timson family,* that huge

*'Rumpole and the Younger Generation' in *Rumpole of the Bailey*, Penguin Books, 1978.

clan of South London villains whose selfless devotion to crime has kept the Rumpoles in such luxuries as Vim, Gumption, sliced bread and saucepan scourers over the years, not to mention the bare necessities of life, such as gin, tonic and cooking claret from Pommeroy's Wine Bar. Uncle Percy Timson, who lived with his wife Noreen in a respectable semi-detached somewhere in the general direction of Kent, had practised for many years the profession of a small-time fence or receiver of stolen property. The business was small, personal and regular: it enabled Uncle Percy and Auntie Noreen to run an elderly Cortina, grow prize leeks and go for an annual holiday on the Costa Brava. They had, it seemed, recently been away for such a package adventure, and the morning after their return, as they sat brewing early-morning tea in their kitchen, Auntie Noreen saw something which caused her to throw the fine Georgian silver tea-pot she was using (part of the business stock) straight into the tidy bin. When Percy joined her at the window he said:

'That new one ... that Detective Inspector Broome's got no bloody manners. When it was old "Persil" White's patch he at least gave you time to finish your breakfast.'

Detective Inspector Broome, known as the new Broome among the disapproving Timsons, was a young zealous officer with horn-rimmed spectacles, a small but aggressive moustache, and views on lawyers which coincided entirely with those which Sir Mathew, the Chief Copper, had been expounding on steam radio. He was at that moment advancing remorselessly on Uncle Percy's garage leading a posse which included Detective Constable Wood, a uniformed officer, and an Alsatian dog. At the garage doors old Uncle Percy came out in his dressing-gown and encountered the D I. His conscience was easy and his manner relaxed. So far as he knew there was nothing of interest to be found in the garage; the load from the Deptford job went the week before, and a consignment of electric blankets was not due till the following Saturday.

'You're interested in buying my Banger, Mr Broome, are you?' Percy asked. 'One owner, and he was the Vicar of Gravesend and only used it for funerals.'

'Open up, Percy.' DC Wood sounded distinctly hostile. 'Or you want us to break the door down?'

'We know what you got there, Percy. We know exactly what you've got,' DI Broome said.

'Nothing, I do assure you, Mr Broome, what's not perfectly legitimate.'

At which, with a confidence which turned out to be ill-founded, Percy Timson unlocked his garage. A huge religious picture, which had been leaning against the door, toppled forward, Our Lord and Saviour, his hand raised in gentle Benediction, was descending on the astonished onlookers.

'Jeesus .. Ker-ist!' said Percy, he was more surprised than anyone.

*

So it happened that Percy Timson found himself in the local nick being interviewed by those fearless battlers against crime, DI Broome and DC Wood. Broome, in the interests of making his case barrister-proof, was after Uncle Percy's autograph on a confession statement, a brief admission of the crime of receiving a religious art-work in his lock-up garage well knowing it to have been stolen.

Meanwhile Mr Bernard the solicitor, who shared with me the honour of being permanent legal adviser to the Timsons, had dropped in on Noreen in answer to her almost hysterical calls, a hysteria brought about by the supernatural quality of the manifestation in the garage rather than by the everyday occurrence of Uncle Percy being taken down to the nick.

'Percy's got too old for it, Mr Bernard!' she told him, over a nice cup of tea from the rescued Georgian silver pot. 'The whole family told him. He's got too old altogether. He ought to retire. Fancy keeping Jesus in his lock-up garage. He's getting that careless!'

'Not sufficiently careless, let's hope Mrs Timson, to give DI Broome his autograph.' At which point Bernard managed to get hold of the Detective Inspector on the phone. The answers he got were only to be expected. Mr Broome was unable to say where

Percy Timson was being held incommunicado. All he could say was that he was not prepared to let Percy see, or speak to, or have any dealings with a lawyer for the reason, which seemed good to the DI, that if Percy were guilty he'd only be stopped confessing, and if he were innocent why did he need a lawyer anyway?

Having satisfactorily disposed of the legal profession Broome returned to where Percy was sitting being fed tea and biscuits by DC Wood (playing the sympathetic role) and briskly informed him that his wife Noreen was in the cells below, about to be charged with conspiracy to receive Jesus, unless Percy at once supplied his autograph. The fact that this statement was an outrageous lie was merely one of the sacrifices the eager Inspector was prepared to make in his devoted pursuit of law and order.

'Tell me,' Broome speculated. 'Just how long is it since your old woman saw the inside of Holloway? We want a statement signed in your own words, Percy.' What were his own words, exactly? Constable Wood read out the composition on which he had been working.

'I received the religious art-work in my garage, well knowing it to be stolen by a person whose name I am not prepared to divulge.'

'Which of them was it, Percy? Which of the Timson family was it, exactly?' Broome asked.

'I am not prepared to divulge.' Although prepared to do almost anything to save Noreen, Percy was not, by nature, a grass, any more than he was a signer of confessions.

'No doubt on the advice of his bloody lawyer,' Broome commented.

'I was intending to dispose of this picture at the earliest opportunity,' Wood read on, and Percy interrupted.

'Like when I went up the King's Elm Saturday and met a few of my contacts. I want that in.'

'Like when I went up the King's Elm Saturday and met a few of my contacts.' Wood read on obediently, and then the document, calculated to stop the boldest, bentest barrister dead in his tracks, was put before Uncle Percy for signature. So, when the brief arrived at my Chambers, I was faced with a clearly signed confession of guilt plus an inexplicable picture of Jesus in the garage. Apart from that little difficulty, the defence seemed moderately plain sailing.

*

As I walked down to the Temple tube station some weeks later, on my way home to Casa Rumpole, I saw a large figure flitting like some bloated white moth through the twilight along the Embankment. It was Julius Kramer, jogging in a track-suit.

'Professor Kramer!' I called out, hoping for news of my son Nick in Baltimore. Nick and I were extremely close when he was a young lad, in fact we formed some sort of unholy alliance against the constant attacks made by She Who Must Be Obeyed on our peace and privacy. Nick would stop her growing restive if I called in at Pommeroy's for a glass of Chateau Fleet Street on my way home, and I would do my best to frustrate her attempts to send Nick to the hairdresser or the dentist, or to other unwelcome destinations. We used to enjoy a good walk across Hampstead Heath, during which I would play 'Holmes' and Nick 'Watson', and we would search for clues. Since Nick married an American girl (a young lady who indulged herself on an extremely dangerous diet of organic vegetation and iced water) and since he took up his lectureship in Sociology, I had seen little of Nick, and to be perfectly frank, I missed his company and that instant rapport it seemed to me that we had when he was about ten years of age.

'Professor Kramer!' I called again; but my voice was lost in the shadows, the cry of the seagulls and the roar of the traffic, and the large man trundled out of view.

When I got home I was amazed to find that She Who Must Be Obeyed not only smiled at me in a way which was clearly meant to be welcoming. She sat me down in front of the glowing plastic coal of our electric fire, pushed a footstool towards my legs and actually poured me a generous G and T.

'Are you tired, dear?' She asked, solicitously.

'Are *you* feeling quite well, Hilda?' I was puzzled enough to ask.

'A day in Court is so hard for a man of your age. Daddy

always said it was such physical labour, standing up in Court.'

'Perhaps that's why your Daddy always sat down so remarkably quickly, particularly if anyone raised the subject of bloodstains. He couldn't stand the mention of blood, your Daddy.'

'Look at the danger to your health, Rumpole,' Hilda continued, unperturbed.

'I know. It's like bloody mountaineering. You take your life in your hands in the law. There's always the risk of falling down the last two steps of the Gents in Pommeroy's Wine Bar.'

'Anyway, Rumpole. You don't want to die in harness. You know poor old Daddy died in harness.'

'Really? I thought he died in the Tonbridge Hospital.'

At which point she produced a bag full of fluffy white knitting-wool and the room was filled with the unusual click of needles.

'Rumpole. You must take things seriously,' warned the gloomy *tricoteuse*. 'You don't want to drop dead in Court.'

I supposed she was right. I didn't fancy the idea of pegging out in the unconcerned presence of Mr Justice Vosper. Harness may be all right, but dying in a wig! To introduce a less depressing topic I asked She what garment she was constructing. Was it, perhaps, bedsocks?

'It's for Mrs Erskine-Brown's baby. Your Miss Phillida Trant as was. That nice girl in your Chambers. She'll have to give up the Bar, now she's got the baby.'

'Birth and death. They silence us all in the end. What are you knitting for it? A dust sheet?'

'No. A matinée jacket. Oh, I forgot. There's a letter for you.'

'Will the baby go to many matinées?' I asked, and didn't get a laugh. Instead She handed me the letter which announced that it came 'From the desk of Prof. Julius Kramer, of Baltimore University,' and continued, 'Dear Mr Rumpole. Your name has long been known to us as a legal luminary. We would wish to invite you, and of course your good lady, to visit us on campus during the autumn semester and deliver a series of lectures on the alienation factor in the psychological aspects of owner deprivation ...'

'What does that mean, Rumpole?'

'Owner deprivation? Presumably nicking things.'

'It's from Baltimore University,' Hilda reminded me, quite unnecessarily, 'Nick's University. What a coincidence!'

There was a further coincidence. Later that evening the phone rang and my son Nick's voice came to me, not frozen by the Atlantic breakers, but clear as a bell. He was flying over to England, it seemed on University business, and he would stay with us. I was, of course, delighted; it was going to be like the old days when he came up for half-term and visited the Old Bailey to listen to one of my murders (always so much more *suitable*, I thought, than the cinema). He could come and watch my performance in Court and I could give him lunch. Life was distinctly improving.

*

The prosecution of Uncle Percy Timson was in the hands of that recent father and married man, Claude Erskine-Brown. As we gathered outside Court Number 2 in the Old Bailey my heart sank. Once again the wheel of fortune had spun and turned up a disaster for the gambler Rumpole. The case was to be tried by Mr Justice Vosper.

As I stood reeling under this blow Erskine-Brown came bustling up and showed me the photograph of a somewhat elderly-looking baby. In fact it looked even older than I felt.

'It's an extraordinarily talented baby. For its age,' Erskine-Brown boasted. 'It has an amazingly powerful grip!'

'That will be for hanging on to its mother's tail as they spring from bough to bough,' I said, forgetting at the moment that the mother was one of my learned friends. Erskine-Brown put away the photograph reluctantly.

'I think it has a remarkably intelligent look. I can't get Philly to see it.'

'Quite remarkable. Any day now it should be picking up a few briefs in the Chancery Division,' I assured him.

'Rumpole. You're not being serious!'

'Perfectly serious! With an expression like that we might find it a place on the Circuit Bench. I shouldn't be at all surprised.'

Erskine-Brown looked at a bench-load of stolid well-fed and dishonest citizens, the Timson family, who had come to lend comfort and support to their Uncle Percy. I recognized Noreen and such old clients as Fred, Dennis, Cyril and Fred's wife, Vi Timson. The men were smartly dressed in blazers and flannels; the women had elaborate perms.

'Are those all your witnesses?' Erskine-Brown asked as the clan Timson gave me warm smiles of encouragement.

'Oh no. My client's family. They're the sort to breed from, the Timsons. Their activities have kept me in work for years.'

'This isn't a fight, is it?' Erskine-Brown asked as we moved into Court.

'Oh, my dear Erskine-Brown. Claude! Shall we say ... just a little skirmish?'

'But the picture was in *your* garage. And *you* signed a confession!'

'That means I start with a considerable handicap. Which is probably fair, considering the difference in our form.' I told him that with an optimism I hardly felt. Erskine-Brown looked disappointed.

'I was hoping for a quick plea. You see, I rather like to get back in time for the afternoon feed.'

'Really? You indulge in a high-tea, Erskine-Brown?'

'Oh no. Not *my* feed. The baby's!'

*

Among the prosecution witnesses Erskine-Brown called a Mr Rowland, a man with a bald, skull-like head, who was, it seemed, an art expert.

'I would say that work is quite priceless,' Rowland told Erskine-Brown, pointing to the picture in the well of the Court.

'But if you had to name a figure ...'

'*How* can you put a price on beauty?' The death's head appealed to the allegedly learned judge.

'It has been done in the past, Mr Rowland, by some quite well-known ladies.' Oh dear, we were all most amused by his Lordship's little jokes. There was obedient laughter in Court.

'Shall we say, a quarter of a million?' Mr Rowland dropped his bombshell, turning poor old Uncle Percy, the small-time fence, into a major criminal. 'Pounds not dollars.' Uncle Percy looked about to faint dead away, and the rest of the Timsons were still whistling under their breath as I rose to cross-examine.

'Mr Rowland. You say this is an undoubted painting by Taddeo di Bartolo . . .' I waved in a casual manner at Our Lord, who had been made Exhibit One, 'nicknamed "Il Zoppo", the lame one.' I gave him back his learning. 'A Siennese master of the fourteenth century?'

'The Quattrocento.'

'The Quattrocento. I'm obliged. And it is a good example of the master's work?'

'I would say an excellent example,' Mr Rowland gave me what might have been a smile had it appeared on a living face.

'Il Zoppo. "The lame one." Is he a painter well known to the general public?' I asked politely.

'He is extremely well known to connoisseurs.'

'Oh, I'm sure he is. I just wondered, if his work was instantly recognizable by the crowd who get in the King's Elm on a Saturday night?'

'My Lord . . .' Erskine-Brown had risen to his hind legs protesting. I ignored him.

'Well. What's the answer?'

'I should imagine . . . Probably not.'

'And . . .' I went on at increased volume, to drown any interruption. 'Any drinker in the saloon bar who did recognize Il Zoppo's work and wanted to buy it would have to be provided with a half a million pounds in his hip pocket to complete the transaction?'

'My Lord. I really don't know what the relevance of these questions is,' Erskine-Brown bleated, and then sat down exhausted.

I picked up Uncle Percy's signed confession and looked at it with disgust. 'The relevance, my Lord, is that in his so-called voluntary statement Mr Timson said he proposed to flog the artwork up the King's Elm next Saturday night! Even judicial knowledge, my Lord, must encompass the fact that the King's Elm is not Sotheby's.'

The judge, however, gave me a brisk return. 'And even your extensive knowledge of crime, Mr Rumpole,' he said, 'must encompass the possibility that your client himself had no idea of how valuable the painting was.'

So, with the score at fifteen-all, a small diversion was caused by Henry bringing my son Nick Rumpole into Court and finding him a seat behind me. Nick had arrived the night before and gone to bed before we had more than a couple of jars, a short chat and some coloured slides of his lovely home, his wife Erica, the swimming-pool and a number of visiting academics cooking a meal on some sort of open fire (although I assumed the house had a reasonably equipped kitchen). Nick had kept his promise to come down to the Bailey for a morning's entertainment and a spot of lunch, and I thought as I turned to look at him, how extraordinary it was that he was so large: I always think of Nick as a solemn boy in a school blazer sitting in silent fascination in the back row of a murder. However I was resolved to give my son an entertaining day at the Bailey, and I entered with enthusiasm into the *mano e mano* with Detective Inspector Broome.

I was asking the officer about the call he had from Mr Bernard, my instructing solicitor. He smiled tolerantly at the jury, as if to warn them that we were now coming to the suspect evidence of bent lawyers, and lied effectively.

'Mr Bernard did not ring me,' he said.

'Mr Bernard will say that he did.'

'I expect he will.' A nudge-nudge, wink-wink at the jury.

'And that he was denied access to his client.'

'Does he say that?' Broome sounded bored.

'You told him that Percy Timson couldn't see a solicitor.'

'No.'

'Would you have allowed Percy Timson to see a solicitor, at the time this precious document was signed?'

'No, I would not.'

I turned and gave Nick a quick smile, and got his nod of approval. Then I re-attacked the witness.

'So if Mr Bernard had telephoned he would have been refused access?'

'Yes.'

'Why?'

'No doubt you were still making your inquiries, were you not, Inspector?' Mr Justice Vosper supplied the answer.

'That is so, my Lord,' said Broome.

'Or was it because you knew that his solicitor wouldn't have allowed him to make a statement?' I asked, and once more the judge interposed himself between the DI and Rumpole's steel.

'I suppose in your experience lawyers don't encourage loquacity in a subject,' he said.

'That is one of their disadvantages, my Lord,' Broome agreed.

'So that this elderly man, with no legal experience, was left absolutely without legal advice?' I did my best to sound outraged, but was somewhat deflated by a dangerous thrust from the judge.

'Are you putting your client forward as a man with no legal experience, Mr Rumpole?' he asked. Well, as Percy had a good fifty years of legal experience in and out of various Courts I could not do that. I decided that it was time for Rumpole to skate off to some thicker ice.

'Well, this elderly man . . .'

'Yes. Clearly he *is* elderly.' Mr Justice Vosper appeared to be enjoying himself. I picked up Percy's admission with renewed distaste.

'Can you explain, Officer, why Mr Percy Timson should have signed this confession, in the absence of his solicitor?'

'I don't know, Mr Rumpole. People sometimes tell the truth.' Broome was delighted by his answer. 'In the *absence* of their solicitor.'

'And people sometimes want to protect their wives, don't they, Inspector?'

'I suppose they may,' the DI sounded less happy.

'You know my client has been married to his wife Noreen for almost thirty years?'

'Are you putting your client forward as a perfect husband, Mr

Rumpole?' The judge weighed in, no doubt sensing danger.

'No, my Lord. Merely as a loving husband.' This shut his Lordship up for a moment and I turned to the witness.

'Did you tell Percy Timson that you had his wife downstairs in the station?'

'It's possible. I can't remember. I do have other cases, you know, Mr Rumpole.' The witness answered carelessly.

'Did you say she was in the station?' I pressed him.

'I may have done.'

'I have here the station book.' I lifted the ledger which the confident Broome had not bothered to read.

'Have you?'

'There is no record whatsoever of Mrs Noreen Timson being taken into the station on that or any other day.'

'I accept that.'

'Why did you lie to my client, Inspector?'

'I didn't lie to him!' The bizarre suggestion that police officers are ever less than a hundred per cent truthful appeared to have disconcerted the witness.

'Why did you tell him Noreen had been brought into the station and charged?'

'I expect I said it, because I intended to do exactly that,' Broome said, as though that explained everything.

'You intended to charge her?'

'Yes.'

'Why did you change your mind?'

'What?'

'You never did charge her, did you?'

'Well, there was no need to after . . .'

'No need to after Percy had signed his statement. Is that what you mean?'

I saw the jury look at Broome as if some of them were beginning to doubt the doctrine of the infallibility of the Police.

'No need to after that. No.' Broome admitted.

'After he'd fallen into your trap, the bait could be thrown away. You'd got what you wanted, hadn't you?'

'What had I wanted?' The defensive position didn't suit DI Broome.

'An untrue confession. Signed in the hope of saving his wife from the welcoming gates of Holloway Prison.'

It was clearly the moment for his Lordship to come to the prosecution's rescue, and he did so with some skill.

'Mr Rumpole?' The politeness from the Bench was icy.

'Yes, my Lord.'

'Aren't you forgetting something? This admirable example of Italian Rennaisance art was actually found in your client's garage! Isn't *that* the point?' At which he gave the jury a meaningful look. 'Yes, members of the jury. Shall we say five past two?'

*

'*Isn't* that the point, Dad?' Nick and I were enjoying a sustaining :teak pie with boiled cabbage, washed down with a pint of draught Guinness in the pub opposite the Bailey. On a corner table the Timson men were consuming brown ales and buying snowballs for their ladies, and in the middle distance the officers in charge of the case were scoffing Harp Lagers and cold sausage.

'But I mean if he's guilty *anyway* . . .' Nick continued to cross-examine his father.

'If he's guilty anyway, why bother to squeeze a confession out of him?' I looked across at the Timson table. 'You see, Nick, I know the Timson family. Their activities paid your school fees for years. They never sign confessions.'

'You'll be able to lecture on that,' Nick was laughing.

'Lecture?' I didn't follow his drift.

'You met Julius Kramer?'

'Was that *your* doing, Nick?' For the first time I got a sniff of some kind of plot.

'You must come to Baltimore. Really, there's a lot of room in the new house. Erica'd be thrilled to have you.'

'Well, if I can get away . . .' I was doubtful.

'Of course you can get away. You've really *got* to get away.'

'*Got* to?'

'Ma says, you've been so tired lately.' Nick was looking at me, concerned. At which moment DI Broome was passing us on his way back to Court, and he stopped for an unfriendly chat.

'Enjoying the pantomime, Mr Rumpole?' he asked.

'Is that what you call it?'

'Don't you?'

'No. I call it a trial. Based on the quaint, old-fashioned notion that a man's innocent until you prove him guilty. This is my son...'

'Oh, really? Following in father's footsteps?' It was clear that the DI didn't consider that such a course would provide Nick with a satisfactory or even an honourable career.

'No ... actually, I'm not.'

The Inspector turned to me, satisfied of Nick's innocence. 'Come on, sir. You know Percy Timson's been a fence for years ...' DI Broome was trying the realistic approach. The Timson family fell silent at their table.

'So what should we do?' I asked politely. 'Convict him on a certificate signed by the Chief Constable?'

'Of course it all makes money for you gentlemen. I suppose you'll still be going through the motions again. This afternoon.'

'Yes. I'll be going through the motions.'

'Man of his age.' The DI looked at Nick. 'I really don't know why he bothers.' On which parting shot he left. I finished my Guinness and lit a small cigar.

'Detective Inspector Broome! The new Broome. Trials are just an unnecessary interruption, in his fearless battle against crime.'

'All the same ...' Nick sounded doubtful.

'All the same what, Nick?'

'Well, it's not as if it was one of the murders you used to take me to. I mean. They were *serious* cases.'

'Yes. You enjoyed those murders, didn't you, Nick?'

'I mean, if Percy Timson really *is* a professional fence ...'

'Oh, he is. Quite professional.'

Nick looked at me, he was smiling gently. 'Well then, why bother really?' he said.

*

The Timson case proceeded slowly, we kept having days off due to the fact that Mr Justice Vosper was dividing his time between us and a Government Committee on 'The Treatment of the Young Offender' (they were discussing the possibility of building a number of detention centres where the less friendly features of HMS Bounty, Devil's Island and nineteenth-century Eton would be combined for the purpose of delivering 'a short salutary shock' to Jamaican teenagers).

Meanwhile a deep-laid plot was going on involving my wife, Nick, and the mysterious Professor Kramer of which I had no more than an inkling. It's true that, when I was alone in my flat, an unknown woman rang the bell, came in and nosed about, asked impertinent questions about the built-in cupboards and the central heating, and then drifted away. I took her for some busybody from a government department; but I suppose I should have realized then that her visit had one clear meaning. 'This flat has been put up for sale.' I only learned months later that Mrs Erskine-Brown (Miss Phillida Trant in real life) had been invited for tea in Gloucester Road, had gone there, received the matinée jacket on behalf of the baby, and been involved in the following conversation concerning the future of Rumpole.

'I really wonder you had time to come over to tea,' Hilda began obliquely, 'what with the baby.'

'They had a day off Court. So Claude's holding the fort. Actually he enjoys it.'

'Rumpole's not having a day off. He's gone for a conference in Wandsworth. Well, he's doing far too much, for a man of his age.'

'He looks tired,' Nick told Phillida. 'Don't you think so?'

'I think he looks . . . well, just as usual.'

'He is desperately tired! We just can't wait to get him away!'

'Get Rumpole away? Where to exactly?'

'America.'

'I want them both to come and live with us. In Baltimore,' Nick said.

'You want Rumpole to give up the Bar?' Mrs Erskine-Brown was astonished.

'Well, to retire. Everyone retires, don't they?'

'Everyone possibly. But Rumpole?' Clearly Chambers had never considered the possibility.

'He's not immortal, you know! Rumpole's hardly immortal. Anyway, not a word to him at the moment. We're luring him across the "Herring Pond" by an offer of lectures in Nick's University,' Hilda told her.

'I've got him an offer from one of our professors. He's going to lecture on law.' Nick revealed the full details of the plot.

'Rumpole? On law?' Apparently my learned friend Miss Trant sounded incredulous.

'Well really, Miss Trant! Surely he knows about the law.' She bridled a little.

The way Mrs Erskine-Brown answered her wasn't entirely flattering, but no doubt it contained a certain amount of truth.

'Hardly anything. Oh, he could lecture on how to tear up paper in the prosecution speech, or how to trick his opponent into boring the Court with a lot of unnecessary cases. That's the one he played on me, when I first started. He knows all about how to cross-examine and which members of the jury to get on his side, but if you ask my honest opinion, Rumpole doesn't know anything about the *law*.'

'But it's only the bait, you see, for getting him over. And I've put this flat on the market. So we'll have a little money, and living with Nick ...' Hilda seemed to see no problems.

'I'm sure once he sees the house he'll stay,' Nick said.

'Nick has a swimming-pool, he was telling me. And a sort of camp fire.'

'Barbecue, mother.'

'Is Rumpole tremendously keen on swimming?' Their visitor was doubtful.

'If you ask me, he's bored to tears with the sort of cases he's doing nowadays.' Nick seemed to have no doubt about the matter. 'An obvious receiver! And the defence is, he didn't do it because he'd finished the last job and was preparing for the next. Now how could that interest anybody?'

'I'm not sure ...' Miss Trant as-was knew me, I'm sad to say, perhaps better than my son.

'Dad's in a hopeless position, with the judge and the police dead against him.'

'Are they? Oh well then. I know exactly how he's feeling ...'

'Pretty depressed, I imagine.' Nick supplied his answer, but the lady lawyer had hers.

'I should think, by now, he's just starting to have fun.'

*

The conversation at that tea-time was, as I say, unknown to me for many months. And unconscious of my consignment, by my nearest and dearest, to the scrapheap of rusty and worn-out barristers I was, in fact, having a certain amount of quiet pleasure in pursuing a line of inquiry with that well-known expert on stolen art-treasures Mr Melvin Glassworth, whom I had gone to visit in Wandsworth, ostensibly to discuss the matter of his appeal.

'Screws treating you all right, are they?' I asked him as we met among the pot plants of the prison interview-room, and offered him a small cigar.

'*Some* of them are rather sweet. But you've got to get me out of here, Mr Rumpole. Sorry I was a bit irritable last time.'

'I'd be a bit irritable, if I'd just got three years,' I assured him.

'*You* can get me out, Mr Rumpole. I know you can.'

'I have been considering your appeal ...' I started judicially.

'I hope to God you've come up with a few bright ideas.'

'I have found at least ten places in which the judge misdirected the jury as to our defence.'

'Then you'll tell the Court of Appeal for me. You will, won't you, Mr Rumpole?'

'I may not be able to take your case on, Mr Glassworth,' I sounded doubtful. 'Pressure of other work.'

'But if you've found ten good points. He's duty bound, isn't he, Mr Barnard?' The plump man, paler but no thinner since his conviction, looked appealingly at my instructing solicitor.

'I'll have to see.' I paused and then said casually. 'Meanwhile, perhaps you can help me. As an expert in stolen art-works.'

'An expert, me? Well, I suppose I am. What do you want to know?'

'A very valuable painting might be too well-known to dispose of?' I made a guess.

'You get that trouble, yes. It's hopeless trying to flog a Goya for instance.'

'Or a Taddeo di Bartolo. Nicknamed "Il Zoppo"?' I inquired casually.

'They're never charging me with that one, are they, Mr Rumpole? *Me?*' Mr Glassworth was appalled.

'Not as yet.' I looked at him, speculatively. 'What would you do if you had a well-known di Bartolo? "The Benediction", for instance?'

'Well. You'd never sell it. Too well-known...'

'No,' I agreed. 'But what would you do?'

'You mean, what would whoever had purloined such an artwork do, Mr Rumpole?' My art expert was cautious.

'Exactly.'

'Dump it!' Melvin Glassworth had no hesitation.

'Really?'

'Only thing to do with it. Of course. It might pay you to let the insurance company know where it got left.'

'Dump it,' I wondered. 'In what sort of place exactly?'

'Somewhere anonymous, I suppose. Somewhere that couldn't be connected with you. The municipal rubbish tip...'

'Has that ever been used?'

'It has been known. Look, about this appeal. It's bloody impossible in here. You can't get a decent shampoo. I wash my hair daily, me!'

I promised to deal with his appeal. He had given me a little help with Percy Timson's case, but I got a lot more assistance when I was met at the prison gates by Mrs Vi Timson (on her way to pay a family visit to her brother Charlie who had just got a two for carrying housebreaking implements by night). Vi said she wanted an urgent word in my ear in private, so I sent Barnard walking up the road and withdrew with her to a corner of the prison wall.

'I'll never forget Mr Rumpole,' she started, 'how you got my young Jim out of that nasty robbery of the Butchers.'*

*See 'Rumpole and the Younger Generation' in *Rumpole of the Bailey*, Penguin Books, 1978.

'Oh yes. Yes, of course. How *is* Jim?'

'Oh, doing very well, Mr Rumpole. Yes, thank you. He's got his own little window-cleaning firm now.'

'Oh dear. I'm sorry to hear it.' Window-cleaning is, of course, the best way to reconnoitre possible breaks and enters.

'The thing is. I wanted to tell you,' Vi burst out, 'I never agreed with what the family done to Uncle Percy!'

'What the *family* did?' I frowned, bewildered.

'Poor old Auntie Noreen. She's up the wall about it. It wasn't all the family exactly. It was Dennis mainly. You know Den was hopping mad when Percy let all that rubber-backed carpet go for twenty pounds ...' The words were rushing out of her, I put a calming hand on her arm.

'Mrs Timson. Vi ... Perhaps you'd better tell me all about it.'

*

The family plot or 'Put-Rumpole-out-to-grass movement' gathered impetus in the next few days. Mrs Erskine-Brown, the baby's mother, told Erskine-Brown, the father, presumably when they met briefly over the Cow-and-Gate tin, that Rumpole was on the verge of retirement. Erskine-Brown told Guthrie Featherstone, Q.C., M.P., and our learned Head of Chambers met Mr Justice Vosper, who was having a drink with his tall, lanky and singularly unattractive son Simon, in their Club, the Sheridan. What had happened then was also something I did not discover till much later.

'Simon's just finished his pupillage,' the judge told Featherstone. 'Naturally he's looking for a seat in Chambers. Aren't you, Simon?'

'Yes, Daddy,' said Master Vosper, whose legal experience consisted in sitting next to his father on the Bench, and industriously sharpening his pencils.

'There might be a vacancy, Judge.' Featherstone was anxious to help. 'Apparently Rumpole's retiring. He's going to live with his son in America.'

'Rumpole retiring!' The judge thought this scheme over and, so Featherstone told me later, approved of it. 'Can't be too soon for me. I've got him before me at the moment. Rumpole simply hogs the limelight. Hopeless case, but you can't stop the fellow fighting.'

Whilst Featherstone was selling my birthright to Master Simon Vosper in the Sheridan Club, I was entertaining the Timson family (all except Noreen who had gone to deliver a clean shirt and an ounce of 'Golden Bar' to Percy in the cells) to tea in the café opposite the Old Bailey. As Vi sorted out beverages I called the meeting to order.

'I wanted to discuss with you, as members of the family,' I said, 'your Uncle Percy Timson's defence.'

'Yes, Mr Rumpole. Has that got two lumps, dear?' Fred was pleasantly co-operative.

'Well. We rely on you, Mr Rumpole.' Cyril smiled.

'The Timson family have always been able to rely on Mr Rumpole,' Dennis assured me.

'Yes. But can Mr Rumpole rely on the Timson family?'

'Mine's the lemon tea, Vi,' Dennis said and asked me. 'What do you mean exactly?'

'As you well know,' I explained, 'half a million nicker and art-works from the Italian Quattrocentro are quite out of Uncle Percy's league. Therefore I shall have to put him into the witness-box to explain exactly what his league is.'

'What do you mean, Mr Rumpole?' For the first time Fred Timson sounded uneasy.

'I mean,' I warned them, 'Percy's going to tell the judge he disposed of four thousand Green Shield stamps for you, Fred. And a couple of lorryloads of nylon tights for you, Cyril. And innumerable canteens of cutlery. And twenty-five yards of rubber-backed carpet from the local Odeon for Dennis. As well as the electric blankets and the three freezer-loads of stolen scampi.'

'I ain't got no convictions,' Dennis protested breaking the appalled silence, and he had the grace to add, 'thanks to you, Mr Rumpole.'

'Oh yes,' I said. 'And I understand you've even got a legitimate job now, Dennis. What is it?'

'Den's a crane-driver,' Cyril said, 'on the municipal muck heap.'

'On the municipal muck heap! Now isn't that a coincidence?' I looked round the embarrassed family.

'What do you mean, Mr Rumpole?'

'I mean that it was on a municipal muck heap that some far more cultivated villain than any of you dumped "The Benediction" by Taddeo di Bartolo. Uncle Percy hasn't been doing too well as a fence lately, has he?'

'Not too brilliant. No.' Freddy admitted.

'Percy's past it.' It was Dennis who said it.

'Getting past it.' I gave it to him then. 'Oh, I know. Letting your hard-won consignment of electric blankets go half-price. Gossiping away in pubs when some minor grass is listening.'

'He got our lad Jim six months, chattering away like that, Mr Rumpole,' Fred was deeply hurt.

'Silly old fool,' said Cyril.

'He's a menace to everyone is Uncle Percy.' Dennis pronounced judgement.

'Is that why you decided he ought to be retired?' I asked them, and was answered by a nasty silence. 'You decided to put Uncle Percy out to grass,' I went on, 'give him his cards. Rusticate him. Put him on the shelf. You all decided Uncle Percy was past it, didn't you? The whole family. So you wanted him to retire, quickly.'

There was another lengthy, and guilty, pause, and then Fred Timson made an admission.

'We couldn't persuade Percy it was time to go, Mr Rumpole.'

'Honest. He wouldn't listen to reason,' Dennis protested.

'The man was bloody dangerous, carrying on at his age,' Cyril told me.

I gave them all a cold look, and told them.

'So Den with the clean record plants a picture on him and rings up DI Broome with the information. Hardly a golden handshake, was it? Not even a gold watch from the company. The trouble with you all is you're none of you Bernard Berenson.'

'We're not *what*, Mr Rumpole?' Fred was puzzled.

'You're not even Lord Clark. You never studied civilization even on the telly. You couldn't tell a genuine Fra Angelico from the top of a box of biscuits. And because of your total abysmal ignorance of matters artistic, Uncle Percy's up on a half-million-pound handling and three-quarters of the way to Parkhurst, Isle of Wight!'

'Well. What are you going to do about it, Mr Rumpole?' Dennis asked uncomfortably.

'No. What are *you* going to do about it, Dennis?' I stood up and prepared to leave the assembled Timsons. 'You'd better think a bit quickly,' I told him, 'Uncle Percy's going to give his evidence tomorrow.'

*

By the time I got back to the flat I was feeling low and somewhat exhausted. I sat by the electric fire, alone in the dark and was roused from a blackish reverie by Nick coming in and switching on the light. It seemed that She Who Must Be Obeyed was out on a visit to the fascinating Erskine-Brown baby. Nick looked at me in the way that relatives look at old people on hospital visits, with a sort of hushed concern.

'A bad day in Court?'

'Detective Inspector Broome wants to reverse the burden of proof, revoke Magna Carta and abolish barristers. Well, that might be all right, if only he could resist gingering up the evidence whenever it suits him. And there's no honour among thieves any more, Nick. I'm ashamed of the Timson family.'

'I've always thought your job must be pretty depressing,' Nick said briskly.

'They wanted to get poor old Uncle Percy to retire, so the family cooked up the most diabolical plot. I don't know . . . I really don't know what things are coming to . . . Drop of G and T?' I shuffled off to the reviving drinks table.

'Thanks.'

'Things have reached a low ebb, Nick. They've even got piped music in Pommeroy's Wine Bar. I have to come home now, to avoid the crooner.'

'How disgusting!'

At which I recalled the good old days, when Nick was about ten.

'Remember when we used to go for walks on the Heath, Nick? I was Holmes and you were Watson, and we used to pick up clues?'

Nick took his G and T, smiled and entered into the spirit of the thing. 'What's the explanation of this half-used box of matches on the path, Holmes?' he said in his Watson voice.

'Someone's either got a hole in his jacket pocket, or he suddenly gave up smoking!'

'You amaze me, Holmes!'

'You can't go for a walk up on the Heath now,' I told him. 'Not a decent Sherlock Holmes voyage of exploration. You keep tripping over the permissive society. I'll never forget those walks. It doesn't matter we don't see so much of each other now, Nick. It doesn't matter in the least. Bound to happen anyway. People growing up and all that sort of thing.'

'Perhaps we can do something about it.'

'Growing up?'

'Not seeing each other. Look, honestly,' Nick protested. 'Haven't you got into a terrible rut?'

> 'Matched with an aged wife, I mete and dole
> Unequal laws unto a savage race . . .'

I started off and my son, God bless him, was on to Alfred Lord Tennyson like a terrier.

> ''Tis not too late to seek a new world'

said Nick.

> 'Push off, and sitting well in order smite
> The sounding furrows . . .'

'You remember it, Nick!' I was delighted, and stood up in a determined manner,

> 'For my purpose holds'

I carried on,

> 'To sail beyond the sunset and the baths
> Of all the western stars until I die . . .'

'You are going to, aren't you?' Nick asked.

'Die?'

'Of course not! Sail beyond the sunset. You're coming to Baltimore?'

'It's a long way from the Old Bailey!' I suppose I sounded doubtful.

'Wouldn't that be a relief?'

'Perhaps it might be.'

'It's still on, you know. The lectures.'

'Oh yes, the lectures.'

'I saw Professor Kramer today. The only trouble is, he's no longer at the Savoy. They've taken him into the Charing Cross Hospital.' Nick broke the news to me as a matter of some seriousness. 'He collapsed while jogging.'

'While jogging, eh? Well, I've always avoided exercise.' I tried to look serious also. 'Exercise is simply an invitation to death!'

*

When I turned up at the Bailey next day I saw Guthrie Featherstone, Q.C., M.P., robed for the Court next door, in earnest conversation with my opponent Claude, the family man. As I drew up alongside Featherstone broke off and looked, I thought, exceedingly shifty.

'Morning, Erskine-Brown,' I said. 'Ready for the battle? I think we may have a little surprise for you today.'

'Ah, Horace. Are you free, by any chance, next Thursday evening?' Featherstone asked in a casual sort of manner.

'Free? I don't suppose so. I'll probably be at home with my wife.'

'Oh, we want Hilda to come too. And your son, of course. I believe he's over.'

'Come? Where?' I was puzzled.

'I'm giving a little dinner at my Club,' Featherstone said, 'the Sheridan. Most of Chambers will be there. Pencil it in, now. Like a good chap.' He went, and I turned to Erskine-Brown for clarification.

'What's the matter with our learned Head of Chambers?' I asked him. 'Has he come into money?'

*

A couple of hours later that doughty advocate, Claude Erskine-Brown, was cross-examining Dennis Timson who had just given evidence on behalf of the defence.

'Let me get this clear,' Erskine-Brown asked with some scorn, 'you found the picture on the municipal rubbish dump?'

'Where I works. Yes.' Dennis smiled at the jury, who were looking, in turn, at the exhibited depiction of Our Saviour giving a half-million-pounds Benediction.

'And you put it in your Uncle Percy's garage?'

'I had a key. Percy lent me his Cortina when they went on holiday,' Dennis explained patiently.

'You put it there at night. Without telling your Uncle what you had done?'

'I did it quietly, like. Not wanting to awaken the old couple.'

'Why store it in Uncle Percy's garage?'

'I didn't have no accommodation. Not for a thing of that size at home.'

'Mr Timson,' asked the exasperated Erskine-Brown, 'can you think of one reason why the members of the jury should believe this extraordinary story?'

'Yes.' Dennis turned to the jury in a business-like way. 'You see, members of the jury. I rang the local nick that night. I said there was this picture, like, and if they was interested they could find it in Uncle Percy's garage. So they was there next morning with the dawn patrol.'

Erskine-Brown sat down on this, and I saw him speaking to Henry who had just come into Court. I rose to re-examine with confidence.

DI Broome had clearly been told by someone that there was something interesting in Percy's garage, and that informant was now revealed as Den.

'Who did you speak to, at the local nick?' I asked.

'I spoke to DI Broome. He'll tell you that.'

'We shall see,' I said, 'if the prosecution recalls him to deny it.' From the whispers from the officers in charge of the case it seemed unlikely that they would.

'You told the Detective Inspector the picture was in your Uncle's garage?'

' 'Course I did.'

'But you never told your Uncle. He remained in ignorance?'

'Total ignorance, my Lord,' Dennis told the judge without hesitation.

'Yes, thank you, Mr Timson. Unless your Lordship has any further questions?'

But by now even Mr Justice Vosper was silent. And Erskine-Brown was busy giving a cheque to our clerk Henry, his contribution, as I later discovered, to the Chambers present to mark the retirement of Rumpole; a handsome clock to be presented at the forthcoming dinner organized by Guthrie Featherstone, Q.C., M.P., at the Sheridan Club.

*

The jury was out for four hours and acquitted Percy Timson by a majority. He went back to work to the great satisfaction of Noreen, and the resigned regret of the rest of the family. On the following Thursday, I duly turned up with my wife and son at feeding-time at the Sheridan. We penetrated the somewhat chilly portals, passed a somnolent and sleepy uniformed figure in a glass case, and went up a staircase to a fire-warmed hall where I was delighted to see my old friend George Frobisher, now a Circuit Judge, and less delighted to see Mr Justice Vosper, and his lanky son Simon. I did my best to ignore the High Court Judge, and greeted the inferior tribunal, His Honour Judge Frobisher.

'George! My old friend. My dear old friend. You've come all the way from Hertfordshire?' I was touched.

'To have dinner in your honour, Rumpole. Of course I have. No hard feelings, about that young schoolmaster?'* George smiled, I thought he was pleased to see me.

*See 'Rumpole and the Course of True Love'.

'Not at all,' I reassured him, 'and I miss you at Pommeroy's. No friendly jar there when the day's work is over.' I sat down, for a moment, on a nearby and inviting settee.

'That's the drawback of being a Circuit Judge, Rumpole. The work's over at tea-time and you're not even allowed to go to the pub.'

'I say, Rumpole. You're not a member here, are you?' Mr Justice Vosper always had to have his two-pennyworth.

'No, Judge. I don't believe I am.'

'Well. You're sitting on the members' sofa! I suppose you plead ignorance?'

'No, Judge. I plead exhaustion.' But I had to move when an elderly waitress appeared and told us that Mr Featherstone was receiving his guests in the small dining-room. So George and the Rumpole family set off in the direction she indicated, and arrived in a room hung with pictures of old actors, judges and best-selling novelists, and found a table lit by candles and gleaming with old silver, with Guthrie Featherstone and all the other members of Chambers, including Henry and Dianne from the clerk's room, chatting merrily and drinking sherry. I was surprised that my entrance produced a sort of awed silence.

Then Guthrie Featherstone stepped forward with a welcoming 'Rumpole!'

'Here he is. The Guest of Honour!' said Erskine-Brown.

'Rumpole of the Bailey!' his wife chimed in.

'Rumpole, my dear fellow. Mrs Rumpole. And Nick. Delighted you could come.' Featherstone did the honours, and I heard Uncle Tom, our oldest inhabitant and non-practising barrister, whisper to Erskine-Brown.

'Are we feeding the entire Rumpole family?'

'What is this, a wedding or a wake?' I asked the world at large, and then moved towards the smiling Erskine-Browns. 'The baby left home, has it?'

'It's actually in its carrycot with the lady downstairs,' our Portia told me, and the proud father added,

'One of us'll have to leave early to give it its ten o'clock feed.'

'*One* of us . . .' I thought that his wife was looking at him in a meaningful manner. I also thought it was time to get off the nappy-chat, so I said cheerfully,

'Well, Erskine-Brown. I thoroughly enjoyed our little scrap.'

'I suppose it's nice for you to go out on a win,' Erskine-Brown admitted grudgingly.

'Go out? Go out where?' I was puzzled. 'Oh, you mean go out for dinner?'

'I didn't enjoy our case much,' Erskine-Brown said. 'I find these days I really prefer paper-work at home. It keeps one with the family.'

'And I love Court!' His wife was enthusiastic. 'Of course, now there'll be such a lot of crime going spare in Chambers.'

'Oh, really? Are you expecting a new outbreak of villainy?'

Before I could fully understand Mrs Erskine-Brown's prophecy of extra work in Chambers I heard a well-known and unloved voice say, 'Rumpole!'

'Oh my God!' I turned at the unwelcome sound.

'Only our judge,' Erskine-Brown reassured me. What had happened was all too clear. Featherstone had invited Mr Justice Vosper and his unlikely lad to dinner.

'I think you know my son, Simon. He's endlessly grateful for the favour you're doing him. Aren't you grateful to Rumpole, Simon?'

'Of course I am Daddy.'

I had no idea what particular kindness, if any, I had unintentionally done young Simon Vosper. Before I could ask for further particulars the judge rattled on.

'I say, that was an outrageous win you had today. Your client should have been potted!'

'I'm sorry you mis-cued.'

'Mis-cued!' The judge laughed mirthlessly. 'Funny that. You'll probably have some outrageous wins too, Simon, as soon as you get your bottom on to Rumpole's chair!'

What on earth was he talking about? His son's bottom on my chair? Was Mr Justice Vosper getting past it? Before I could inquire further the antique waitress called us to the trough.

'Come on, Rumpole,' Featherstone called to me. 'I've ordered pheasant. Game chips and all the trimmings. The best that the Sheridan can offer!'

'The last time I remember having pheasant was in old Willoughby Grimes's day. We had a Chambers dinner here and they dished us up pheasant.' Uncle Tom was reminiscing as we moved to the table.

'The occasion was Tiny Banstead's being appointed Recorder of Swindon, which was considered a great honour at the time.'

'Dinner's ready, Uncle Tom,' Mrs Erskine-Brown called from the table. But our oldest inhabitant insisted on finishing his story.

'Well, poor old Tiny got one of those little pheasant bones stuck in his gullet and they rushed him to hospital. Death by suffocation! He never sat as a Recorder. Quite a disappointment to his wife . . .'

A couple of hours later, during which I had been speculating about a mysterious cardboard box in front of Featherstone's place, the learned Head of our Chambers beat on a glass with a spoon and rose to his feet to address the cigar-smoking, port-swilling company who were all still present, save Erskine-Brown who had slipped away mysteriously after the pud.

'Just a few words from me,' said Featherstone. 'Horace Rumpole has become part of our lives in Chambers. Like a valued piece of antique furniture which we see every day, and only notice perhaps, and miss, when it's gone.'

Well, that fell into that category of things which could have been put better, but I let him carry on, seeing that he was about to open the box in front of him.

'But I hope, Horace, I sincerely hope that you and Mrs Rumpole will accept this clock as a token of our affection and respect. May it tell many happy hours in the future.'

As the handsome time-piece was thrust into my hands, engraved as it was with the names of all the members of Chambers, including Henry and Dianne, and as I fondled their gift, and as their voices were raised in asking Rumpole for a speech in reply, the pieces of the jigsaw, as they say in detective stories, fell into place. I saw clearly that there had been a plot against me as ruthless and well-planned as the Timson family's scheme to dispose of Uncle Percy. I was being retired, and their clock was my parting gift. I had little time to consider the participation of my wife and son in this conspiracy. My final speech was expected of me, and I gave it.

'If your Lordship pleases. Hilda, Nick, my friends. My old friends. This occasion has cheered me considerably!' I drank port, and my audience smiled pleasantly. 'There have been times lately, during the long hours in your Lordship's Court . . .' I went on, and Vosper J. called out, 'Pretty long for me, Rumpole.' However, I ignored the interruption. 'Listening to the constant attacks on our profession by the police, there have been times, I must confess, when I wondered if I hadn't been getting into some sort of rut.'

'That's exactly what I've been thinking!' I heard Nick whisper to George. And then I gave them the first whiff of Tennyson:

> 'Matched with an aged wife, I mete and dole
> Unequal laws unto a savage race,
> That hoard and sleep and feed and know not me . . .'

Members of Chambers all looked at Hilda in a friendly fashion; and she smiled and said, 'Really Rumpole!'

'In such moods, I must confess, I have been tempted to chuck it all in. To retire. To go out to grass.' Here I paused and looked round at them all gratefully. 'But your support, your affection, and above all this very generous gift, have made me change my mind.'

There was a moment's puzzled silence; but before they could ask a question I had launched into the final great passage of the old Laureate's *Ulysses*.

> 'Tis not too late, to seek a new world . . .'

I told them,

> 'Push off, and sitting well in order, smite
> The sounding furrows: for my purpose holds
> To sail beyond the sunset . . .'

'A new world?' George whispered to Nick. 'Perhaps he's going after all.'

'Of course he is!'

> '... And the baths
> Of all the western stars until I die.'

I went on, and I heard Hilda assure Mrs Erskine-Brown, 'he's definitely going'.

> 'It may be that the gulfs will wash us down'

I told them,

> 'It may be we shall touch the Happy Isles
> And see the great Achilles, whom we knew.
> Tho' much is taken, much abides; and tho'
> We are not now that strength which in the old days
> Moved earth and heaven: that which we are, we are ...'

'What are we?' Uncle Tom was asking.

'What we are, apparently,' George assured him.

> 'One equal temper of heroic hearts ...'

'He still makes a good final speech, old Rumpole.' This was Featherstone muttering to Mr Justice Vosper, to which the judge replied, 'Goes on a bit long.'

> 'Made weak by time and fate, but strong in will
> To strive, to seek, to find, and not to yield.'

I paused. There was a smatter of applause.

'Well. Is that it?' Uncle Tom asked, but I had the final clear announcement to make.

'This handsome time-piece will encourage me, my old friends,' I told them, 'to forget all thought of surrender and retirement, and not to yield in all my future cases at the Old Bailey, London Sessions, Luton Crown – or even before the Uxbridge Magistrates! And I shall never be late. This will always get me to the Court on time!'

I was standing, holding the clock proudly whilst the assembled company stared at me with mingled hostility and amazement. At last Uncle Tom spoke, to no one in particular.

'If Rumpole's *not* retiring,' he said, 'does he really mean to hang on to our clock?'

FOR THE BEST IN PAPERBACKS, LOOK FOR THE

In every corner of the world, on every subject under the sun, Penguin represents quality and variety—the very best in publishing today.

For complete information about books available from Penguin—including Puffins, Penguin Classics, and Arkana—and how to order them, write to us at the appropriate address below. Please note that for copyright reasons the selection of books varies from country to country.

In the United Kingdom: Please write to *Dept. JC, Penguin Books Ltd, FREEPOST, West Drayton, Middlesex UB7 0BR.*

If you have any difficulty in obtaining a title, please send your order with the correct money, plus ten percent for postage and packaging, to *P.O. Box No. 11, West Drayton, Middlesex UB7 0BR*

In the United States: Please write to *Consumer Sales, Penguin USA, P.O. Box 999, Dept. 17109, Bergenfield, New Jersey 07621-0120.* Visa and MasterCard holders call 1-800-253-6476 to order all Penguin titles

In Canada: Please write to *Penguin Books Canada Ltd, 10 Alcorn Avenue, Suite 300, Toronto, Ontario M4V 3B2*

In Australia: Please write to *Penguin Books Australia Ltd, P.O. Box 257, Ringwood, Victoria 3134*

In New Zealand: Please write to *Penguin Books (NZ) Ltd, Private Bag 102902, North Shore Mail Centre, Auckland 10*

In India: Please write to *Penguin Books India Pvt Ltd, 706 Eros Apartments, 56 Nehru Place, New Delhi 110 019*

In the Netherlands: Please write to *Penguin Books Netherlands bv, Postbus 3507, NL-1001 AH Amsterdam*

In Germany: Please write to *Penguin Books Deutschland GmbH, Metzlerstrasse 26, 60594 Frankfurt am Main*

In Spain: Please write to *Penguin Books S.A., Bravo Murillo 19, 1° B, 28015 Madrid*

In Italy: Please write to *Penguin Italia s.r.l., Via Felice Casati 20, I-20124 Milano*

In France: Please write to *Penguin France S.A., 17 rue Lejeune, F-31000 Toulouse*

In Japan: Please write to *Penguin Books Japan, Ishikiribashi Building, 2–5–4, Suido, Bunkyo-ku, Tokyo 112*

In Greece: Please write to *Penguin Hellas Ltd, Dimocritou 3, GR–106 71 Athens*

In South Africa: Please write to *Longman Penguin Southern Africa (Pty) Ltd, Private Bag X08, Bertsham 2013*